Aisulu tilted up her chin. Above her—high above her—was the eagles' nest. Aisulu was a mountain child. She could climb. But she could also fall. What would happen if she fell and broke a leg? There would be no one to help her.

"Stop thinking about that," she said out loud. There was a baby eagle up there, and it would die without her. She hoisted herself onto a stone at the base of the outcrop and began to climb.

Stand on the Sky

Erin Bow

HOUGHTON MIFFLIN HARCOURT
Boston   New York

hmhbooks.com

The text was set in Adobe Caslon Pro.
Cover design by Whitney Leader-Picone
Interior design by Whitney Leader-Picone

The Library of Congress has cataloged the hardcover edition as follows:
Names: Bow, Erin, author.
Title: Stand on the sky / Erin Bow.
Description: Boston ; New York : Houghton Mifflin Harcourt, [2019] |
Summary: Twelve-year-old Aisulu defies the expectations of her Kazakh family and
tradition to train an eagle in order to save her brother, Serik, and
prevent her family from giving up their nomadic life forever. |
Identifiers: LCCN 2018052137 (print) | LCCN 2018056301 (ebook) |
Subjects: | CYAC: Family life—Mongolia—Fiction. | Sex role—Fiction. |
Eagles—Fiction. | Nomads—Fiction. | Kazakhs—Fiction. |
Mongolia—Fiction. | BISAC: JUVENILE FICTION / Animals / Birds. | JUVENILE
FICTION / Girls & Women. | JUVENILE FICTION / Social Issues / Self-Esteem
& Self-Reliance. | JUVENILE FICTION / Family / General (see also headings
under Social Issues). | JUVENILE FICTION / People & Places / Asia.
Classification: LCC PZ7.B67167 (ebook) | LCC PZ7.B67167 St 2019 (print) | DDC
[Fic]—dc23
LC record available at https://lccn.loc.gov/2018052137

ISBN: 978-1-328-55746-9 hardcover
ISBN: 978-0-358-43420-7 paperback

Manufactured in the United States of America

2 2021
4500839879

For my late sister Wendy, who was Serik when I was Aisulu. Kiddo, it's a little late, but I wanted to say that I would have done anything to save you.

Chapter One

THERE WAS NO SIGN of Serik's horse.

Aisulu and her brother, Serik, had searching for almost two hours. They'd followed footpaths and goat paths, tracked through sand and skulls and sharp-cornered stone.

"Well," said Serik. "That's it. Dulat's going to kill me. I'm going to die."

Aisulu slung an arm around her brother's shoulders. "You think that's bad? I'm going to have to do *embroidery*."

They were standing together on top of a shale outcropping, which they'd climbed to use for a lookout. Above them the sky was high and huge and bright, wheeled with birds. Below them the mountain swept away, fierce and dry and the color of foxes. They could see up to the snow line and down to the power lines and the road. They could see the tracks of the goat herds and the hollow with the three tent-houses—the gers—where their herding family lived. What they could not see was any trace of stupid horses that had wandered off while their riders lay napping in the sun.

And the trouble they were going to be in was feeling less and less like a joke. Aisulu had been fetching water when Serik had come to her for help. Water was her job because she was a girl. She'd hauled pails of water up the mountain so many times that the wire handles had left raised yellow lines at the roots of her fingers.

Right now, Aisulu was meant to be bringing that water back. She was meant to be doing the morning milking of the yaks. Was meant to be churning that milk into butter. There was no chance she hadn't been missed. Their mother, Rizagul, was probably already planning the embroidery project that Aisulu would have to start when she returned. Rizagul never missed a chance to school Aisulu in girls' work. Aisulu did not mind girls' work, but she liked other things too: tending the solar panels that powered their light bulb and their radio, studying math, and riding fast with her arms stretched out like wings. In a land where girls are supposed to have hearts made of milk, Aisulu had a heart made of sky.

And as for Serik ... Aisulu might have needlework waiting for her, but Serik might have the whack of a folded belt. At fourteen, he was really too big to take a beating — but if he lost his horse their uncle Dulat might make an exception.

On top of the shale outcrop, Serik stood with his head

tipped back. He was watching the birds circling overhead. They were huge and black against the sky, a pair of golden eagles. Aisulu knew them well. She'd seen them all season, swooping in and out from a certain crag high up the mountain. For a while there had been only one eagle — the father — but now there were two again. That meant their eggs had hatched.

She watched Serik watching the birds. Serik, her brother: in their faces, they were almost as alike as twins: the same moon-roundness, the same eyes like sunlight through dust, the same wind-burned cheeks, dappled as red as the sunny side of an apple. In the last year, Serik had suddenly grown tall — sprouting in both height and awkwardness — while Aisulu had remained small for twelve, though wiry-strong, and sure-footed as a cat. But as little children they had been inseparable as a pair of puppies. Even now, at an age when girls and boys were pulled apart, they stuck together.

Except. Serik was watching the eagles with a look she didn't understand, a longing so fierce it was almost like pain, or fear. His hand was squeezed tightly around his leg, above one of his knees.

"Hey?" Aisulu elbowed him. "Lost horse? Remember?"

Serik shook himself. "Strong Wind!" he shouted.

It was unusual among their people — the Kazakhs of Western Mongolia — to name animals, but children did it, of course. Serik had named his horse Strong Wind because, he said, the horse was fast. Aisulu had agreed to call him that because, she said, the horse was also prone to farting.

Serik cupped his hands to make a megaphone. "Strong Wind!"

Only the regular wind answered. The sun was warm but the air was turning chill.

Serik dropped his hands. "Now what?"

"I don't know," said Aisulu. "Maybe we could follow his smell?"

"Shut up," he said, brotherly. Then he sighed. Together —bracing each other and offering hands—they edged and slid down the shale face. Back on the ground, Aisulu slapped her coat to shake the dust from it. The coat was her brother's old shapan, knee-length and made of corduroy. It had been black when Serik had worn it, but now it was so faded that it looked like a chalkboard covered in eraser marks. The scant bits of embroidery around the collar were fraying, and the wind whipped the gold threads into her black hair.

"Your horse," she declaimed, helping Serik down the last step, "is dumb as two bags of rocks and a Russian tourist." She wrinkled her nose and tucked strands of loose hair behind her ears. To her mother's endless exasperation, Aisulu had trouble keeping her hair neatly braided. "What next?"

"We should check the high meadow." Serik bounced a bubble of air from cheek to cheek. Under his jean jacket, he was wearing a Mickey Mouse sweatshirt. Mickey alone was smiling. "But—the herd was up there. We'll probably run into them."

He meant their father and their uncles.

He meant their oldest uncle, Dulat, with the empty eyes.

The bounce drained slowly out of Serik. He smeared his hands down his jeans. As he did, Aisulu saw something. There was a place in his leg—the place he'd been squeezing—and when he touched it, he flinched from his own hands, like a horse with a sore mouth overreacting to the reins. As she watched he squeezed again, seeking measurement of pain in a way that only humans do.

She'd seen him do this before. She'd seen a shadow of a limp that was beginning to change Serik, to darken him. She did not think anyone else had seen it. He hid it, and she did not blame him for that. They lived in a hard country. A goat with a limp got no help, except perhaps into the stew pot.

Serik caught Aisulu watching him and dropped his hand from his leg. He tugged his skullcap down and rubbed a knuckle into the middle of his forehead. "Look, Aish. You don't have to come. I can walk up."

"Serken, don't be stupid." He'd used her childhood

nickname, and so she used his, though he'd almost outgrown it. They were on the edge of something, some big change. For a moment they looked at each other. "Look, we'll go up together, okay?" She offered him a fist to bump.

He hesitated, and then bumped her fist back. "Okay."

Aisulu whistled, and her horse, Moon Spot, came trotting. "See?" She grinned at Serik. "You can teach them to come when you call!"

"Oh, shut up," he answered, and slapped her arm.

She hit him back, because she loved him, and because he was her brother.

And then they rode up together, toward the high meadow, into the empty sky.

Doubled up on Moon Spot's back, Aisulu and Serik followed a goat path all the way to the high bowl. It was where their family herd had been that morning, but when they finally reached its rim, there was not a goat or an uncle in sight. Just an empty meadow of green grass and blue poppies.

"They're not here," said Serik.

"You're kidding! Really?" said Aisulu. But her heart wasn't in the teasing. Meeting their family would have gotten them into trouble—but not meeting them meant there was something wrong. Why would the herd not be here?

The grazing was good—it was June, and in Mongolia that meant earliest summer, a time when the high meadows were soft but the weather was breakable.

The weather was breaking now. Overhead, shining streaks of cloud were sweeping past them like ribbons flung into the wind.

"I don't get it." Serik got down. "Where else would they go?"

"Farther up? Or back home?" Aisulu dismounted and climbed up to the rim of the meadow to look back the way they'd come. And from there, she saw it: Clouds were banked behind the ridge of mountains across the valley. Snow reached down from them with long purple fingers. A summer blizzard. Aisulu froze.

Serik had come up beside her. "Aish . . ." Her shortened name puffed out like a prayer. "We should go."

Yes. They should go. The blizzard might come fast. Their parents had taught them: Find shelter and you'll be fine. Don't and you could die. They needed to get back to their camp. But Aisulu said: "Without your horse?"

Serik chewed on his lip, and his hand sought the sore spot in his leg again. Aisulu watched him squeeze it. She could almost feel the stabbing throb. To lose a horse . . . The thought bruised her heart.

Moon Spot was eating poppies while the wind pulled

her mane and tail like banners. She made a picture: a gray horse with a black mane among the blue flowers. Moon Spot was not afraid. Aisulu tried not to be afraid either. "Home is down," she said. "But to look for Strong Wind, we should go up."

On the far side of the bowl was a high pass, where the mountain rubbed shoulders with another mountain. A faint track of bare sand and clay ran up it. There was another meadow on the other side of that pass, she knew. When last she had snuck away riding, she'd found it full of globe thistles, a favorite of horses. They'd been tight as fists then, but they would be open now. A horse might be drawn to them.

Aisulu whistled Moon Spot over and mounted. "Strong Wind would go up," she said. "Because otherwise we would have met him on the way down." That wasn't true—the mountain was full of folds and hidden places. After all, they'd somehow missed the whole goat herd. But Aisulu thought a horse like Strong Wind would follow the paths, because he had no brains. She thought he would go to the thistles.

Serik squeezed his leg again, as if he'd forgotten she was watching. "We'll climb to the pass and look." He did not say *and then we will go home*, but she could hear it in his silence.

We will check one place and then we will leave my horse. That was the thing he was not saying.

There was pain in Serik's face.

Aisulu understood it. They say in Mongolia that mares don't win medals — meaning that girl horses are slow and girl riders are slower. Most girls couldn't ride, but Aisulu could. Her father put his horses in the great fall races every year, and when Serik at nine had grown too big and heavy to ride them, Aisulu at seven had learned to make them fly. She was fast the way foxes are fast — she had quick ears and eyes, and she could make a gallop swerve sideways without even shifting in her seat. And she had won medals, a few, that hung on a square of velvet with her father's old wrestling medals and snapshots of her grandfather holding his great hunting eagle.

She loved horses. She loved Moon Spot. If Aisulu lost Moon Spot, the way Serik was losing Strong Wind . . . It was the biggest thing she could imagine losing, and even the brush of the thought was crushing.

But she had no time for such worries. She pulled her brother up onto the horse behind her. With the blizzard chasing them and their bodies pressed together, they rode fast. They swept across the bowl of poppies and climbed toward the pass. Moon Spot's muscles bunched and surged between Aisulu's legs. The horse's body felt warm, suddenly, because the wind had turned cold. The smell of the air sharpened.

At the highest point of the pass was a shrine to the sky. It was made of stones — from small boulders to fist-sized rocks — that were heaped up into a pile about thirty feet across and fifteen feet high. Poles were thrust into the top of the pile, wound with scarves and banners of blue silk. Aisulu and Serik skirted the shrine until they had a view of the northern slope.

Behind them, across the valley, the nearest peak wrapped itself in gray clouds like a woman wrapping up her hair. Beside them the banners of the shrine tattered and snapped. Before them the high meadow swept downward.

The storm was at their backs, but north-slope meadow was still sunny, crossed by quick-moving shadows from streaming clouds. It was full of songbirds, and full of thistles, and on the far side was the thumb-sized figure of Serik's horse.

Serik got down and dashed forward, a staggering limp in his run. He put two fingers in his mouth and stretched it to give a sharp whistle.

Strong Wind's head came up.

Strong Wind's head went back down.

He went back to his thistles.

"Two bags of rocks . . ." said Aisulu.

". . . and a Russian tourist. I'm not arguing! Strong Wind!" Serik shouted at the top of his lungs, but the wind whipped and tattered his words away.

From the back of her own, much better horse, Aisulu snorted. "That will never work. We'll have to go get him."

Serik turned and looked at her. Then he looked past her, and his eyes went wide.

Aisulu turned, and there was the blizzard, close and solid as a wall.

"Wait here!" she shouted. "Take cover!"

She squeezed her knees and stretched her body over Moon Spot's back. She dug her heels in hard. They ran.

Moon Spot streaked across the meadow, and Aisulu, bareback, moved in the way she remembered from the great races, so that it was all effort and no impact. It felt as if they were skimming across the ground, hearts beating hard, hooves hardly touching the earth. Strong Wind saw them coming. He lifted his dull brown head and whinnied. He had a racing name, but Moon Spot had a racing heart.

Horse and rider looped around Strong Wind like a dog around a stray cow. Moon Spot swept into a tight turn, and Aisulu leaned far into it, her knees squeezing in, the horse's huge muscles surging as if they were her muscles. The speed was contagious: Strong Wind caught it. Moon Spot ran back toward the sky shrine and Strong Wind ran behind her, reins flying, his saddle blanket sliding under its strap. They were back to Serik just as the blizzard struck.

Serik grabbed Strong Wind by the reins. "This way!" he shouted, pointing.

The snow was suddenly all around them. From her height on horseback, Aisulu could not even see the end of Serik's fingers. But she followed him as he dragged Strong Wind around toward the sheltered side of the shrine. Aisulu saw that Serik had not just been waiting for them—he'd saved them. He'd shifted the rocks to make a V-shaped cove in the stones.

She swung to the ground and ran to help him, making the cove bigger and deeper even as the needles of snow pierced her fingers. Serik was wearing a sweatshirt and a denim jacket, jeans, and sneakers with the Velcro worn out. Aisulu's hand-me-down shapan was just corduroy and felt padding. The shapan might have been warm when it had been Serik's, but now the padding was lumpy and thin. Neither of them was dressed well enough to survive a blizzard. They both knew that.

The cove that Serik had opened was tiny. Aisulu thrust herself to the back of it and kept moving stones. Even though she was tucked down, the wind swirled stray hairs from the crown of her head. Serik worked beside her, their shoulders knocking. In just a few moments they had made a niche in the stones big enough for both of them.

"It can't be big enough for the horses," he said. They could not enlarge their shelter that much without tools, without time. Aisulu knew that, and yet she wanted to try.

"They'll be all right, Aish," said Serik.

Moon Spot was a wild little thing, still shedding her winter coat. Both horses were sturdy, shaggy, small, and wild: Mongolian horses, hardy as the plants that grew in the cracks of cliffs.

Aisulu told herself that as she left them in the cold.

Aisulu usually rode bareback, but Serik used a folded rug in place of a saddle. Now, he unstrapped it from Strong Wind and brought it into the cove. His elbow jabbed Aisulu as he unfolded it. The rug was not much bigger than a prayer mat—two feet across, four feet long. It was stiff with dirt and horse sweat, but it was made of thick felt and it would be warm. Serik shoved it into her hands and darted away. In two steps he had vanished into the snow, but in five breaths he was back. He had stolen the blue silk from the sky poles.

They bunched the silk up under them. They huddled down and pulled the blanket up over their bodies and their heads. Darkness fell.

Aisulu and Serik huddled under the saddle blanket with the summer blizzard raging above them. The wind slipped in around the edges, and the blanket began to grow heavy with snow. Cold soaked up from the stones, but the silk protected them from the worst of it. Above them the blanket made a tiny tent. In it they lay face-to-face in dimness, their knees tucked together, their breath steaming.

It was cold, but not deadly cold. They were not going to die.

Aisulu made a soft fist and banged Serik in the heart, because he was her brother and he'd saved them. "Good thinking, with the rocks."

He hit her back. "Good finding, with the horse." He breathed out hard. "I think we'll be okay."

"Okay?" She made her voice light to cover her nerves. "This is perfect! We're not even going to get in trouble." When they came staggering down out of the storm, brave and clever survivors, their parents would simply be glad to see them.

Or at least, they would be glad to see Serik.

Kazakhs nomads live in big families, ruled by the eldest brother: in their case, their uncle Dulat, who was fierce as a king. But Dulat had no children, and so if he was a king, then Serik was a prince. And if Serik was a prince, he was a shining one. He was fast, and sweet, and funny. He could ride anything from a billy goat to a bull yak, and his name had been Aisulu's first word: she'd learned it because her mother was always shouting it across the steppes. *Serik, get down from there! Serik, come back!*

And yet, for Serik, their mother's scolding had never been truly angry. Serik was a handful, but a handful was what he supposed to be. Aisulu was a handful too, but that was different.

She was not sure her mother would be quite as happy to see her.

But that was for later. For now, they lay together. The blizzard went on. Serik kept shifting and shifting, which let the cold come in to brush against Aisulu with its blue hands. "Hold still," she said when a shift tugged the blanket up to expose the nape of her neck. Serik held still for a while. But then he shifted again, slowly, as if trying to sneak the movement by her. Aisulu realized: he was lying with his weight on the painful spot in his leg. "Do you want to switch?" she asked.

It would be risky for them to roll over. It would let out all the heat they'd hoarded. Serik did not seem to understand. He said nothing.

"Turn over," she said. "Take the weight off your sore leg?"

She felt how her words hit him. He pulled a breath in and held very still. "There's nothing wrong with my leg."

"Nobody sees it."

But she saw it.

For a moment they were both speechless, breathing into each other's faces. They were very close together. They loved each other. Surely they could say anything. "How long has it hurt?" Aisulu whispered. "Have you told anyone?"

Aisulu's nose was full of her brother's smell: boy sweat and horse sweat, but something else, too, something sharp and angry, a smell that made her heart twist. Something— he was sick, she realized. The thought punched the air out of her. It was the kind of blow that is so bad that for a moment all you feel is numbness.

Aisulu felt numbness. She felt tears make her eyes wide.

"It's nothing," Serik mumbled.

"It's not!"

"It will heal itself."

"But what if it doesn't? Serik, what if something is really wrong? We have to tell someone. Tell Mother—tell Father."

"Don't you dare. *Don't you dare.*"

"But it might be . . ." she said, then stopped. She didn't know what the limp might be. It wasn't as if they had diagnosed all those doomed limping goats.

Serik jerked out of her arms and thrust the blanket up.

He pulled himself into a stiff crouch. The blizzard swirled in. The gathered snow slid onto their shoes. "Switch, then," he said. "If you know what's best. If you think you've got all the answers. Let's just switch."

Silent, Aisulu rolled into his space. And then he lay down again, in her space, still facing her, but this time on his other leg. It was cold for a little while, and then it warmed again.

"Serken . . ."

"Don't you get it?" Serik's voice was low and rough. They were so close that she could feel the hitch in his breath. His hands were curled into fists between them, but he did not hit her—whatever this pain was, it was not one that could connect them. "Don't you get it, Aish? I can't—I can't stay here if I'm limping. I can't ride with the herd, or wrestle the goats, or—any of it. They'll send me away."

Serik, the golden child, the prince. He wanted the life that left Aisulu wanting more. But how could a boy with a limp rule a nomad family?

"They won't—they'd never—" She curled a hand up and tapped it against his heart. "Serken—together. We'll tell them together."

"No!" The space between them was tiny, but his arms stiffened in it. He was pushing her away. "Don't you dare, Aish. I'll lose everything." The stones under them were hard. The snow over them was heavy. "If you tell, I'll lose everything," said Serik, and Aisulu knew he was probably right. "And I'll never forgive you, Aish. I'll hate you forever."

Aisulu fell silent. Her throat felt as if it had been wound up in wire. It got tighter, and tighter, until she thought it might stop her breath. She huddled with her brother in the darkness as the wind howled and the snow fell, weighing them down.

Chapter Two

THE SUMMER BLIZZARD WAS SHORT—an hour, perhaps, or two. It was hard to judge the time. The world seemed to grow quieter and quieter as the snow covered them, until it was so muffled that silence rang in Aisulu's ears. But now, she thought, the wind had stopped.

Serik had been shutting her out by pretending to sleep, but the new silence made him stir. The light was dark brown. Aisulu could barely see her brother, but she could feel him judge the silence. She did too. Without needing to speak, they moved together and pushed the blanket off.

Light pierced them. The pocket of damp warm air in which they'd huddled snapped into icy fog.

Aisulu and Serik both eased themselves up, sore from huddling on the stones. The light was so bright that it was like looking into emptiness. Serik lifted a hand to shade his eyes. Aisulu blinked and blinked.

First they found the shapes of their horses, close by, shadows against the white air. Moon Spot came to lean against Aisulu. Snow was matted like felt into the shaggy places of her coat. But she seemed fine. Both horses were fine.

And finally Aisulu could see again.

The meadow was ice hard, wind glazed. The sky had pulled up and lost its colors. The air was still.

Serik strapped the blanket back onto Strong Wind, then picked up the blue silk he had stolen. He still hadn't said a word to Aisulu. He climbed up the piled rocks to return the silk to its poles. She knew she should help, but she watched him instead. She watched the way his leg bore his weight. She watched the way he moved, which reminded her of a horse with a stone in its hoof. She was watching him so closely that Moon Spot managed to sneak up on her. A cold wet nose found her neck and ear.

Aisulu turned. "Moon." She scratched the mare under the jaw, working her fingers into the matted snow and pulling it free of Moon Spot's coat. Then she leaned her forehead against the horse's forehead. "Oh, Moon."

She and Serik had lived. Their horses had lived. But something had broken between them. Aisulu knew it. Something was wrong. She looked down the northern slope. She saw the meadow blazing white, shadowless. Then she saw that scattered across the hard snow were birds.

Little songbirds, sweet grass birds, summer birds. Like Serik and Aisulu, they had sought shelter. They had scooped hollows in the hard drifts and huddled in them together. But they had not made it. The shining snow was dotted with the feathered bodies. "Oh," said Aisulu. "Oh, birds . . ."

They were dead.

They were all dead, hundreds of them, scattered everywhere. And still there was not a breath of wind.

"Look!" Serik was at the top of the shrine, looking down at the meadow on the other side of it. "Aish!" His call was half cry, half whisper. "Quick—come look!"

Fox-quick, Aisulu scrambled up the pile of stones, past the offerings people had left: horse skulls and crutches and vodka bottles. Serik was standing at the peak of the shrine, holding on to the sky pole. With his other hand he grabbed her arm. "Look at that!"

The meadow on the far side of the shrine was also blazing snow, and also beaded with dead birds. Dancing from body to body was a great golden eagle.

An eagle.

Aisulu's family had always kept eagles: her oldest uncle had hunted with eagles, and her grandfather, and her great-grandfather, back and back. Her people were nomads who moved with their herds across the mountains of Western Mongolia, and their life could be harsh. And yet it was glorious, and it was sweet, and it had eagles. In the summer the men in her family had kept the eagles in the camp, and had stroked them like kittens. In the fall they went to the Eagle Festival and came home with medals and honor. In the winter they rode deep into the bitter mountains and came home with foxes and hares: fur to keep their families from freezing. And everywhere they went, men named them "burkitshi," which meant "eagle hunter," but also meant "great man among Kazakhs."

Seeing the eagle now, so close—Serik was frozen, his hand on Aisulu's arm. Aisulu, unthinking, cupped her hands in front of her, as if in prayer.

"From the pair at the high crag," Aisulu breathed. "It's the female."

"How do you know?"

"She's bigger." Female eagles are bigger than males, and fiercer. Mares might not win medals, but eagle hunters always took female eagles.

Serik's hand was still on Aisulu's arm, tight as a baby's fingers. He had forgotten to lie about being fine. He was standing with his weight off his sore leg, clutching the sky pole. His face was aglow. "Just look at her."

The eagle was feasting. She had her wings spread like a grand embroidered coat. She hopped about on her feathered legs as if she were wearing stiff new boots.

The lowest feathers of those boots were stained red. The eagle's beak was hooked and fearsome. When she saw Serik and Aisulu watching, she glared at them with strong and wild eyes. But she didn't stop eating. Two tears and three gulps was all it took her to finish a dead songbird. A flounce and four hops found another.

Great silence gripped the mountain. The silk in Serik's hands did not stir. The dead birds did not sing. It was as if the world were braced for something.

Aisulu could hear the eagle's stiff feathers folding over each other. She could hear the meat tear and the beak click as the eagle ate.

"We could catch her," said Serik. His voice was high, excited. "This is one way they—one way the eagle hunters take their birds. They wait for them to be fully fed, to be too stuffed to fly. Then they—"

"No."

"Why not?"

There were a dozen reasons why not: Serik wasn't an eagle hunter. They had no net. The eagle would kill them. The eagle chick would die . . . Aisulu looked at the eagle and saw the eagle looking back at her, with eyes that could see for miles. The eagle was holding still, suddenly. Aisulu could hear the creak of flexing talons biting into rock. There were a dozen reasons why not, but Aisulu could name only one of them: "Because she is an eagle, Serik."

Serik yanked his hand away from her, so violently that the horses behind them stirred and cried questions. "And what am I, Aish?"

The limping prince. The goat for the stew pot.

"Burkitshi," said Serik. "I could be an eagle hunter."

Never mind the prince of her family. A burkitshi was a prince of the people. Serik's limp could cost him everything —could an eagle give it all back?

"But—" Aisulu thought of the strange moment in the snowstorm when something like a smell had hit her in the pit of her stomach. That smell and this moment. They added up, somehow. To something bad. To disaster coming. "You can't catch her like this, Serik."

"And you can't stop me," he spat. He dropped the blue silk and whirled. Little stones clattered and skidded out from under his feet as he dashed down the rock pile toward the horses.

"Serik!" Aisulu ran after him. He yanked free of her reaching fingers and she tumbled forward onto her belly in the heaped stones. The breath whooshed out of her. For a moment, her eyes were swamped with bright blobs. When she could see again, Serik was on his horse and riding away.

Aisulu pushed herself to her hands and knees, then surged to her feet. Her stomach still felt punched: it wanted to come right up her throat. But she stumbled the last few feet off the shrine. Moon Spot pushed on her shoulder and made a worried noise. Aisulu put a hand on the mare's neck, as much to steady herself as to calm the horse down. She had to climb back onto a stone to mount. Moon Spot didn't like it. Her ears kept swiveling.

"Easy," whispered Aisulu, then coughed. "Moon Spot, easy. Let's go after Wind — easy and go."

Belly spasming, Aisulu guided Moon Spot around the shrine, over the crest of the path.

In the south meadow, Serik was trying to get Strong Wind to ride toward the eagle. The eagle, still on the ground, was watching them with a tight stillness, poised like a hunter with his rifle raised and his breath slow. Deadly, ready.

A golden eagle could kill a wolf. Horses were generally too big to be eagle prey, but Strong Wind seemed to have his doubts. The horse pinned his ears and leaned backward, stiff legged, almost as if he might fall on his tail in the snow. But he kept putting one foot in front of the other. The eagle kept staring.

"Serik," whispered Aisulu. But her brother wasn't listening.

The moment was poised on the edge of a cliff. It was going to jump.

The eagle took off. It swooped past them, flying low. Aisulu felt the great rush of air as eight-foot-wide wings brushed almost by her ears. Moon Spot reared. Aisulu had to throw her body along the horse's back and wrap her arms around the damp neck.

The eagle swept past, and Serik came after it. His hat flew off behind him, a splash of blue and gold in the wind.

Moon Spot reared again, and Aisulu could only hang on.

"Serik!" she shouted, but it was no use shouting.

She gathered handfuls of black mane and leaned forward. "Fast, Moon. Let's show them fast."

Moon Spot took off after Strong Wind. They went fast: two sure-footed mountain horses and the two mountain children, chasing the eagle, leaving the high snow and their home mountain and the whole of their old lives behind.

The terrible thing was that Serik was right. The eagle was so full of songbird that she was flying low, sometimes hardly flying at all. She pulled out far, far in front of them, but never up and away, never quite out of sight as they galloped down mountain, through the snow drifted in the folded places, across ridges scoured bare by the wind, farther and farther from their home. Far ahead, the eagle alighted on an outcrop, beating her wings in warning. She was huge, and she looked bigger on the ground than she did in the sky.

Over and over, the eagle perched and rested, and then took off again as they came close. But she rested longer each time, and let them get closer each time. And when she flew again it was not as far.

Serik tore after her, and Aisulu galloped alongside.

The wind of their motion slapped and howled in Aisulu's ears. "Serik, wait!" she shouted. "Serik!"

But her brother's heart was hurting so much that he could not listen to her. So Aisulu stopped calling. The eagle, watching them come, had bad-luck comets for eyes.

Every time they came close, the eagle rose on heavy wings. The wings made a noise like their mother shaking out a rug. With her voice, though, the eagle made no sound. Every time she let them come a little closer.

Finally, at the bottom of the mountain, the eagle alighted on a heap of bones—the twisted ruin of a camel skeleton —and did not rise again. Her beak was open and glinting. She looked at them. Her eyes were perfectly round.

Aisulu reined up beside her brother and looked back into those yellow eyes. She was hot under her shapan, with sweat running down her backbone. But there was a tight cold place where her stomach should be. This eagle was broken. Something so large and wild—broken.

"Serken," she whispered. "Let's just go."

The broken eagle twitched her head toward Aisulu's voice. But Serik didn't even look at her. He slid down from the horse like a cat round a corner, both sneak and swagger.

The eagle watched Serik. Suddenly she hacked and shuddered, and then threw up a mass of songbird. She spread her wings—her huge wings, wider than Aisulu was tall. But even having made herself lighter, she could not lift. She did not rise.

The sky over them was big and lonely, as if the five of them—horse and horse and girl and boy and eagle—were the only creatures under it. It felt bad to Aisulu. Cold and bad, as if the world had already gone wrong. The mountain tilted at her back, alight with new snow. A little wind whispered and curled around her ankles.

She thought wildly: *Burkit makes burkitshi*—the eagle makes the eagle hunter. She'd heard that all her life. *The eagle chooses,* she thought. *The eagle.* And this one—

"Serik," she said again.

"Shut *up*, Aisulu."

The eagle's head jerked toward Serik's shout. Still she did not rise.

Serik started to take off his coat. Aisulu could see that he meant to throw it over the eagle, because of course they had no net. He kept his eyes on the bird's eyes and fumbled with the metal buttons. One, two, three, four. He eased one shoulder forward and free. But then, as he twisted to free the other shoulder, his limping leg made him waver a little.

As he wavered, the eagle struck.

The eagle screamed—a huge high wild sound—and rose and swung her talons out. They were curved like crescent moons. They were sharp as blades. They could take down deer.

Serik shouted and staggered backward.

And then something snapped. It sounded like a branch breaking. But it wasn't a branch. It was Serik's leg.

He tumbled down and started screaming.

"Serken!" Aisulu ran toward him—toward the claws of the eagle too. Boy and eagle were both down. Serik was twisting under his half-off coat, and the eagle was flapping under her exhaustion. Aisulu skidded to her knees. Strong Wind screamed and reared, hooves crashing into the loose stones beside her hand.

Horse and boy and eagle all screamed. But Aisulu didn't. She wanted to, but there was no one to hear. No one at all under all that sky.

She grabbed Serik under the armpits and dragged him back.

Her brother's voice came out as a wordless thing between gasp and shout—she knew she was hurting him. But the eagle was gripping the grass and flapping, as if trying to stay perched on top of struggling prey. Its big wings almost brushed them, and Aisulu didn't dare stop so close. She dragged Serik one pace, two paces, three, four, away from the wings and talons. His feet left grooves in the sand, and in snow that made scales on top of the sand. He was stiff and gulping down screams, but then they bumped over a rock and he went limp in her arms.

Aisulu fell backward, Serik's body tangling her legs. "Serik!" She struggled out from under him. "Serik!" His golden-brown skin had gone gray. There were beads of sweat as big as raindrops all over his nose and forehead. She could see the pulse struggling between the strained cords of his neck.

"You're alive," she gasped. She pushed the sweat off his face with both hands. "You're alive. Serik.

"What do I do?" Aisulu sometimes talked to the sky

or the flowers, but now she was talking to nothing at all. "What do I do?"

Five paces away, the eagle looked at them with cold, cold eyes.

"I'll splint it," said Aisulu. "I'll splint it, and . . . and . . ." There would have to be a next thing after that, and she didn't know what it was.

The eagle looked at them.

It held Aisulu in its eyes as if she were the whole world. It was as if the air had turned to glass. She couldn't move. But her brother. She had to save her brother. And the way to do that, the next thing to do, was to make a splint.

The eagle would not strike again — she thought it would never move again. Aisulu tore herself from its eyes and bolted sideways. She needed branches. There was a little stand of larch in the wrinkled dip that probably marked a streambed. She ran for it like a rabbit running for a hole. She broke into the larches, thrashing through the leaves.

The light was dappled there, green and strange. There were fallen branches — there were poles. She gathered them and dragged them back to Serik, a tumbling run, the poles bouncing along the ground behind her. Serik lay where she'd left him, an awkward heap of a boy, his body half twisted out of his coat. His eyes were open and wet.

And five paces away —the eagle. The great bird sat still on the ground. Her shoulders were hunched. Her tail was spread out. She was blinking big slow blinks. They had broken her, and she was blinking down to death.

Aisulu laid the branches on either side of Serik's thigh. Her too-big shapan was belted to keep it warm: she fumbled with the buckle, her hands shaking. "I'm going to splint it, Serik. I'm going to splint it and tie it to the other one." She put her hand on the break. Even through his jeans Serik's leg felt hot.

He stirred at her touch, and his breath whined.

"I've got you, Serik," she said. "Why don't you—" She looked up at the slowly blinking eagle. "Close your eyes."

She could not bear to look at Serik's face. She looked straight down at her hands as she tied on the splint, and her brother screamed.

When he stopped, she looked up. He'd passed out. Slivers of white moon eyes showed behind tangled black eyelashes. "Serik," she whispered. She looked up, and the eagle was slumped on the ground now.

Its eyes were open; it was looking at her. But it was motionless. It almost looked calm.

Aisulu let herself kneel there, one breath, two breaths, three breaths. She was that frightened. The wind was cold in her sweaty hair. But then she put her hands on her thighs, and she got up. She stood up straight as an Imam saying a blessing. Then she picked up the larch poles.

The eagle didn't move even as Aisulu whistled the nervous horses back over and built a drag sled of larch poles and flat leather reins and Strong Wind's rug-saddle.

Then she tied the whole contraption to Moon Spot's back—Moon Spot, whom she would trust with her life. She used every scrap of rein and bridle she could pull off Strong Wind. In that moment, she didn't care whether Serik's horse followed them home or fell off a cliff. She needed Moon Spot, and she needed the leather rope.

The sled was built. Getting Serik onto it was an ugly business of pulling and rolling. Serik's hands fisted and breath whistled past his teeth. His skin was cold and gray. Sweat soaked his hair. She tucked his coat under his chin like a blanket and tried not to look at his leg.

Moon Spot snorted and kept stepping backward and forward. The sled rocked. Serik moaned. "Easy, easy," said Aisulu, to her horse, to her brother, to the eagle with its gold fixed eyes. "We're going home."

As she coaxed Moon Spot into a slow walk, she looked back.

The eagle was still lying there. Watching them.

There were wolves in that country, singing in the darkness. There were corsac foxes, golden and clever. There were snow leopards that moved like ghosts and rumors. An eagle that could not fly would quickly be something's dinner.

Aisulu looked at the eagle. She took two steps farther away from the eagle, toward her home.

Then she stopped, and she darted back to the eagle's side.

Chapter Three

THERE ARE THINGS TOO BIG to have words about.
Things that leave the heart as empty and wild as the sky.

For Aisulu: her broken brother, the broken eagle.

Her brother, gray and loose-eyed. Her brother, tied to a
drag sled.

The eagle, wrapped as if in a straightjacket. The eagle,
dead weight under Aisulu's arm.

She'd scooped the eagle up and it had not resisted. She'd
taken off her shapan, wrapped it around the wings and
claws, and tied the sleeves up tight. Wedged under her arm
now, the eagle was still. The eyes and the beak were frozen
and open. It was as if fear and exhaustion had turned the
bird into a statue.

Aisulu felt too heavy and too light. As if her gut would
knot itself up. As if her heart would come right up her
through her mouth. She didn't have words.

But she could keep walking.

So she took Moon Spot's lead in her free hand, and she

walked for home. The sweet horse followed, her nose nearly on Aisulu's shoulder. The drag sled carrying her brother rocked along behind. The sun was bright, but the wind, blowing off the new snow, was cold as metal. Aisulu shivered without her shapan. The eagle under her arm seemed to grow heavier.

They had chased the eagle all the way down the north slope, around the western flank of the mountain. It was not a place Aisulu knew. The land in the mountain's rain shadow was rocky and dry—too dry for grazing—though crossed right now by rivulets of snowmelt. There were no herds in sight, no dwellings. No help. Aisulu and Moon Spot went step by step, seeking the smooth way, crossing the sandy, scraggly slopes and the softening fingers of new snow. Strong Wind followed, farting occasionally.

At intervals she put down the eagle and checked on her brother, crouching to see his face. She gave him water, tipping a canteen to his lips. She tucked his coat close. She told him he would live.

Even those times when his eyes were open he said nothing.

His eyes were strange. Pain had changed them. They had the look of the eagle's eyes, almost: they seemed both lifeless as glass, and looking at things that were far, far away.

Serik could not hear her, and Aisulu could not speak.

She shifted the bundled eagle to her other arm. It surged once inside the fabric, for a moment panic and strength and then utter stillness. Serik groaned. Aisulu could feel her heartbeat pushing against her eardrums, *thump thud*.

Step by step. Around the mountain, under the indifferent sky.

It was sunset before — finally — they came over a rumpled crest and looked down on their home. There were three gers, the canvas walls and roofs round and gray and weathered, cupped in the high hollow like eggs in a nest. Around them was the happy clutter of gear and animals, the threads of smoke rising slantwise in the cold wind.

A family group of gers is called an aul, and this was theirs. Their aul. Their summer camp. Their home.

Aisulu paused at the crest of the hill, because it seemed right to pause. She put the eagle down and wiped Serik's face one more time. His weird eyes looked at her. "We made it, Serken," she whispered. "We're home."

Serik's hand moved. He was tied to the drag sled and he could not lift his arm. But, peeking out from under his coat, his hand moved. He reached for her, the inch the rope let him reach.

She put the water down and took his hand in hers.

"I know. But we made it."

She was only hoping that he understood her. His eyes

37

seemed to have pain stirred into them, the way salt is stirred into tea. She hoped he would say something like *good*, or *thank you*, or just her name. But what he said was "Don't tell."

"Don't?" she began, confused. "They'll see, Serik—"

He was so hurt, so changed—she was dragging him in a sled—of course everyone would see what had happened.

"Not that," he whispered.

Did he mean the eagle? But that, too—she was carrying the eagle, and they'd see that, too. She felt sick with what they had done to the eagle, but they would have to tell. There was no way not to.

But Serik said: "The limping, Aisulu—don't tell."

What he had said in the blizzard: *I'll lose everything*.

At that moment, Strong Wind came to the crest beside them and realized where he was. He took off down the slope and galloped into the aul, his tail high, as if *he'd* saved someone. A bolting, saddleless horse: Aisulu could imagine how scared that might make her mother and father. She pulled free of Serik's hand and stood up, shouting and waving an arm above her head. Her voice sounded small, washed away in the empty bigness of the sky. She was sure she would not be heard. But in the next moment people came streaming toward her. They were so far away they seemed small, but they ran toward her, not just her parents and her aunts and uncles, but other people too. All the people of the mountain.

She crouched back down to help her brother. The snow here was thin and blown into scales and bare patches. "Here they come, Serken. Just hold on."

Serik's throat worked as if he were swallowing a stone. His breath came out in lumps. And then a lump of words: "Aish, please don't—"

"Serken . . ." She did not know what to say. Her eyes broke from him to watch the people running. Their mother came fastest. Soon Aisulu could hear what she was calling. It was: "Serik! Serik!"

Aisulu was the one who had shouted. She was the one who had brought her brother home. But no one was saying her name. She felt herself get smaller even as she rose and stood up straight.

"My boy, my boy—oh, what happened?" Rizagul fell to her knees beside Serik. Her jerking hands made Moon Spot snort and shift. Rizagul looked at Aisulu, desperate. At the eagle, confused. "What happened?"

Aisulu had no chance to answer. Suddenly she was in a press of people and voices. There were second cousins, and people from the lowland gers. Someone cut the drag sled free. Someone lifted one end, someone lifted the other end, and they carried Serik down the hill. The family swallowed up Serik and the stretcher, and left Aisulu standing speechless on the crest of the ridge, holding a broken eagle.

Because she was not the one hurt, she was forgotten. But ten steps down, her father turned around.

"Aisulu," he said. Which was enough. Which was perfect. She just needed to hear her name.

She dashed toward him.

"Little fox kit—what on earth are you holding?"

"It's— it's an eagle. Serik and me—it's hurt."

Her father was already looking away, watching the others carry Serik into their ger. "Well," he puffed. "Well. Dulat can take a look."

Dulat was his older brother, the ruler of their aul. Once, he had been a burkitshi, an eagle hunter. He wasn't anymore.

Aisulu would think about that in a moment. Right now, her father, whose name was Abai, put one big hand on her head and gathered her against his coat. She trembled a little. His voice rumbled against her ear. "I went up the mountain as soon as the snow stopped. To find you. Everyone has been looking . . . since the storm . . ."

The neighbors and cousins. The people of the mountain. Helping to look.

"Your mother was so worried, but I knew you would be safe. You are so smart. I knew you and your brother would find each other and keep each other safe."

"Ake," she gulped—it was a child's word for *father*—

Serik was . . ." Aisulu did not know how to explain. Even the one word of her brother's name made a rock in her throat.

"You did well, my Aisulu, my fox kit, to bring him home. You did it just right."

But she had not done right. Under the blanket, in the blizzard, she had felt something wrong stick in her like a swallowed bone. And nothing had been right since. They had hurt the eagle. And Serik—he had begged her not to tell.

Abai let out a huge puff that might have been a laugh or a sob. "When I saw his idiot horse . . ." He patted Moon Spot's neck, and then closed one big hand around Aisulu's little shoulder and squeezed. "I was very glad, Aisulu, to see you."

She knew he meant "and Serik." But he didn't say that. He said her name.

The crowd of people carried Serik into his own home, into the little ger with the yellow door.

From outside the open door, Aisulu could see the glow of the stove and a single light bulb over the table. They put her brother on that table. From the doorway, Aisulu watched the jostling crowd of backs as people bent around him—the darkness of men's hair, the bright knots of women's scarves tied at the napes of necks. Someone knocked the light bulb: shadows swung. Objects flurried from hand to hand—leather straps and broom handles for a better splint; city medicine wrapped in white plastic, torn open in someone's teeth. The flash of the syringe.

Aisulu took three steps backward into the cold twilight.

There was nothing for her to do. She didn't want to do the things that the men and women were doing for Serik. They were awful. The things that were hers to do—the penning up of the baby goats, the spreading of dung to dry, the churning of the mare's milk fermenting in its blue plastic barrel—none of them seemed important.

Inside, the people pulled Serik's leg straight. A scream struck her, and then the silence.

Shuddering, Aisulu sank into a crouch, clutching the eagle to her chest. She looked at the yellow door. She looked at its raised orange panels with their painted turquoise scrolls and curlicues. The color was fading from them as the light went down.

And then, in front of her nose, boots.

Big black boots, dusty and scuffed with work, and jeans, and curled hands that looked as if they wanted to grip something.

Dulat, her uncle.

When Aisulu's grandfather had died, a year before,

Dulat had been summoned home from his work in the far-off capital city. He was the eldest son: he had a duty. He had brought with him a foreign wife. What he had left behind, Aisulu could not even guess, but she thought it was something. Dulat seemed hollowed out, and his empty insides sometimes filled up with bitterness. He ruled the aul, but he did not yet seem to fit into it.

In front of his boots, Aisulu could not get out a sound —but she held up the wrapped and frozen eagle.

In the thickening dark, Dulat crouched down. Now she could see his broad face and thick mustache, his eyes glittering as he took the bundled eagle from her and set it between them on the ground. He pulled a flashlight out of his pocket and stuck it between his teeth. In the jittering light he undid the tied sleeves of the straightjacket-shapan.

The next instant the flashlight beam was full of whirling, flapping, slashing wings. Then the eagle fell still again. Its beak was open, yellow-edged and blue-gleaming. Its feathers looked almost black. Its pointed tongue protruded.

Dulat grunted around the flashlight and pushed the eagle against the ground with one hand. He ran the other hand over the wings, across the tail. The eagle was no longer the sleek creature in the embroidered coat she had been among the songbirds. Feathers were bent up and sticking out everywhere. One wing was flopping. The eagle looked as disjointed as if she had already been slaughtered.

Dulat looked up at Aisulu and the flashlight caught her in the face. She jerked back, blinded. "It's hurt," said Dulat, into her blindness. It seemed as if his voice had come loose from the rest of him. "It's damaged."

There was a pause. Aisulu saw her uncle's bulk shift. She heard a sound—like Serik's leg-breaking sound, a meaty snap. Then there was stillness.

Dulat stood up.

When Aisulu could see again she found the eagle lying in the dust at her feet. It was dead.

The eagle and her brother—her brother and the eagle—

Horror seemed to trickle down her spine like snow down her collar, and then she was frozen everywhere. She was so frozen that her heart felt stopped. Hurt. Damaged. Dead.

Dulat put his hand on her head. "It would not have flown again," he said roughly. The hand pressed and ruffled her hair. He was making it stick out, like the eagle's broken feathers.

"Come on." Dulat lifted the eagle by its feet, and he headed for his own ger, the big ger that had once been his father's. Aisulu's mother and father and her other uncle were in the little ger helping Serik. The rest of the family —Aisulu's two aunties, her little cousins—were gathered outside Dulat's big ger. Dulat strode toward them, and they watched, silently, as people might watch a king coming.

The eagle's head scraped across the ground.

Long ago, before he had left for the city, Dulat had flown eagles in the great festivals. He had hunted in partnership with eagles in the long winters. He had carried eagles on top of his arm. Now, the eagle dangled. Dulat kicked the curious dogs away from it with the side of his boot.

No one spoke. Only Dulat's wife came forward. She was Tuvan, an outsider among the Kazakhs. The Tuvans spoke a different language, and worshiped strange spirits instead of Allah. Dulat's Tuvan wife had a name no one could get their mouths around: Kara-Kat-Kis, the blackberry woman. The family did not call her that. They called her the Fox Wife. It was not a compliment. It meant demon. Trickster. Shapeshifter. Witch.

"Dulat," she said, and she seemed to speak from the bottom of a well, her voice weird and echoey. "What have you done?"

Aisulu had been small when Dulat had left for Ulaanbaatar, Mongolia's capital city. Serik said he had been different before he left, but Aisulu did not remember that.

She remembered the picture of him and his father, her grandfather, each holding an eagle on top of his arm.

Golden eagles can live for thirty years or more, but a hunting eagle is set free when it is ready to have its own eagle family, after five or seven or ten years only. The only thing Aisulu was sure she remembered about Dulat was him coming back from releasing his eagle with tears streaming down his face. The next day he had flown away to the city, to the university, where he had studied and studied. Now he was back, and he was different.

He was now the kind of man who would drag a dead eagle through the aul, its beak leaving a groove in the snow and sand.

"Dulat," said the Fox Wife again, and he reared back from his name. For a moment Aisulu thought he would cuff his wife like a bear. But he did not.

"Take care of it." He tossed the eagle onto the ground at her feet. "Tourists will pay money for eagle feathers."

The Fox Wife picked up the dead bird, folding its wings together and cradling it in one arm. She made a little crooning noise and joggled the eagle as if it were a baby she was trying to send deeper into sleep.

Aisulu's auntie Meiz, who actually was holding a baby, stiffened and stared. Her other children bunched close and clung to her. There were whispers about the Fox Wife, and this was the worst of them: that she forgot the difference between the living and the dead, and in her hands the dead sometimes forgot too.

"You killed it." The Fox Wife slipped the fingers of her other hand into the circle made by the eagle's clenched yellow feet and curving black claws. "Dulat, why would you do this?"

"It was hurt," he said. "It was not going to fly again."

Aisulu wrapped her arms around her body, shivering.

Meiz shifted the sleeping baby on her shoulder. "What's happening with Serik?"

"Broken femur," said Dulat—a university word. "Broken thighbone." He glanced around at Aisulu. "It's a bad thing to break, but it's closed and clean. You did well to get him home."

Aisulu could not meet Dulat's eyes. She stepped back, and back again, until she was standing against the canvas wall of her own ger. Through the thick fabric came a murmur of voices, with no words carried. It was like listening to the blizzard through the blanket. She thought *Closed and clean*, but she knew it wasn't true. *My brother is sick,* she thought. Aisulu's people were herders and riders and nomads. They lived a long way from help. They knew how to set a broken bone. That was what they were doing for Serik: setting a bone. They did not know about the limping.

They didn't know what she knew: that he wasn't just *hurt*. He was *sick*.

Serik had begged her — he had grabbed her hand and begged her.

Dulat and the rest of the family were staring at her.

She spun away from how they were looking. Her ger was almost at her nose. It was made of a lattice frame wrapped outside with thick felt and then covered with canvas. The bottom inch of it was left open on summer days but wrapped in the evenings. One of Aisulu's jobs was tucking the ger in for the night. She usually did it with Serik — it was the one task they shared. She did it alone now, so that her brother would be warm. She dragged the heavy canvas strip around the ger. She tucked it in under the tension ropes. She made her home safe and snug. The blizzard had been only that morning; the darkening wind was cold. But she would keep her brother warm.

That tucking in the ger also pulled her away from Dulat's eyes — she told herself she wasn't thinking of that.

Her father, Abai, was there she reached the place where the lattice wall was strapped to the wooden door frame. He stood outside the door, staring out at the herd, which still needed to be penned up. His canvas hat was squashed in his thick hands. He looked old. Aisulu had never before thought that her father looked old. But he held himself carefully, as if his joints hurt. His face looked wet in the light that spilled from the ger behind him.

"Ake," she called softly.

He turned, squinting into the dimness. "Aisulu? I asked Dulat to find you— Take a look at—"

"He killed it," said Aisulu.

"What?"

"He killed the eagle," she rushed on. Her heart said: *Hurt. Damaged.* "I wrapped up the ger. Serik will be warm, because I wrapped up the ger."

"Little one . . ." Her father's big voice sounded so sad. "This is too much." He shrugged out of his canvas coat and wrapped it around her shoulders. It was warm, and it smelled like safety: like cooking smoke and horse and him. "Aisulu. You should rest. You should eat."

Aisulu pulled the coat closed around her. She ought to have been starving, but her stomach was twisted and cold. There was a difference between hurt and sick. She should tell her father, but Serik had begged her.

"I am sorry about the eagle," Abai said. "But your brother will be all right. You saved him."

For just a moment she was frozen. When eagle hunters trained eagles, they tied live rabbits to leashes. Sometimes the rabbits ran, leaping into the air at the end of their ropes, at the end of their lives. But more often they stood still, the way she was standing. They froze, as if that would save them.

It never did.

And she was not a rabbit. "Ake," she said. "Serik is—he was limping, before he broke it."

"Before?"

Her father sounded so innocently puzzled that Aisulu almost did not explain. But she would not be the rabbit on the leash. "Ake," she said. "Serik has been limping for a long time." Aisulu put her hand on her leg and squeezed it. "He puts his hand on his thigh," she told her father. "He squeezes. I think it hurts him very much. And then it broke, in the place that he squeezes."

Aisulu's words settled on her father, and on her own heart, and began to make changes. She could feel the changes. She knew that after this moment, her life would never be the same.

"He asked me not to tell," she said, and though she was trying to be brave, her voice was little. She closed her eyes.

Her father's sudden hug surprised her. He crushed her against his chest. "Oh, Aisulu," he said. "It is good you did."

"He begged me not to tell." Her voice felt broken. The roof of her mouth ached. She fisted her hands against the sheepskin of his vest. "Ake," she whispered. "Will he be all right?"

For a long moment, Abai did not answer. She could hear his heart talking under her cheek, saying *Ser-ken, Ser-ken.*

"We will take him to town, to the clinic," her father said, and pulled away from her. "We'll find a doctor." He brushed his thumbs up her cheeks and tucked her wind-stroked hair behind her ears. "It is good that you told, Aisulu. It is good."

Then he went striding off like a man with business. Aisulu took a few steps after him, then stopped. She sat down on a stone, between the night herds and the empty mountain. The sky kept falling. It grew thicker around her. High overhead the Milky Way opened like a great wing.

After a little while she heard an engine cough, catch, and growl—a motorcycle. Its one headlight came on, and her father drove away until the falling sky swallowed him.

The night fell around Aisulu as she sat there, and the gers around her began to glow at their doors and smoke holes, faint and warmly gold.

She was tired, but she was not sure where to go. The ger with the yellow door was her home. She did not want to go in there. Serik was there. He had begged her not to tell, and she had told. She did not want to face him.

She sat.

She sat for such a long time that sleep fell slowly around her. Like the falling sky it was soft. It made things blink and blur. Her head dropped and jerked. She dreamed of eagles. While she was dreaming, an arm wrapped around her. She stood up inside the arm and walked leaning on it. Before her was the big ger, the blue door looking black in the darkness. The ger that had been her grandfather's, the newlywed home of Dulat and—

The Fox Wife.

The Fox Wife took Aisulu inside and set her on the bed that was for guests. She peeled the coat from Aisulu's shoulders. She was singing something tuneless and endless, the way the wind sang.

"Thank you," said Aisulu.

The Fox Wife smiled—a gleam of teeth in the dimness—and her hand fumbled upward to find the light switch. The one bulb came on. "You *are* awake."

"Sort of."

"Then go back to sleep. It's very late." Her accent made her words rock and swing. Aisulu blinked at her. The Fox Wife reached around behind the back of her own neck and untied her headscarf, unwrapped her hair. It came swinging and tumbling down to her waist. It was not black, but dark, dark red, like blackberries. Like dried blood.

"Kara-Kat-Kis?" Aisulu used the Fox Wife's real name because that seemed polite. "Do you have brothers and sisters?" *A brother* was what she really wanted to say. *Do you have a brother?* What would it be like to be without one?

The Fox Wife smiled. "I was twins once. A good sister and an evil sister. Only one of me survived. I forget which."

"Oh," said Aisulu, shivering. She was half asleep and thought she might be dreaming. The Fox Wife had laid her in a place of honor, which was not right. She was only a girl. Above her, two eagle wings were spread against the crown of the ger, tied open. The bird Dulat had killed. The body gone. Had they eaten it? Had it tasted bitter?

"That's what they say, anyway," said the Fox Wife. Aisulu looked at her. She was framed against the canopied opening of her marriage bed. The edge of the canopy was hung with pelts, the gold and red pelts of corsac foxes. They seemed to sway. Or was Aisulu swaying?

"You have done everything that can be done, child," said the Fox Wife, her accent tilting and blurred. "The herd is home and the stars are watching us. Go to sleep."

So Aisulu slept.

The next morning her mother woke her up to do the milking.

Waking in the Fox Wife's ger was so strange and her mother was so normal that for a moment Aisulu thought she was still dreaming. Had she dreamed all the terrible things: the blizzard and the broken bone and the thrash of the flashlit eagle? Rizagul's face was scrubbed and her head-scarf was tied straight and tight. "I let you sleep through the yaks," she said.

Yaks were milked at dawn, and it was broad daylight. Aisulu pushed herself upright and blinked, her eyes gummy.

"The men must take the herd out," said Rizagul. "Come on, now."

"Eej," said Aisulu, a small word for *mother*. "Eej, I didn't mean to—"

They never got up like this. They got up in morning when the world looked half made; they washed and prayed together and stood together in front of the speckled mirror while her mother brushed and brushed Aisulu's unruly hair.

But now her mother was already heading out the door. Aisulu put on her boots in a hurry. She did understand: milking does not stop simply because the world has ended. The goats needed to be milked before they went out to graze, and they needed to graze all day, so they needed to be milked now. If they did not graze, they would not give milk, and if they did not give milk, her family would be hungry.

The aul was quiet. The herd was drifting up one side of the hollow. The baby goats were milling about in their night pen. The neighbors who had searched the mountain and helped her hurt brother were gone, off to tend their own herds. The morning was bright and thin; the sun glinted fiercely off the new snow on the mountains.

Aisulu trotted to catch up with her mother, bits of icy snow scattering and shattering under her boots, empty pails rattling in her hands. Her aunties were already sorting the goats into strings, one belonging to each brother. They were late. Her mother walked fast and stiffly. But how could they worry about being late, when Serik was still—

Serik was nowhere in sight. Aisulu thought of the morphine, the syringes that were kept in a tin box under her parents' bed.

She began capturing the nanny goats bearing her father's mark—one notch in their left ear—and wrestled them into a line, looping leather thongs around their necks. Her mother squatted to begin the milking before this was even finished, and that was not right: they roped the goats together, and then they milked together.

Aisulu could only see the nape of her mother's neck, and the way her hair was tangled in the knot of her headscarf, which was yanked tight. Her own braids were a mess— sleep-crushed and wind-shredded. She tucked them behind her ears and crouched opposite her mother.

Rizagul was pulling hissing streams of milk into her pail.

"Eej—" said Aisulu. "Is Serik . . . ?"

"Sleeping," said her mother. Behind her, Aizulu's auntie Meiz was getting trouble from one of her goats. Meiz grunted and swayed into a different squat—she was pregnant again, just showing—then slugged the offending nanny goat in the udder.

"Your father has gone to borrow a truck," said Rizagul. "We'll take Serik to the clinic. Or maybe a hospital."

There was no hospital within a hundred miles—a distance that seemed almost impossible to Aisulu. The stones that had pressed into her in the blizzard were making her feel as if she'd been hit all over.

"While we're gone you'll have to do the milking, and the churning, and . . ." Rizagul trailed off. She seemed to be looking at the white blankness of the mountain peak, which stood against the sky as if something had been erased. "I know you can manage, Aisulu. You are growing into a fine young woman. I know you'll make me—"

Aisulu could only hope that the next word would be *proud*. Her mother did not say it. Instead, she stood up, suddenly, shielding her eyes. A truck was coming up the mountain.

It was a hay truck, with an open pen on the back. It was a strange color, the color an old Soviet storybook might paint the sky: a flat ugly blue. No sky in the world had ever been that color. The truck growled up the mountain toward the aul. Black Dog and Yellow Dog lunged, snarling, at the tires; the yaks bellowed. Her father swung through the open space where the passenger door had long since been removed. He went into the ger where Serik was sleeping.

The cousin who was driving shut off the engine and a bird-song silence began.

"Finish this," said Rizagul, thrusting the half-full pail of milk at Aisulu.

Pail dangling, Aisulu stood and watched her mother stride down the slope. When she could move again, she started milking—badly, but fast. As she milked she watched. In the aul things were happening like a movie, like something she couldn't touch. The cousin hopped down from the truck, leaving the driver's door open behind him. He took off his baseball cap and hit it against his leg to knock out the dust. He put it back on. He stretched.

Meanwhile, her mother and father moved quickly—jerkily—in and out of the ger, carrying things. Her father brought rug after rug, the thick felt rugs that could be wall or mat or even saddle. He spread them across the bottom of the truck bed. Her mother brought a cloth bag, probably full of bread or dried cheese. She brought a suitcase, and then another.

The bed of the truck was big enough to hold a whole ger, poles and covers and rugs and all. With only the rugs and the two little suitcases in it, it looked empty. The slatted sides cut the sun into beams, gold with the dust raised by the rugs. The truck sat there, full of light and nothing. From the top of the slope, where Aisulu was trapped, milking, it looked like a toy.

Then her father and her uncle Dulat carried Serik out. He was still on the stretcher Aisulu had built. He was sleeping—still drugged. Abai lifted his son from the stretcher and settled him on the felt rugs. He bent over and kissed Serik's forehead.

Serik didn't move. Their father straightened up. Their mother climbed into the back of the truck. The cousin was turning the crank at the front. The engine started with a cough and a roar.

They were going.

They'll send me away, Serik had said, and they were, but they were going with him. They were leaving her behind. She hadn't dreamed that they would all go, and so quickly, that she wouldn't get to say goodbye. But they were.

Aisulu dropped her milk pail and started to run.

Her father climbed up into the passenger seat. He leaned his head out and said something to Dulat. Aisulu couldn't hear it. Dulat nodded. The truck pulled away.

She wasn't close enough. She was left with dust and diesel fumes, and no goodbyes.

Chapter Four

AISULU WATCHED THE TRUCK until she couldn't hear it, and then until she couldn't see it, and then until its dust plume faded into the haze of distance. Her brother, going. There was a thought that kept trying to rise and block her throat: He was going away to die. He would never be coming back.

Her aunties were coming down the slope with the milk pails. They had finished the milking—even hers—and untied the strings of goats. The herd was milling around the hollow. Her small cousins were letting the goat kids out of the night pens, and the baby goats streamed toward their nannies, baaing and bouncing happily. Her younger uncle, Yerzhan, was already on his horse, ready to take out the herd.

"All right, Aisulu?" That was her older uncle, Dulat, hovering behind her. His eyebrows were scrunched down, and he was looking at Aisulu as if she were a difficult math problem.

She could not speak to him. Even looking at him made her feel a jolt like the flashlight hitting her, the moment when he'd snapped the eagle's neck.

Then she thought: *The eagle.*

She and Serik had stood on the shale outcrop and watched the eagles. And she had thought: *Their eggs must have hatched.* The great eagle eating songbirds—she had been a mother eagle. Freed from sitting on her eggs, she had been feeding herself, and gathering food for her chicks. But now she was dead, and the sky was empty.

They had killed a mother eagle, in the season for eaglets.

They had killed the mother eagle, and so the eaglet would die.

Unless she went to save it.

Aisulu found herself standing very still. It was as if her heart had stopped.

She knew what she should be doing—what her mother would want her to do. Milking and churning milk into butter and making milk into cheese. Her mother wanted her to be a young lady. Her mother wanted her to manage.

Her mother had left without saying a word.

Aisulu did not pick up the milk pail. Instead, she put a ball of twine in her pocket. Instead, she found a sack that had once held five pounds of flour: cotton cheaply printed with pink roses. Instead, she found her horse.

Her uncles, Dulat and Yerzhan, had taken the herds up the mountain. Her auntie Meiz was busy with her small herd of children. The Fox Wife stood at the door of the big ger and watched Aisulu mount, saying nothing. No one scolded Aisulu. No one said *Stop*. And so, for the second day in a row, she rode up into the high hard sky.

She'd always envied her brother's freedom to ride out with the herd every day, to ride into high places and stand in the wind. Maybe this was that freedom, but she didn't feel free. She felt like a kite with its string cut.

Her path took her past the sky shrine where she and Serik had weathered the summer blizzard. The snow was still there, but little trickles of meltwater were running over the rocks. Patches of stone and green were opening. The bodies of the little birds no longer looked like beads on blank fabric. They had each melted a little hole in the snow, sunk into it like gray footsteps. She could hardly see them.

Snagged on a branch of a dried thistle was Serik's hat. Aisulu leaned out and grabbed it. It was blue velvet, worn thin, with gold embroidery around the band. Aisulu held it in one hand for a long while, then stuffed it into her other pocket.

She kept Moon Spot to a walk. They cut sideways along the snow line, through folded meadows, across ridges of stone. Always they went toward the crag where she had seen the eagles.

Finally there it was, rising in front of her: an outcropping of shale, and it stuck up from the loose skin of the mountain like an old skeleton, like the backbone of the camel where the eagle had perched. The outcrop was taller than any building she had ever seen—three times as tall, four times, five times, ten times. It got bigger as she rode closer to it. The sky above it stayed empty. She started to be afraid.

A kite with its string cut doesn't fly. It falls.

Aisulu coaxed Moon Spot to the base of the crag. There, they stopped. Without the sound of Moon Spot's hooves, it was quiet. The sharp-edged stones whistled and moaned as they sliced into the wind.

Aisulu tilted up her chin. Above her—high above her —was the eagles' nest. It was taller than she was, wider around than her outstretched arms. The bottom layers of it were gray, but the top sticks were fresh. Eagles have many nests, and come back to them across many years. But the fresh sticks meant the eagles had come to this nest in this season.

Nevertheless, the sky was empty.

The mother eagle was not in the sky, and it was not in the nest. They had killed it. She and Serik. Dulat had finished the job, but they had killed it.

They had left an eagle baby motherless, up in that nest. And it would die.

Aisulu dismounted and walked to the base of the outcropping. The shale was the color of dried blood, brown and brown-red and almost-purple, crusted with lime-green lichen. It was steep. The squares and chunks of it were like blocks.

They were like stairs.

Aisulu was a mountain child. She could climb. But to climb a shale outcrop . . . Shale cracked. It shifted. It could shift under her. What would happen if she fell and broke a leg, as Serik had broken his? She had helped Serik. There was no one here to help her.

"Stop thinking about that," she said out loud, and even her voice sounded small. She was a girl who did things. So she did this: She hoisted herself onto a block at the base of the outcrop. She wedged her fingers farther up the crack. She began to climb.

Aisulu put her feet onto this block and into that crack, choosing each step. Soon she was five feet up, and then ten. At twenty feet, a stone gave way under her boot. She yelped and grabbed tight, one foot pedaling over emptiness before she found a place to put it. A chunk of stone the size of her skull fell away. It made a clicking, cracking noise as it bounced downward. It sounded like bones breaking.

Her eyes followed the falling stone. She could see the worn cuffs of her hand-me-down jeans, gone to frazzled white loops at the heels where she stepped on them over and over. Beyond that there was only air.

A lot of air.

Below her Moon Spot whinnied like a worried mother.

"I'm okay!" she shouted down. "It's okay," she told her hands, which were curled into claws and hooked into a crack. Yarrow grew from a fissure there, wire stemmed and sharp smelling. "It's okay," she told the yarrow. She stopped looking down.

She looked up.

There was the eagles' nest. Ten more feet.

Aisulu blew through her lips like a horse and climbed another step.

The nest was wedged into a crack in the cliff face. Aisulu climbed to the crack and began to inch sideways along it. Both her palms were skinned, and one of them was bleeding. Her fingers felt as if they were made of knotted leather. Her mind said to them: *Open*. But they didn't open. She had to put them in her mouth and pull them open. They even didn't feel like hers.

She was so afraid that her toes curled against the bottom of her boots, but she kept moving. The sun-struck shale was warm. The wind was cold. She could smell her own sweat. She could smell something else, now, as she came close to the nest.

Old blood. Death.

The crack deepened then, became almost a small shelf cave, a ledge floor and an overhang roof. Aisulu got down on her knees and crawled forward until she could look into the nest.

And there it was: the baby eagle.

Only one. It lay limp. It smelled like death. Its eyes were filmy, like death. She thought: *It's dead.*

And then its eyes opened.

Inner eyelids rolled sideways. It was those eyelids that had made the eaglet's eyes look dull. Now they were bright. They looked right at her. They were eyes that could see for three miles, but instead they were looking three miles deep into her.

"*Masha-Allah,*" Aisulu breathed. *Thank God.* The baby was alive.

The eaglet's eyes were a dark contrast to its white coat of fuzzy down. They were not quite black—just brown enough that she could see the pupils dilate. *Alive.* Aisulu had never seen anything more alive.

And in front of her, it was dying. It was a baby, as she'd thought it would be—no bigger than a rabbit, gawky and fuzzy in its coat of white down. Its skin beneath the down looked bruise purple. Its yellow feet were clenched. It was not sitting up, but leaning limply against the side of the nest.

It kept looking at her for a moment; then it opened its beak and made a *kree* noise.

Aisulu *kree*d back to it, softly.

Kree, said the baby eagle. It had a folded, pointed tongue. Aisulu held perfectly still.

The eaglet lurched up away from the side of the nest. It was splay-legged as a baby with a full diaper. It wobbled. It spread its stubby, useless wings. And it tottered toward her.

Toward.

Kurr, it said.

"Hello," Aisulu whispered. Its mouth was yellow, like its feet, but the hook of the beak shaded to a bluish black.

The eaglet looked a mile deep inside her. She thought it could see that she had killed its mother. Its long black talons —already they were as long as her pinky—were wrapped up over its fisted feet. It wobbled on them like a man with frostbitten toes. She reached out and touched it with one fingertip. It was soft, softer than felt, softer than a newborn lamb, softer than a goat's ear. It was softer than anything she'd ever touched.

"Little soft," she said to it. "Hello. I'm glad I came for you. Hello."

The eagle tipped back its head and opened its beak.

"You're hungry," Aisulu said. She had no meat, of course. She was kneeling between the sheer stoneface and the drop, and she had nothing at all. "We killed your mother, little soft. My uncle. My brother and me. She's not coming back.

"And so . . ." Moving slowly, Aisulu pulled the sack out of her pocket. The little eaglet looked at her. The upper corners of its eyes were marked with a puff of tawny color, like eye shadow. The filmy eyelid slid across the dark eyes, side to side—alien, but sweet. Sleepy. *Kurr*, the eaglet purred.

Aisulu picked it up and stuffed it in the sack.

It weighed far less than she thought it would—less than a rabbit, about as much as a week-old kitten. Like a kitten it was fuzz and body warmth and bones. Fragile. But it yelled and thrashed with surprising power. The sack swung from side to side. Curled talons needled through the fabric, through the cheap roses. The blue-black point of the beak followed. Aisulu held the sack away from her body. It screamed.

"Yes, you're welcome," she murmured. She held the honking, swaying sack away from her body and spoke to it sternly. "Now, look: if you scratch me, I might fall. I might even fall on top of you, and then we'd both die. No one wants that."

The sack screamed again.

Aisulu gave up reasoning with it. She tied it to the back of her belt and began to climb down.

Moon Spot would do anything for Aisulu, but she had second thoughts about baby eagles.

The young horse came prancing to her side as she reached the ground. She snorted and blew warm and damp onto Aisulu's ears and cheeks, fussing like a grandmother.

"You're right, you're right, that was stupid," said Aisulu. "That was so, so stupid."

Now that she was on the ground, she was starting to feel every inch of the climb she had made. More: she could feel every inch of every fall she had not taken. She began to shiver, then shake. Now that she was safe, she was afraid.

She reached behind herself to retrieve the sack from her belt. The screaming had grown quieter during the climb, but she was still scratched across her back, where her shirt had pulled free and baby eagle talons had found bare skin. She'd been scratched through her jeans, too—she'd jerked and had nearly tumbled to her death, as promised.

Aisulu held the bag at arm's length. Moon Spot took a whiff, as if expecting apples, then arched her head away, wrinkling her lips up so far that her gums showed. She huffed in and snorted out. The look she gave Aisulu was pure betrayal.

"I know, he smells. Or she smells."

Bumffff, said the horse, a lip-whiffling sound of disapproval, of concern.

"And you don't like it. I know. But we need to take him. He'll need—"

At this point, Aisulu realized she did not know what baby eagles needed. Meat, presumably. But then what? She had no idea what to do. Her father would know; he was an eagle hunter's son. But her father was gone. Dulat would know, but she could not ask him, not after the flashlight and the snap.

"Let's just go," she said. She grabbed a fistful of wiry mane, ready to mount, but Moon Spot twisted sideways. Aisulu tried again, and again the horse sidestepped. "Really?" Aisulu released Moon Spot and put her free hand on her hip. "I've got enough to deal with right now, Moon."

The sack swung in her hand and whistled forlornly. Moon Spot looked up, tilted her head, and then went back to grazing, as if she had every intention of letting Aisulu walk away.

"You're bluffing," said Aisulu. "Come on."

Liquid green poop shot out the bottom of the sack and

Aisulu dodged, thrusting the sack away from her. The poop went a surprising distance and splattered into the grass with force.

"Please, Moon Spot," said Aisulu, and the horse snorted as if to say *oh, fine*.

Aisulu mounted. The sack screamed. Moon Spot swiveled her ears backward, like radar dishes. But she responded to Aisulu's knees, to the touch on her neck. They started for home.

Riding with her knees alone, Aisulu took her brother's hat out of her pocket. She sniffed it to smell her brother. Then she turned it upside down, reached into the sack, and retrieved the baby eagle. The sack was horribly sticky, and the little eagle was sticky too. She set it in the cup of the hat. It screamed at her for a second — *ker-reep, ker-reep, ker-reep* — then snuggled itself against the velvet.

Serik's hat didn't have a brim. Holding it was like holding a bowl. Little silver bobbles lined the edge. The eaglet worried one with its beak. It made the *kurr* sound again — a loving, lovely sound.

Then it pooped in the hat.

"Really?" said Aisulu.

The eaglet craned its long neck toward her, opening its beak wide. Aisulu tried to feed it some dried cheese. It turned its tiny head away, sighed, and closed its eyes.

It was an hour's ride back to the summer camp, and the little eagle was hungry. It woke and begged; slept and woke and begged. Every time it begged, it begged with less brightness. Its eyes got duller. Its neck stretched less far. How long could it go without food? How long had it been without food before she found it?

What did it need to eat?

What was she going to do?

By the time they got to the aul, Aisulu's arms ached from holding the hat steady. She was very tired, the kind of tired that was like heavy shoes. She stopped by the solar panels and dismounted, trying to think. Moon Spot leaned in, looking down her long nose and into the hat. She bumped against Aisulu's shoulder and sighed—a *what now?* sigh.

The eaglet was still asleep. Aisulu ran one pinky from the corner of its closed eye to the top of its round head. The little creature cracked an eyelid, but this time it did not lift its head.

"You will not die," she told it fiercely. "You will not."

But what could she do to save it?

Almost without thinking, Aisulu took the baby eagle to the last place she herself had found shelter: she took it to the Fox Wife, to the big ger that had been her grandfather's, whose dark blue door was blazed with painted roses. The door was propped open. Aisulu hesitated on the threshold. "Kara-Kat-Kis?"

The Fox Wife was standing in the dimness by the stove. She was silent. She was so still that she might have had antlers.

In the doorway, Aisulu lifted the hat in both hands, like an offering.

"It's an eagle," she said. "Will you help me?"

There was a long pause. Then the Fox Wife came into the square of light thrown by the door. Shadow spilled onto the floor behind her, seeming to start from her back, like a pair of wings. The Fox Wife looked down into the hat, and then up.

She smiled.

"It will need to eat something with bones," she said.

Chapter Five

"LET ME TEACH YOU," said the Fox Wife, "how to catch mice."

Aisulu sat on a wobbly stool with the light from the ger's open crown streaming down all around her. The table in front of her was covered with a plastic cloth. On the table sat her brother's hat. Inside that was a baby eagle. It was asleep. Maybe it was dying. "What does it need?" Aisulu put a finger beside one closed eye. This time it did not open. But she could feel the warmth of the creature, and the pulse that pounded through it, as if its body were one big heart. "What does it want?"

"Warmth," said the Fox Wife. "And meat." She picked up a poker and rattled up new flames from the smoldering dung fire. A puff of grass-smelling smoke rose. The Fox Wife turned and took a stone from her dresser.

Aisulu was not sure why there was a stone on the dresser. But then, the dresser mirror also featured the antlered skull of a reindeer—complete with bright blue bridle, because the Tuvan people rode and herded reindeer—a pair of heavy plastic glasses hooked by their one remaining ear piece, a wolf's anklebone on a string, and a headband of dark beads and red tassels. A stone did not seem so strange, compared to all that. And it was an ordinary stone: river-smooth and the size of a fist, black but crisscrossed with pale lines. The Fox Wife set it on the cookplate.

Then she turned and filled the kettle from the bucket by the door. The bucket—Aisulu looked at it. "I saw you go," said the Fox Wife. "I fetched the water for you."

Aisulu blinked. She was not sure what she had expected from her strange auntie, but simple work, simple kindness —fetching water—that wasn't it.

The Fox Wife handed Aisulu the heavy kettle. "To catch mice," she said, "you must find their holes. I will show you how they look. And then you pour the water into the hole. When the mice come out, you hit them with a stone."

The stone from the dresser was still sitting on the stove. "With a . . . hot stone?" Aisulu asked.

"With any stone," said the Fox Wife. "A heavy one is good. The biggest one you can swing hard."

"Uh," said Aisulu, who did not really want to become the doom of all mice. Her nose felt flared and tight with the thought.

"The little eagle will eat the mice. He is not big enough

for goat bones. He needs mouse bones. He will eat three mice at a time, ten times a day."

"That's a lot of mice," said Aisulu.

"He must grow into a lot of eagle. And he does not have long."

"Is it—is he male? How can you tell?"

"He's male now, because he will ask everything of you," said the Fox Wife. "But maybe he will grow into a great female eagle, a hunter's eagle."

The Fox Wife turned to her marriage bed, dark beneath the canopy of hanging fox furs. There was an embroidered bit of red silk covering the pillows. She took this and wrapped the hot stone in it. Then she put the whole thing into the upturned hat, beside the baby eagle. She lifted the limp body and draped it across the red warmth.

She turned to Aisulu. "Bring the kettle," she said. "Come."

The summer camp, it turned out, was a great kingdom of mice.

Aisulu had seen mice around, of course, usually being snapped sideways in the jaws of Yellow Dog. But she had not known there were so many. The Fox Wife led Aisulu beyond the well-trod circle of the gers. The snow had already vanished, leaving nothing behind but a darkness in the sand, a chill hiding in the places where the spindly plants clumped up. She dropped into a squat, her skirt sliding up over her knees, her eyes bright and fixed forward, like a predator's. "There," she said, and pointed.

Her finger parted two clumps.

She was pointing into a divot in the ground, no different from a thousand other divots. It had a dark hole in it, small as Aisulu's thumb.

"How did you find that?" said Aisulu.

"First you don't see them," said the Fox Wife. "And then you see them. Give me the kettle."

Aisulu passed it.

The Fox Wife poured a ribbon of water into the dark hole. She poured for a count of five. She waited for a count of three.

A mouse came shooting out of the hole, its brown fur black and oily with water.

The Fox Wife hit it with a rock.

She put the little body into an orange plastic basket. She stood and handed the kettle and the rock to Aisulu. "Now you."

Aisulu, without much optimism, took three steps and crouched. The soil was sand and pebble, and the plants were tough as wires. There were rumples and dips everywhere. She looked at them until she felt cross-eyed, but found nothing. She took another three steps and looked in another place. But still she didn't see any mouse holes. They needed to find mice. They had to find mice, or the eaglet would die.

The Fox Wife crouched down beside her. Aisulu could see the raw bones of her knees through the holes in her thick dark stockings. "Here," she said, and put a finger into the grass.

Mouse hole.

Aisulu took a deep breath and lifted the kettle. She poured. The mouse came out. She smashed. The mouse squeaked and crunched. The Fox Wife lifted it by its tail and put it in the orange basket. They both stood up and took three more steps.

The brown beast Aisulu called Curious Yak came wandering over. The yak bellowed and blew huge warm grass breath down the back of Aisulu's neck as she crouched again, and again could find no hole.

Snorf, said Curious Yak, and licked the back of Aisulu's hair, right up the part between her braids. Aisulu slapped the beast away without turning, squinting into the weeds and rocks. She did not see a mouse hole. But the Fox Wife stabbed with her fingers into the roots of a clump of irises. "Here," she said. She twisted a little. "And here. And here. And here." In a moment she had found five mouse holes.

Aisulu picked one, poured, struck, and winced at the

crunch. For the eagle, it was for the little eagle. She had promised to save it. She would save it.

They moved on without hunting in the other four holes. "Take one here, one there. Like a fox does." The Fox Wife's smile showed she knew very well what they called her. "Like catching the wild horses. You take one mare, and you leave the herd."

Away from the gers, step by step, they went, and the yak followed them. Every time they crouched, the Fox Wife could show Aisulu three holes, or four, or five, or six.

And the tenth time they stopped, something changed. The world seemed to slide and slip into place, and suddenly Aisulu could see the mouse holes too. She knew what they looked like. She knew where they were.

"Good!" The Fox Wife clapped in delight, like a little child. "Now you have eyes!"

Curious Yak made a low yak noise that meant either *Hurrah!* or *Milk me.*

"I have fox eyes," said Aisulu, grinning.

"Oh, no," said the Fox Wife. "You have the eyes of an eagle."

When they came back with the mice, the motherless eaglet was asleep but not dead. His whole body seemed to heave with his breath. He looked so fragile.

Aisulu put one finger on the soft down of the eaglet's head. He did not stir. "Hello, little," she coaxed. "We brought you food."

"Split it open," said the Fox Wife, handing Aisulu a mouse and a knife. "That's what his mother would do, while he's small. And he is weak. Split it, and give him the heart."

Aisulu again felt her lips and nose tighten up. Taking care of an eaglet involved more stickiness and crunching stuff than she had imagined. But she would not let the eaglet die. She spread a mouse out on the plastic tablecloth. As she lifted the knife, she found herself murmuring *"Bismillah,"* as if beginning the slaughterer's prayer, the one her father said to thank the goat for the gift of its life, and Allah for his gift of the goat. But she did not know the slaughterer's prayer, and she was only saying under her breath: *Live, live.*

She opened the mouse skin as if it had a zipper and peeled it back from the tiny ribs. She plucked out the heart, little as a knot in yarn, and put it on her fingertip. She eased the heart into the eaglet's limp beak.

For a moment nothing happened.

Then the beak quivered. And closed over the mouse heart.

The Fox Wife handed her a long splinter of wood, and

using this, Aisulu feed the eaglet bits of mice. Scrap by scrap: livers smaller than pinky nails, and grass-thin bones.

Slowly, the eaglet woke up. Strength came into him like butter forming in a churn. He got his splayed legs under him. He extended his funny long neck — so long he looked like a tiny sock puppet — and started to snap at the food.

When he had finished the third mouse, he looked up at Aisulu.

His eyes: they were dark, dark brown like hers, and bright like hers, like water that moves quickly. Those eyes looked at Aisulu as if she were taller than the sky and twice as beautiful.

Again, the world seemed to slide into a new vision.

Aisulu stroked one finger down the softness of the eaglet's back. "Toktar," she breathed.

The eaglet opened its sharp beak and called, a high, pure whistle.

Toktar meant "he will live," and it was the eaglet's name.

Only later did she think about her brother, and the blue truck vanishing into a plume of dust and distance.

Aisulu took Toktar back to her own ger, her family's ger.

It was just as her parents had left it. The blue plastic barrel that held the fermenting mare's milk, the kumiss, was still pulled into its nighttime spot close to the stovepipe, and wrapped in an old sheepskin vest like a fat uncle. Her father's prayer rug was left unrolled by the westmost curve of the wall. The loose sheet of linoleum that made the floor of the ger was filthy: the syringe wrappers from the previous night's catastrophe lay scattered about in a wild smear of footprints.

No one had swept. That was her job.

The fire had gone out. That was her mother's job.

Everything was normal but nothing was normal. Her parents were gone. Her brother was gone. The little ger that was all of theirs, together, was empty, and quiet, and cold.

If she had not had Toktar, the strangeness of that afternoon would have crushed her. But she did have Toktar, and so she was busy. On any ordinary day, she had to do milking, and churning, and cheese making. But on this day, she went from milking to mice; from churning to mice; from cheese making to mice. She had to run to keep up with it all, banging in and out of the little ger without feeling what was missing from it. Instead, she felt what was new. Every time she came through the door, Toktar would raise his head. He would cry and whistle, sounding much sillier than a grand golden eagle had any business sounding. He was loud, too —louder than a baby yak.

He could not be a secret.

Even if he had not made so much noise, the aul was too

small for secrets. But for that one afternoon, no one discovered them. Her uncles were out with the herds. Her small cousins had a summer cold and were too sick to come bursting through the door.

So through that single afternoon, Aisulu held Toktar secret in her heart. This lively, needy, greedy, smelly lump of an eaglet. He was hers, and only hers, and he helped her feel whole even though her brother was hurt and her parents had left her without a word—whole even though her entire world had gone.

And then it was evening.

The mountain threw a long cape of shadow over the aul. Down the slope came a roll of dust and noise as her uncles came in with the herd. Two hundred goats, a hundred sheep, two men on horses. Aisulu and her aunties went out to meet them. The men used their flails to herd the animals against a ridge of shale. The women waded through the herd, sorting the nanny goats into strings for milking. Aisulu waded in with them and tied the rawhide line to a bracket pounded into the ground. She grabbed her family's goats by the horns and dragged them over, looping the leather around their necks, tying them cheek to cheek, tight as good embroidery.

The milk goats were food animals, and so they did not have names, but Aisulu knew them all anyway: Dreadlocks,

Soft Ears, White Witch, Little Brown. There was one who always sat down on top of the milk pail, the one Aisulu privately called Next Week You're Lunch. There were twenty-seven of them in her family's string. The goat milking was the biggest task of the day, and Aisulu had done it with her mother since she was big enough to walk.

Now she was doing it alone.

Her mother had said she'd have to manage. That she could manage. Alone.

Her mother had said she was growing into a fine young woman. That was what her mother wanted: a fine girl, a fine young woman, a fine daughter whose life would be full of milk.

Aisulu's life was full of milk, but she felt hollow. She paused in her milking to tug her brother's shapan closed.

Each of the three families of the aul had a string of goats to be milked. Aisulu and her mother always finished first, because they were two. But on that day, Aisulu finished last. She unstrung her goats. She carried the pails of milk back to the shed outside her empty ger. The pails felt heavy. They rubbed against the yellow lines on her hands. She washed her goaty hands at the outdoor sink and let the traces of milk sink into the good earth of her aul.

She waved off her auntie Meiz's offer of supper, thinking that though she could not hear Toktar, he must be hungry. There were a few mice left in the basket, so she went inside to feed him. He was looking right at her when the door opened, his eyes shining.

Toktar ate, and then Aisulu ate. Had she ever eaten alone before? Cheese in her pocket, under the wild high skies, yes, but like this, at a table? She did not know. Should she eat alone, or should she have gone with Meiz and the little cousins? Where did she fit, without her parents, without her brother? Where would the eagle fit?

She lifted Toktar out of her brother's thoroughly ruined hat. He weighed nothing in her hands, like a meal made of one piece of bread. But he wriggled. She could feel the prickle of his strong claws. Alive; he would live.

One-handed, she grabbed one of the big tin bowls they used for gathering dung fuel. The eaglet would poop in it, but it could be rinsed. Her mother kept a kindling basket —grasses, scraps of paper and shreds of rags—by the stove. Aisulu added these to the bowl. The eaglet would poop on them, but they could be replaced.

She put the bowl on top of the kumiss barrel beside the stovepipe and tucked the eaglet into it. Toktar hummed and plucked at the grasses with a quizzical sound. Aisulu unwrapped his stone and set it on the cookplate. Then she had to restart the fire. It was near the longest day of the year, but the wind off the mountain was cold, and with the fire down, the empty ger held a chill.

Her mother would never have let the fire burn out like this.

Aisulu rubbed her hands together and tucked a cotton cloth over the eaglet, as if he were dough that needed to rise.

Kerr! objected the wriggling lump she'd made. *Keeeeer-rrrr!*

It was a carrying sound.

Aisulu took the blanket off.

The eaglet looked at her: *What did you do that for?*

"To keep you warm, little thing," she explained.

Ka-rear! Toktar shouted, a piercing cry that must have carried half a mile.

"Well," said Aisulu. "I guess you aren't going to be a secret."

Kerr? he said.

"Yes," she said. "Soon I will go and murder mice for you."

Kurr, he purred, contented as a well-loved king.

She took the warm stone from the cookplate, wrapped it in its red silk, and put it in the bowl.

Toktar attacked it, trying to tear the red silk like meat.

His beak went *click*. His claw tangled. His head cocked. He spent a half second puzzled, then lay down against the warm stone and went to sleep.

She put one finger on the pulse of his soft head. She stood for a moment like that, in the empty ger.

And then the door opened. It was Dulat.

"I thought I heard—"

Toktar jerked upright and began to *screep*. Doors opening, in his tiny mind, meant mice.

Dulat spotted Toktar and froze. He was carrying milk—her milk, her family's milk—and for a moment he stood so quietly that she could hear it slosh in its pails. "An eagle," he murmured at last. "I came to fetch you, and I thought I heard an eagle."

Aisulu was standing, still as if she'd grown roots. Power seemed to surge up from her feet, and made her speak. "The orphan," she said. "The eagle Serik—the eagle you killed was his mother. I rescued him."

"You?"

"I rode Moon Spot up the mountain. I found the right cliff, and I climbed it. I found the baby eagle and I saved him."

Aisulu's words felt hot against the roof of her mouth. Telling her ake about her brother's limp had seemed half wrong. This felt all the way right.

Kerr! said Toktar, because no one had given him mice.

"You cannot have an eagle," said Dulat.

"But I do have an eagle," she said.

Ka-rear! shouted Toktar.

Dulat put down the milk pails—so fast and so carelessly that some of the milk sloshed onto the floor.

No one spilled milk, not ever. Milk was life. A milky pail or milky hands could not even be rinsed in the river: they had to be rinsed where milk-water could fall into the earth of the aul and give them all strength. Milk was life, and Dulat was taking Aisulu's, and he was careless with it. What was wrong with him? What else might he do?

"You cannot have an eagle," he said. He sounded less angry than stunned. He gave his head a shake. "You are too young, and a girl. You cannot."

"But I do." She should tuck her head for her uncle, but she lifted her chin instead.

Dulat crossed the ger to her, going counterclockwise as if he belonged there, as though he were family. He *was* family. And yet she could not remember him ever coming into the little ger. He was the oldest. They went to him.

Dulat reached toward Toktar. The little eaglet's neck snaked out and he snapped his tiny beak shut around the pad of Dulat's thumb.

Dulat yelped and yanked his hand back.

They both stood then, silent. Aisulu could see Dulat's hands curling up as if to make fists. "You should not be alone, with your father gone, with your mother gone," he said at last. "That is what I came to say. I will take you in. You will come with me, and Kara-Kat-Kis will look after you. She will help you with my brother's milk. We will take care of you."

As oldest brother, Dulat could rule the aul like a king. Aisulu had no ground on which to stand if she wanted to stand against him.

"My eagle . . ." she said.

His hands were still curled up. "I will keep the eagle," he answered.

Chapter Six

Dulat was having trouble with the milk.

He was a man who liked to stride, and Aisulu thought he wanted to be striding now. That he wanted to herd her across the aul like a goat. Instead, she carried Toktar's bowl like a priestess in a procession, and Dulat walked like a horse on ice. Even on his way into his own ger, he banged into the door.

"What are you doing? Put those down!" scolded the Fox Wife. "You'll spill them!"

She was standing by the stove, churning the barrel of mare's milk to make kumiss. She straightened up, arched the kink from her back, and pushed the kumiss barrel closer to the stove. Her voice went soft and kind. "Here, Aisulu."

Dulat looked at his wife with pure husbandly bewilderment. "You knew about this?"

"I know things," she answered with a smile.

Aisulu put Toktar's bowl on the barrel, and for a moment the three of them stood looking down at the fuzzy white eaglet. When Dulat put his hand out, the eaglet flattened, pressing his body to the bottom of the bowl.

"Oh," said Dulat. "It's frightened." He pulled his hand back.

Of course he's frightened, Aisulu thought. *He's a baby. He's such a little thing, and he's in such a strange place. Of course he's frightened.*

Dulat sucked the pad of his thumb where Toktar had bit him. "I took my first eaglet from the nest, but she was not so young. They should not be taken so young."

"If I hadn't taken him," said Aisulu, "he would have died."

Dulat smoothed one hand down his face, and it looked almost like prayer. "So small—it might still die. You should prepare for that."

"He might die," said the Fox Wife. "But he might not." She got a third bowl from the cabinet and started the tea. "Dulat, give them space."

Dulat surprised Aisulu by stepping back, and then astonished her by helping to set out the food: women's work. He laid out baursak and butter, cheese and clotted cream. And he spoke softly. "I climbed down a cliff to find her—my first eagle."

"I climbed up," said Aisulu.

"Down is better," he said. "Someone above can hold the rope."

"There wasn't anyone."

"There could have been," he said, which made Aisulu wonder if that were true. Would Dulat have helped her?

With the food laid out, Dulat sat down in the man's place, the place of honor, facing the door. Over his head hung a pair of photographs: the one of her grandfather and Dulat each holding up his hunting eagle, and another of two little girls riding a single reindeer: Kara-Kat-Kis and her lost sister. The pictures were hung even with each other.

Dulat said a brief *Bismillah* over the food and then seemed ready to make sweeping proclamations again. "The eaglet must be kept warm," said Dulat. "And it will need a great deal of rabbit."

"Mice for now," said the Fox Wife.

Dulat frowned. "Where will I get mice?"

"I'll get them," said Aisulu.

Dulat's eyebrows folded down. It was a look like a guard dog getting ready to run off an intruder.

"Aisulu must get the mice." The Fox Wife paced around out table, pouring the tea. She served Dulat first, as was the Kazakh way. "The eaglet must be fed while you are out with the herd. Four times, five times during the daylight, while he is so small. And that much at night." She let her hand touch Dulat's.

Dulat's eyebrows relaxed, and turned his hand over so

that the Fox Wife could touch his palm. They sat touching hands, as Kazakh people rarely did. Dulat seemed to catch Aisulu looking, and explained the one thing she wasn't curious about: "Kara-Kat-Kis studied . . . she is a conservation biologist."

"And I know things," said the Fox Wife. Behind them was their marriage bed, hung with a dozen dead foxes.

Dulat put a lump of dried cheese in his tea to soften it. "Well then. How will *Aisulu* get mice?"

"Great hunts can be made," said the Fox Wife, "with a kettle and a little stone." She lifted her bowl of tea, her bright red bowl. It was like the red smile of a creature four times her size. "Eat quickly, child. He's getting hungry."

After tea, Aisulu went out to murder mice and then came in to feed the eaglet.

Dulat had been whittling a matchstick into a toothpick. He handed it to Aisulu as an eagle-feeding tool and started on another one. "It's good that you can do this," he said, pointing at her with his pocketknife. "The eaglet will need to be fed often. It will grow quickly." Then he stopped as if he'd thought of something. "Was there a second chick in the nest—a larger one? How do you know this one is male?"

Aisulu considered. The Fox Wife's answer—he is male because he will take things from you—did not seem like a good thing to say. She settled for, "Kara-Kat-Kis knows things."

"I do," said the Fox Wife, sounding wicked.

"She does!" Dulat half laughed. "It's a pity it's not female, though."

"Yes," said Aisulu, and as soon as she could, she fled outside, to do the work of a girl in the evening, and then to murder more mice. There was a lot of work, and a lot of murder. It was nearly dark by the time she went in to feed the eaglet.

She gutted the mice at the table. The bare light bulb cast hard shadows. The Fox Wife was bent over the stove making the evening meal, the meat meal: boiled goat and plain noodles, without even an onion to spice it. Dulat flipped on the radio, which for just one hour every evening broadcast in Kazakh, their language.

Dombra music. The weather forecast. The Mongolian national anthem.

Dulat sat on a stool by the stovepipe, his arm wrapped around his wife's waist, his eyes on the little eagle. "My first eagle was called Crooked Claw," he said.

"This one is Toktar," said the Fox Wife, as if the sky had told her so and there could be no argument.

Aisulu tried to remember if she'd told the Fox Wife Toktar's name.

"Hmmm," said Dulat, and nodded slowly.

"Good evening, radio listeners," said the distant voice, and began to spread the news. If there was a wedding, a festival, a funeral to go to, they would hear of it now.

Aisulu listened for her brother's name.

That night was the first night with Toktar. Dulat's ger was big: it had a second bed, plus the futon by the table, where men and honored visitors might sit, and sleep. But Aisulu choose neither of these. Instead, she piled thick felt rugs on the floor.

The light bulb was still on, but Aisulu was exhausted. She pulled the rug pile toward the stovepipe. "I'll trip over you," grumbled Dulat, lifting a curl into the top rug with a nudge of his boot.

"It's to keep Toktar warm," said Aisulu. She set the eaglet's bowl on the edge of her rugs.

"He'll need feeding four times in the night," said the Fox Wife to Dulat. "Isn't it better if he wakes the girl instead of you?"

Dulat snorted like a yak, which was not quite agreement. The radio switched from Kazakh to Mongolian. He flicked it off, and with bad grace unrolled his prayer mat to make the day's last prayer. But he did not pick up Toktar's bowl, or move Aisulu's improvised bed. She lay down with the eaglet in the scoop of her arm.

She slept badly, of course. In the strange place. On the hard rugs. She was kept half awake by her fear that she would roll over and crush the eaglet. Three times that night, Toktar's whistling peeps woke her. She fed him in the starlight, in the breathing silence. And when she put her fingers over the edge of his bowl, he leaned into them and slept warmly.

The night was too long and her sleep was too short, and the next day was hard. To do her work, and her mother's work, and to care for the eaglet—Aisulu had worked hard all her life, but this was more than she had ever done.

Aisulu went and came, and came and went. She had to milk the yaks at dawn, and the goats after. She had to milk the horses five times a day. She had to spread dung to dry and gather the dry dung for the fires. She had to help her auntie Meiz make cheese. She had to take a turn at churning butter. She had to fetch the water, running down the path to the bottom of the mountains with her empty buckets flying. Looking for time, for mice, for mice and for time to murder them.

Toktar ate the mice, recovering his strength. Just one day of food had made him strong enough to lift his little pointed rump above the rim of the bowl and send his white poop shooting five feet through the air. Strong enough to peck at the red silk that wrapped the warm stone nestling like a sister beside him.

He ate and pooped, and pooped and ate. The big ger started to smell funny.

By the second day, fatigue was making Aisulu's hair feel heavy and her blinks feel slow. By the third day, she found herself leaning on the yaks as she milked them, even falling asleep with her forehead resting on a shaggy flank. She woke only when Curious Yak twisted around to see what she was up to and dumped her face-first into the dirt.

At least she didn't spill the milk.

On the fourth day, Aisulu attracted attention: her little cousins, her auntie Meiz's children. They'd been confined for three days with their cold but they were better now, and they made a gaggle like goslings. They followed her around the sandy bowl of the summer camp as she hunted. Temir and Balta, twins of six—two boys named after iron and axes— squeaked and squealed when the wet mouse met hard stone. Enlik, four, a girl named after the most delicate bloom on the mountains, was fearless about mouse murder, and when she squealed, it was with delight.

Aisulu gave Temir the kettle, Balta the basket, and Enlik the stone.

When the orange basket was piled full of mice as, in

another place, it might have been piled with French fries, she took her cousins inside the big ger to meet the eaglet.

Toktar still felt like a secret to her, like something she should hold close to her heart. But there was simply no way to keep a secret like that. He was growing stronger, and his voice was a loud, a ridiculous whistle.

Aisulu stood at the table cutting up the first mouse, and the goslings gathered around the kumiss barrel, still wheezy and snotty with their summer cold, but as full of wonderment as a choir of angels. They pushed close and looked down at the eaglet with bright eyes. The eaglet looked up at them, and opened its beak.

Kree! said Toktar.

"I'm working on it," said Aisulu.

Eeep! said Toktar. He threw his head back, stretching his sock-puppet neck, twisting and wiggling from foot to foot.

"Yes, yes," said Aisulu. "You are the prince of the birds, the khan of the mountains."

"You can't keep an eagle," said Temir, the squeaky. "You're a girl."

"He's Dulat's eagle," said Balta, the snotty, wiping his nose on his sleeve.

Four-year-old Enlik rolled her eyes as if she were fourteen. "Brothers are so stupid."

Brothers—Aisulu sucked in breath. The whole world just *stopped*, as if the air had turned to concrete in her lungs, pushing against her ribs and making them ache. It was a moment before she could force that air out again in lumps, before she could breathe and blink and make the world move. She turned to Enlik: "*Your* brothers are stupid."

Temir and Balta both whined—"hey" and "but"—but both of them shut up as Aisulu fed Toktar the back quarter of a mouse, leg and all. The eaglet tilted his head back, gulping. Aisulu ran a finger down his crop until the tiny paw disappeared inside the yellow beak. The beak shut with a click, and as one, her cousins cooed, "Ooooh." The little eaglet was so cute, in a bloodthirsty kind of way.

"But, Aisulu, you can't—" said Temir again.

Aisulu interrupted him. "Do you want to kill mice for him or not?"

"I will!" said Enlik. "Me!"

Glep, said Toktar. And that was settled.

On the fifth day, the twins hunted mice as if it were a game. They even tossed dead mice to Yellow Dog to make him leap and twist in the air. They gloried in it—when they did it. Sometimes they simply forgot. But little Enlik was as single-minded as a supervillain. She pulled a fraying felt rug into the middle of the meadow and laid her baby brother, Naizabai, on it—watching the baby was what she was supposed to be doing. Instead, Naizabai went scooting on his belly to the edge of the blanket, over and over, to play unsupervised with pebbles and goat droppings, and Enlik went ranging like a little fox, murdering mice by the basketful.

Enlik's mother, Aisulu's auntie Meiz, watched all this. She would straighten from her churning or her milking, put her hands on the small of her back, and arch so that her face was to the sky. Once she had smiled at the sun, she would smile at Enlik. Five months pregnant, Meiz was beginning to be round-bellied like a hail cloud—and she was unstoppable as weather. Aisulu would be glad if she could get her auntie Meiz on her side.

After the mouse hunt, Meiz came to see the eaglet. She sat on a stool, nursing baby Naizabai and watching Toktar wobble about on the table. Enlik put scraps of peeled mouse on the end of a matchstick and Toktar snatched them eagerly. Meiz beamed at her little daughter, beamed at the little eagle, and looked around her brother and sister-in-law's ger. It was the great family ger, which had belonged to Dulat's parents before they died. The lattice walls were covered with the dead woman's embroidered pieces, with thirty-seven winters' worth of stitching. The Fox Wife had not added a new embroidered piece yet. Aisulu had often heard Meiz wonder if the foreign woman could even stitch, and once, in a mutter, if the foreign woman could have children.

There were no children of Dulat in the big ger. There was no new embroidery hanging that would make it clear it belonged to the next generation now. And yet, Dulat had hung their diplomas on the wall, side by side, higher even than his string of eagle-hunting medals. And Kara-Kat-Kis had hung the reindeer skull over the mirror where once Aisulu's grandfather had straightened his eagle hunter's hat. Kara-Kat-Kis, who spoke to the dead. Who, the whispers said, could stop a heart—or start one.

Meiz looked into the reindeer's eye sockets and then back at the Fox Wife.

"We can share the churning, eh," she said. "To make it manageable."

"I will churn," said the Fox Wife. "You make the cheese."

Another smile dawned slowly on Meiz's face. "We could even get the twins to sweep."

"Like girls," said little Enlik, and fell into a fit of giggles. Toktar finished the scrap of mouse meat and went on to attack the matchstick, and then a red flower on the plastic tabletop.

Meiz finished nursing her baby and tucked him up over her shoulder, swaying him and patting his back rhythmically. "Take your eagle off the table, Aisulu," she said.

Aisulu took note of that word: *your*. She picked Toktar up. He fit into her hand, warm, and heavier than the day before.

The Fox Wife swiped the plastic tablecloth clean. "*Tsai oh?*" she said. This meant "drink tea." It was the first coin of Kazakh hospitality, a deep and basic invitation to fellowship. It was one phrase where the Fox Wife's accent did not show.

"*Tsai oh,*" agreed Meiz. "Let us have tea."

It was like an alliance being sealed.

From that day forward, Aisulu found herself at the center of a new circle: one made of women and children. Enlik did the mouse hunting. Meiz and the Fox Wife did the cheese making and the churning—even Aisulu's churning. Once or twice the twins were bullied into sweeping. And though Aisulu still had her hands full of all the usual things —fuel bowls and water pails and milk buckets—she was no longer run to exhaustion.

Aisulu had always been a little wild and a little strange. She was a girl who could ride horses. She was a girl who liked the top of the mountains instead of the hollow of the aul. She had always been on the edge of what was proper, and though her father loved her for it—though her father and her brother and maybe even her mother loved her for it —she had still been on the edge.

Now she was in the middle.

It took Dulat—who thought *he* was the middle— a while to notice this. After all, he and his brother spent the whole day out with the herds, and came back to butter already churned and cheese already drying.

Even Aisulu did not notice until she let the boys feed the eaglet one day, Temir holding Toktar and Balta bravely manning the matchstick. It was going fine until Toktar pooped on Temir, with force, the poop splattering up and backward, clear of his imaginary nest, right into the little boy's face. Temir shouted and dropped the eaglet on the table. Toktar began to totter back toward his matchstick. Balta was giggling uncontrollably.

"You should be careful," said the Fox Wife, "when the eaglet is so small. The one who handles him now will have his heart." As if she were merely getting the table ready for tea, she picked up the eaglet—and handed him back to Aisulu.

Aisulu felt Toktar's whole body pulsing, and thought: *I have his heart.*

And he has mine.

But every night when the radio came on, she listened for her brother's name.

Chapter Seven

TOKTAR, TOKTAR. AISULU COULD MAKE a song out of it, a little two-string melody. She said it on every breath, as if it were a prayer. *Inshallah,* toktar: If it pleases God, let him live.

Toktar lived. He ate and ate, and he pooped and pooped. He grew.

Within a week he'd outgrown the dung bowl. Dulat dug out his old eagle perch — a three-legged stool made from the snarled root of a pine tree and painted blue. He put it on a tabletop, and Toktar sidestepped up it like a parakeet and hopped down at will. The Fox Wife sighed and put a dishrag on the table to be handy. Toktar promptly attacked it.

Aisulu eyed the drop from table to floor. "He won't fall?"

"Never," said Dulat. "They're born on cliffs."

Toktar did not fall. Dark brown feathers began poking through his white down, like iris sprouts coming out of the snow. He learned to cheep — *ker-honk, ker-honk, ker-honk* — whenever Aisulu came into view.

And between the feathers and the voice . . . well. Golden eagles are the great birds of the Altai Mountains, the khans of the air. But apparently no one had told Toktar he was meant to be majestic. Those first feathers ruffling his down made him look as bedraggled as a wet sheep. His high loud voice made him sound like a kitten stuck inside a bullhorn. Wandering the tabletop world of milk, investigating the butter and cheese and clotted cream, he was utterly ridiculous.

And Aisulu loved him.

But sometimes when she was out of the ger and in the high wild air, she felt empty, and as lost as a kite cut free.

In the mornings, Aisulu put Toktar on the dresser as she brushed her hair. He liked to prance among the Fox Wife's talismans. It was hard for her to say which of them was more awkward. Aisulu's hair was finer and curlier than was common among Kazakhs—it was wind-wild and would not stay in its braids. Every morning for as long as she could remember, her mother had brushed her hair. Her mother would brush and brush and brush, a hundred strokes, even though there was so much to do. She would oil the brush and tug and turn the strands, plaiting them into two long braids, glossy and smooth. *There,* she would say. *Now you look like a fine girl.* Then she would pour her own hair into a scarf, and they would face the day together.

Without her mother, Aisulu could not make her hair behave—especially not when Toktar attacked the swinging ends of it. Weeks went by, and she felt as if she were slowly growing farther from a fine girl. As if she were slowly becoming more lost. Wilder.

No word came from her family.

She kept thinking it would. Summer was a time for long light and for visitors: women tracing the water paths, men on motorcycles making the dogs go crazy. Every time someone came, Aisulu stood straight and silent and waited for them to pull out a letter, deliver a message. Over and over there was nothing.

The visitors brought shimin-airkh: a homemade vodka that tried to fume its way free of old Fanta bottles. They brought Choco-Pies and hard candies from the village shop. They brought gossip and rumor. But they didn't bring word from her family. They didn't bring news about her brother. When she asked, they looked at her in a way that made her face flush and prickle. So she stopped asking.

Then came the day when one visitor brought the rumor that Serik had been taken from the clinic in the nearest town to the hospital in Olgii City, a hundred miles away. Aisulu had known Serik might be taken to the hospital: her mother had said that, before she had left. But—her family had been close, close as the nearest town, close as an hour's ride. They had been that close, and then they had gone that far. And they had not sent her a single word.

Aisulu bolted out of the ger.

She whistled for Moon Spot and she rode and rode and rode, trying to escape whatever it was she was feeling —like she'd been kicked in the stomach, stabbed in that inside place where a swallow starts. She ran her horse up the mountain, and then on the downward slope, faster and faster, so fast that tears streaked backward to pool cold in her ears. She pretended that they were tears drawn only by the wind. She rode until the wind deafened her and the pounding hooves made her numb to her pain.

When she finally came straggling back, it was evening. She had missed the goat milking—a great sin. Her auntie Meiz, named for sweet golden raisins, looked sour as bad grapes. The Fox Wife stared at her and tilted her head, like a cat considering. Aisulu thought she might speak in her bottom-of-the-well voice, her spell caster's voice, as she had when Dulat had killed the eagle. But instead, very slowly, she stretched out one arm. She wrapped it around Aisulu's thin shoulders and gathered her in.

Aisulu stiffened. The hug was lopsided. Rigid as a camel's backbone. Nothing like her father's hug, or Serik's—

She shoved the Fox Wife away and didn't even care that

the woman's face crumpled. Or she told herself she didn't. She darted away and thrust herself through the door like a whirlwind.

Dulat was sitting at the table, and there was a school notebook open in front of him. He looked up when she entered the ger.

"Aisulu!"

"What?!" she snapped. "What?" She was slowing down, staggering to a stop. On the table, Toktar *ker-honk*ed at her. As if he'd missed her. As if he wanted news.

Her uncle lifted the notebook and waggled it at her. Toktar weaved his head about, following the motion. The notebook was not one of hers, but it was well used: the cardboard cover gone soft, the spiral wire binding spinning loose on one end like a young vine. "Look here. I think I can prove that the little eagle is female."

Aisulu answered without thinking: "He's not. He's my brother."

Toktar struck out and tore a corner from a fluttering page.

"Bold da!" Dulat said to the bird. "Stop that!"

Toktar *screep*ed and pooped in answer. He let the scrap drop, then pretended to kill, crumpling it up in one foot and squeaking with delight.

"Look here," said Dulat, turning his back on the playful eagle. "The rate of growth, the speed at which the feathers come in . . ." He flipped the notebook around and showed her hashmarks arranged in a table. They were not enlightening. "If it is female," said Dulat. "If it is female, then I can hunt with it. I can fly it this fall, at the great festival. There is a prize, even."

The radio voices had talked about the Eagle Festival, had had news about foreigners coming from some American television place. Aisulu had paid no attention. But now—

Dulat snapped the notebook down onto the table, making Toktar jump back. "We must start tonight."

"Husband," said the Fox Wife gently: she had been watching from the doorway. But Dulat was already bustling around.

The family stored the things they did not use every day in a pile of stiff-sided suitcases, big on the bottom and little on top, draped at each step with lace and embroidery. Dulat pulled one out from near the bottom, rumpling its lace cover. He threw open the chrome catches and began retrieving eagle hunter's gear: The jeweled leather ankle cuffs. The little straps that hooked to them—jesses, these were called—that would tie Toktar to a leash. The hood that would cover his head and eyes to blind him and keep him calm.

The eagle hunter's glove, a heavy thing like an oven mitt that came halfway to his elbow, made of thick leather padded with felt.

"Dulat," said the Fox Wife.

But he didn't answer. He began to fit the cuffs onto Toktar. The eaglet turned his head upside down to watch. The ankle cuffs must have been Dulat's father's once. They were old, the leather black and crackling, the silver embellishments tarnished. Dulat padded them with scraps of Astroturf. Toktar instantly began trying to eat them, but they were built to be eagle proof. The green shag, peeking out from under the leather, contrasted with the dirty yellow dinosaur scales of Toktar's growing feet.

As Aisulu watched in silence, Dulat hooked a leash to Toktar's jesses, then lifted him onto the glove. For an instant, the little eagle froze, his eyes wide as pinwheels. Then he threw himself away in a desperate effort to escape. The leash was clamped firmly under Dulat's thumb, and the eaglet did not get far. He fell and hung upside down in a whirlwind of feathers and flapping.

"Don't—" said Aisulu, starting forward.

"It's all right. He'll get used to it. Watch." Dulat recaptured the dangling eaglet and set him back on the glove.

Toktar threw himself down again, and again burst into violent, useless flapping. Tears sprang to Aisulu's eyes.

Dulat set Toktar upright on the glove again, and again the eaglet threw himself away. He hung upside down as the dead eagle had done, swinging and flapping. Down flew everywhere. Kara-Kat-Kis put her hand in the middle of Aisulu's chest and pulled her close.

The fourth time Dulat set Toktar on his wrist, the eaglet stayed up.

Aisulu put her hand over Kara-Kat-Kis's, over her own heart. And none of them—eagle, woman, girl, and heart—none of them moved at all.

For the next few weeks, it was like that. In the evenings, Dulat picked Toktar up and set him on the glove, and then lifted him from the table. He spent hours rolling his forearm back and forth to build Toktar's balance.

During these hours, Toktar would hold still, his feathers so tight to his body that it looked as if he'd been shrinkwrapped. Aisulu remembered the Fox Wife's warning: *The one who handles him now will have his heart.* Toktar did not look as if he were giving his heart. If he looked at Dulat at all, it seemed to be to gauge whether or not he could take out an eye.

But he never struck. He never moved at all.

Aisulu could watch no more. One day, when Dulat was away with the herds, she found a private space between fetching the water and milking the beasts, and borrowed her uncle's eagle glove.

The glove came up to her elbow, and it made her feel clumsy, as if she were wearing a cast. Her wrist would not bend. Her thumb could barely reach the thumb hole. Suddenly she remembered that her grandfather had let Serik try his glove when he was no bigger than the twins, when she was no bigger than Enlik—she remembered her bright-eyed brother cocking a hip and thrusting his fist to the sky.

Serik. "Stop," Aisulu barked at herself. Toktar flinched from her. His eyes were on the glove, his feathers tightening. "I'm sorry," she crooned. "I didn't mean to yell. You know I'd never hurt you. Here. Look." Fumbling because of the stiff leather, she held out one of Toktar's afternoon mice in her gloved hand.

Toktar saw the food at once. He came to the very edge of the table and stretched his neck toward it, his scraggly feathers tight, his eyes shining. He opened his beak and *screep*ed.

"Well, I know you can't reach it," she told him. "Jump for it, Toktar. Come here."

She did not want to pick him up as Dulat had. She had always heard *burkit makes burkitshi*: the eagle chooses the eagle hunter. She wanted that. She wanted her eagle to come to her. To choose her.

But he didn't. He whined and chirruped. He stretched. One foot shot out, fast as a snake. She felt the claws brush her glove, but he could not quite reach his treat.

He looked at her, full of birdish bad mood. It was like being glared at by a half-stuffed pillow.

"It's one step, beauty. Toktar. Come on."

The mouse was perhaps two inches away from the eagle's outstretched neck. But leaving his nest—or in this case, his table—was a big step. Deep in his feather-ball brain, Toktar knew he was not ready to take it. He was a nestling, and she was asking him to leap.

He did not leap.

He paced. He complained. He stamped his feet. But he did not leap.

Day after day, he did not leap.

Maybe he was her eagle, her heart. But night after night, it was Dulat who held him.

For Aisulu, those first weeks of Toktar's training were hard. The rumors and the glances from visitors. The Eagle Festival news on the radio. Her eagle on someone else's hand. She could not shake the feeling she'd had when the flashlight had struck her, how she'd been blinded and frozen in a whirl of eagle and fear.

The snap-bone sound.

Her parents had abandoned her. Had left without a word. Had sent no word.

Serik, thought Aisulu, over and over, and found herself saying absolutely nothing, because she was afraid of saying her brother's name.

And then, one evening, her father came home.

It happened during the evening milking. Along the track that wound between the roots of the mountains came a motorcycle. Aisulu heard the sputter of the tailpipe as it slowed, the grind of the lower gears as it left the track and begin to weave up the slope toward them.

Even before she could see the rider's face, Aisulu knew that it was her father, and she would not be left on that slanting slope a second time. She stopped mid-milk, she put her pail down, and she ran.

They reached the aul at the same time. Abai knocked the motorcycle's kickstand down with his heel. And then he just sat there. The dogs milled around him, barking righteously.

"Ake!" Aisulu called. Her voice quavered, filled with hundreds of questions.

Abai turned, speechless, and climbed down from the motorcycle as she ran and threw herself into his arms.

"Ake," she sobbed.

"Aisulu. Aisulu!" He crushed her against his chest. His hands were in her hair. The smell of him—she'd almost forgotten how he smelled. "You were right," he said. "Oh, child, you were right."

She had to know. She had to know right away. "Serik?" She pushed away from his chest so that she could see his face. "What happened? Is he—?"

"He's alive." Abai took a deep breath. "Aisulu, your brother—" He stopped. His face looked a dozen years older than it should. "Come inside. I will tell you everything."

He was almost leaning on her, as if his leg were broken. He opened the yellow door of his ger, Aisulu's home ger, the empty ger. It was stale and cold, the fire unlit for weeks, the table laid with dust. Abai stopped and blinked.

"Ake?" Aisulu whispered.

He staggered forward and sat, not in the place of honor, but on a rickety stool between the stove and the table. In his hands was a packet of Choco-Pie sandwich cookies. Chocolate and marshmallow flavored, crumbly dry, Choco-Pies were what you brought back from cities. Choco-Pies were normal, but they looked so strange. Abai set them down, red cellophane crinkling, put his elbows on the table, and scrubbed his face with his hands.

For a moment Aisulu could only watch him, and they were alone in the dusty empty ger. Then Dulat came through the door, and Aisulu's other uncle, Yerzhan, and then the Fox Wife, who was carrying kumiss in a pail, and Meiz with children and bread and butter. The women wiped and laid the table. The little cousins crouched nearby, big-eyed and solemn, the twins whispering and poking each other.

The Fox Wife ladled kumiss into bowls for all of them — the best drink, the gathering drink, the drink of summer greetings. They gathered, tight. And yet when Abai began to speak, it was as if he and Aisulu were alone.

"You were right, Aisulu." His voice clotted up and he took a drink of the kumiss. "You were right about Serik's limp. You have saved your brother's life."

The room held its breath.

"But."

The word hit Aisulu in the stomach. She could not breathe. In her hand, the bowl of kumiss rippled as she shook.

"He has . . ." Abai reached inside his vest and pulled a square of paper from his pocket. It was folded, and soft on the folded edges, as if he had pulled it out and opened it many times. He unfolded it now. He stared down at the words as if lost in the immensity of them. After a minute he slid the paper over to Dulat.

"Osteosarcoma," said Dulat, pulling the syllables apart carefully. "It's a cancer. A cancer in the bones."

"They took his leg. When they realized. The second week. They cut it." Abai bounced the blade of his hand restlessly on his own leg, just above the knee. He had to stop and swallow.

Aisulu felt the whole world freeze. Like a blizzard striking. *I will lose everything.* Serik had been right.

"They cut off his leg and they gave him medicines. And now they say he is better. But if he is to walk, we must take him to Ulaanbaatar." He named the Mongolian national capital, a city a million people strong, a thousand miles away—an impossible place, an impossible thing.

"Beskempir said she heard you took him to Olgii," said Meiz cautiously. Visitors and gossip, that was all they'd had to bring them word. But it made sense: Olgii was the provincial capital, and was much closer. There was a hospital in Olgii.

Abai shook his head. "They've done as much as they

can in Olgii. But he needs . . ." He gestured helplessly at the paper.

"A prosthesis," said Dulat, reading it. "That means an artificial leg. Physiotherapy—training to use it."

"The medicine made him sick. And his—" Abai made the chopping gesture again. "And his, his leg. It is still healing. But he needs a good new leg to walk. And to use the new leg, he needs this training."

Then Dulat said, "What about the money?"

"That's why I've come. To— I don't know what we must do. Sell the ger, sell the herd. We need to get to Ulaanbaatar, and we need to live there . . ."

"And then what?" said Yerzhan. "If you sell your portion of the herd, you'll have no way to come back."

"It's not good for Kazakhs in Ulaanbaatar," said Dulat. The capital was a Mongolian city: Kazakhs were a small minority there, and not one that people liked.

"You went," said Abai.

Dulat sat up straighter and lifted his chin, mustache bristling. "To school. Where I became an engineer. You'd be at the slaughterhouse, at the coal plant, on the streets."

Aisulu felt as if she'd been spinning around and around: sick and sloshing. To leave the gers—to leave her cousins and aunties—to leave Curious Yak and Yellow Dog and

Moon Spot—to leave her creatures and her mountains. To leave *Toktar* . . .

"Brother," said Dulat softly. "You'll be trapped. Don't— Are you sure it's worth it?"

"Of course I'm sure," said Abai fiercely. "Of course I'm sure! He's my son. My *son.*"

And—Aisulu felt ashamed of her selfishness, but just once, just for once, she wished someone would call out: *My daughter.*

Chapter Eight

So Abai began a sad and strange business: counting his creatures and tallying what they were worth. He counted the goats in milk, counted Dreadlocks and Soft Ears and White Witch and Little Brown as if they were just one, two, three, four. He counted the male goats that could be slaughtered when the cold came. He counted the sheep and estimated yards of felt. He counted his one yak and two cows. He counted the milk horses, and the riding horses, his and Serik's. He counted Moon Spot.

He measured their ger and found it eighteen feet across, with its yellow door sturdy and its top ring strong and painted red.

The counting was a terrible time.

But there was one bright thing in it.

After that first gathering in the little ger with the yellow door, Dulat had led his brother outside. "Come with me," he said. Abai looked at him, stunned like an owl in the daylight.

"Aisulu has been with me. You should come too. Both of you should stay with me."

He opened his blue door.

Toktar, on the table, *ker-honk*ed and opened his beak, because you never knew who might have a dead mouse handy. He hopped down from his perch and came fearlessly to the edge of the table.

"Dulat," said Abai. He crossed the ger in a daze, struck with wonder. "It is an eagle."

"It is an eagle," repeated Dulat. Behind him, on the wall of the ger, the diploma had been moved down and the ribbon of eagle hunter medals up. They were newly wiped, gleaming on the red silk.

"Oh," said Abai. "When you killed the one Serik captured, I thought . . ." Aisulu knew what he'd thought: the way Dulat had dragged the eagle through the dust had been a violation, a rejection. It had shown his heart scraped empty. But now, Abai smiled, though heartbroken in the smiling: "Father would be so pleased."

Dulat stroked his mustache and for a moment looked almost bashful.

Abai ran a finger down the back of Toktar's neck. The eagle preened. "She's a beauty."

"Aisulu insists we must call it male." Dulat glanced at

Aisulu and shrugged, but somehow it did not look mocking. "Male, but big enough to fly. She calls him Toktar."

"Aish?" Her father looked around at her.

"Toktar is—" She hesitated. "He is the orphan of the one Serik and me captured. I climbed up to his nest to rescue him."

"Aisulu! That crag—what if you'd fallen?"

She could have been hurt. She could have been killed.

"I had to— It was my—" It had been her fault that the mother eagle had died. Hers and Serik's. Though sometimes, when she looked at Dulat holding Toktar, she would hear again the snap-bone sound the eagle's neck had made. Aisulu was desperate for her father to understand. "Did Serik tell you? How we caught the mother eagle?"

The memory made something bitter push its way up the back of her throat. The eagle staring while she made Serik scream and scream.

"He told me," said Abai.

"Does he talk?" She'd not meant to say that—it just bubbled up, like water welling through a crack in the ice.

"Oh, he talks and talks," said Abai. "He is going to get a new horse and ride it everywhere, he is going to get a new leg, he is going to get the best new leg and race in the Olympics."

"It will have to be a smarter horse," said Aisulu.

Her father gave a haunted smile. "Yes. A much, much smarter horse."

Screep! said Toktar. He opened his beak and hopped from foot to foot. Abai stroked him absently.

"Your brother will be all right, Aisulu."

Aisulu looked at her father and tried to believe it. There was a grayness in Abai that she did not remember. He looked like a man who had seen ghosts. Aisulu herself felt flashlight blind, and her heart was frozen.

On the day Toktar pooped in the cheese dish, the Fox Wife threw her hands open. "Enough," she said. She whisked the cheese away, but that was clearly not the end of it.

The four of them were having dinner, the meat meal. Dulat sat with his knife, digging scraps of meat from the nooks between bones and passing them out to Abai and Aisulu and Kara-Kat-Kis in turn. Toktar sat immediately in front of him, his eyes on the meat as it moved on the knife point, his head weaving like a snake's.

The Fox Wife stalked back to the table. "I am not much of a housewife, I know, but there are some limits."

Dulat slipped a hand around his wife's waist. "Blackberry, you are just fine."

The Fox Wife softened, curving into the hand, but did

not stop regarding Toktar. "His feathers are all but in. He is ready to be outside."

"Do you think so?" Abai asked Dulat. "It looks a little young to me."

Dulat moved his knife in a figure eight to make the eagle's head turn upside down. "I trust Kara-Kat-Kis on these matters."

Abai did not push it, but Aisulu—the thought of the change, of Toktar lost in the wind, abandoned—that thought made her shiver. "Are you sure?"

"He's an eagle," said the Fox Wife. "He deserves a sky."

Dulat flipped the scrap of meat to Toktar, who squealed and attacked it. "He is ready to be outside." He smoothed his mustache and nodded to himself, as if he had made a decision worthy of Suleman. "Yes. The eagle must go outside."

The next morning, Dulat commanded construction of an eagle pen: a long rectangle of low walls that that would keep Toktar safe from careless yaks or hungry wolves. They could use the night pen wall for one of the sides, but the other three would have to be built fresh, and built of stone, because there was so little wood in the mountains.

The men took the herds out, and Aisulu worked alone through the day, piling stones between the churning and the milking, between the sweeping and the cooking, between the fetching of water and the boiling of whey. Dulat came back with the herds in the evening, moved the bigger stones, and then took all the credit.

It was tiring work. On the first day, Aisulu's hands changed. She had smooth hard calluses from her daily work of milking and hauling water, but the stones made them as rough as if they'd been sandpapered. When Dulat held her eagle that night, it was hard to make her hands close. It was hard to do nothing.

On the second day, Aisulu was so tired that it felt as if she had a rock instead of a heart—but that was all right, because she still had Toktar. He was like her heart outside her body. When Dulat held her eagle that night, she could feel the bird pulse inside her, beating fast.

On the third day, Aisulu left the rocks to themselves and went to sit inside the ger with Toktar. The next day he would be moved outside. It felt as if he were being moved away from her. "It will be all right, though," she told him. "You'll have the wind, and you'll have the stars. And Kara-Kat-Kis is right: an eagle really ought to have a sky."

Were there stars in Ulaanbaatar? A photo from a textbook haunted her: a huge city, huddled between low mountains and hung with coal smoke. It was black and white. It was gray.

Aisulu shook herself and mentally shut the book on the

city. She fetched a lump of butter and sat at the table to rub it into the rough places of her hands. Toktar came and watched her. She would rub one hand and his head would tilt left to watch. She would rub the other hand and his head would seesaw right. His feathers were nearly in. He looked as if he were wearing brown suspenders on top of his white down. His scruffy head went tip-tock.

Aisulu watched him—delighted, sad. The bright ger wrapped all around them. "I think it will be frightening, to go outside," she said. "But—"

She could not think of a but.

A huge city, hung with smoke, where eagles could not go.

Her hands were as good as they were going to get, but there was still butter left, and she'd spoiled it for eating. She fetched the eagle glove and began to rub the fat into its stiff crackling leather—it had been packed away for so long. Toktar watched, his feathers relaxed and fluffy, his neck soft. He tipped his head and kept tipping it, until he was looking at her with his head upside down, as if this would reveal any hidden mice.

Aisulu huffed something that was meant to be a laugh —and Toktar seemed to laugh back, fluffing up like a dust mop, wiggling his rump.

She rested her gloved hand on the table to work the butter into the cracks around the thumb.

The young eagle waddled over. He stretched his neck down to peer at the glove close up, sneaked a look at Aisulu, and gave the glove an experimental nibble.

"It's not food," she said. "Come on."

Nibble, went Toktar. *Nibble snap.*

"*Bold-da,*" she scolded him. "*Jok.* Come on, no. I'm tired." She scooted the glove away and he took a pace after it. She scooted it away again. "It's not food, Toktar. Not everything is food."

He put one foot on her gloved thumb.

Aisulu stopped moving.

Toktar put the other foot on her glove.

She could feel his whole weight pressing her hand into the table. She did not lift him. It seemed like too much.

With her bare hand, she stroked his tummy, feeling the strong ridge of his breastbone, where all his flight muscles began. She ran a hand down his back, which was softer than fox fur, sleeker than freshly brushed hair. The young eagle raised all his feathers, puffing up like thistledown, and then gave himself a shimmy to settle them sleek. It was the eagle equivalent of a happy sigh.

"Look at you, on the glove."

Toktar looked down at his toes, then back up at Aisulu. He whistled.

"Yes, and you're not dead. Look how brave you are, Toktar."

He tipped his head at his name. She sat there for a long moment, just being with him, not pushing him further.

"You're so brave," she said. "And it's going to be all right." She was thinking, again, that tomorrow they would take him outside: that it would be for him like entering a new world. "Things change sometimes, that's all. Things—" And then suddenly her voice caught. She had slept in the wrong ger, she had cared for an eagle, and now she must leave both. Go to Ulaanbaatar so that Serik might walk again. But leave Toktar.

A memory cried out: *I'll lose everything.*

"Things change sometimes," she told her eagle. "But I'll be there. For as long as I—" She gulped down the next word and laid a hand on his head. He ducked and turned as if he were leaning into a kiss, and rubbed the edge of his beak over her thumb.

Then she let her head lean against him. He smelled like the dust and iron, like the sun on stone.

That evening, Dulat helped her finish building the pen. Her father had gone visiting neighbors. Aisulu knew he was look-ing for a buyer for their animals and ger. She was almost glad he was gone. She hated the way his face looked as he planned to leave everything. Dulat was breaking his back moving stones, but he looked less pained than her father did. He lifted a big one and stopped to puff a moment, putting an arm around Aisulu. "You've done well with this."

She nodded, silent.

"You've done well with this, and well with that eagle."

At that, she did not even nod.

"I was your age when I took my first eagle. I was young, so I gave her a name—I called her Crooked Claw. She caught a wolf, once, a huge gray beast like a monster from a tale. I swear he was half as tall as a horse. She hurt a talon doing it, bent it all the way backward. And the wolf spun her and snapped at her in the air. But she never let go of his throat." He held up his own hand and made it into a tight claw. "She squeezed the life out of him. She was half snake, I think. Half snake and half arrow, the deadliest thing in the Altai."

Aisulu said nothing. Toktar was not a snake, and he was not an arrow. He was her heart.

Twilight was coming on. Together they watched the shadows of clouds sweep up the mountains. Finally, and against all tradition, Aisulu spoke first.

"Will you tell me about your eagle?"

Dulat laughed, surprised—and surprisingly, answered.

"Crooked Claw—she was a glory. I took her from the nest when she was about the age of your eagle now."

Aisulu noted that word again: *your*. She held her breath, but Dulat did not seem to notice what he'd said. "I trained her that summer, and in the fall we went to the Eagle Festival. I was so proud—and we did well enough. We won one of the little medals. But Crooked Claw wasn't made for festivals. She was made for hunting. Festivals are fine, but hunting . . ."

He stopped, as if a memory had snagged him.

"My father took us out the day of the first snow. We went into the mountains. We rode for days. It was so cold that the snow squeaked, and nothing moved anywhere but the wind with the snow in it." His fingers traced ribbons in the air. "We were hunting foxes. It was days before we flushed one, and it was too quick, even for Crooked Claw. It was gone almost before I could thrust her into the air. And then we could not find another, not all day. When we did find one, it turned at the last minute—they'll do that, foxes, turn on your bird. And Crooked Claw did not strike it. She did not make her first kill.

"I thought . . . I wondered then if she was meant to be a hunting eagle. If I was meant to be a burkitshi, if I was meant to be a true eagle hunter. We'd been traveling so long, and I was so cold, so tired."

Aisulu found herself nodding. The blizzard, rescuing Serik, rescuing Toktar. These rushed together in her head. She'd been so cold, and so tired. She'd been desperate and doubting. It all came back into her body as Dulat told the story of desperation and doubt.

"And then," said Dulat. "The third beast we flushed was not a fox at all. It was the wolf."

Again he made his hand into the tight claw in the air. Aisulu bent her fingers. They were tight and strong.

"She struck him like a thunderbolt, Aisulu," said Dulat. "She left my glove and she never wavered. She hit the wolf so hard he rolled over. And he rolled her and snapped at her, but she never let go."

His voice sank. "I killed the great wolf and I cut out his heart for her. And my father tied the body to my saddle, and he said to me: *Now you are a man of your people.* He took off his big glove, he put his bare hand on my head, and he said: *I knew you had the heart for an eagle. Now you are a man of your people.*"

Aisulu looked up at him, dark and upright against the high orange sky. He looked different—or she was looking at him differently. Like time the Fox Wife had told her: *You have the eyes of an eagle.*

"I was your age," Dulat said. "I was your age, and I had the whole world in front of me."

Her uncle with his heart overflowing. Her father selling their life. Her brother without his leg. Her eagle—

In her new eyes, the sky tilted. Something was changing. Something had changed.

Chapter Nine

AT LAST CAME THE DAY for Toktar to go outside.

In the evening, after the milking, Dulat picked Toktar up and set him on the glove, then popped the hood onto his head from behind.

Aisulu flinched. Her father patted her hand.

She was expecting Toktar be spooked by the hood. It was such an alien thing, though a beautiful one: dark leather goggles set with garnets where the eagle's eyes would be, attached over the top of the eagle's head with a leather cap. It was as strong and simple as a ger, and it weighed less than a coin. The eagle hood was older than Aisulu—probably older than Dulat—and when Toktar wore it, he looked indeed like a khan in his crown, like a blind poet with his eyes covered. He was only two months old, with white down still showing through his flight feathers like a boy's undershirt. But in the hood, he looked ancient and powerful.

He also looked calm.

"Eagles hunt with their eyes," said Dulat, his voice again

that soft voice, the heart-for-an-eagle voice with which he'd ended the story of the wolf hunt. "They look for danger with their eyes. An eagle with its eyes covered feels safe. Open the door."

Abai opened the door, and Dulat brought Toktar out into the open air. Aisulu trailed them, helpless.

The young eagle sat on her uncle's arm, his feathers tight, his body still as a statue. "That's my bird," murmured Dulat. "There." He stepped so carefully that he seemed to glide. In that way, he crossed the aul, swung over the new wall, and put Toktar on the ground inside his pen.

Then he took off the hood.

The whole world hit Toktar at once, and he flattened under its weight. He spread himself out like a badger and pushed his body against the ground. He was silent. His feathers were tight. The wind tried to ruffle them, but the eagle did not move.

His eyes were open and terrified.

"Oh, there," said Dulat. He made chuckling noises as if to a fussy baby. He stroked a hand down Toktar's neck. The bird stayed rigid. "There. You're safe. Stop this now. You're safe."

But Toktar did not move.

Dulat had left a slaughtered rabbit in the pen earlier. He offered Toktar the heart.

But Toktar still did not move.

"Stop this now," said Dulat. Louder, harder.

The mountaintop world was huge. The cries of the goats and sheep, the rattle of the sharp wind. The sky was all around them.

Aisulu watched, her hands tight on the top of the new wall, her father like a windbreak, right behind her. And Toktar did not move.

"I'm here," Aisulu whispered. "Things change sometimes. But I'm still here."

As if her voice were warmth, the eagle relaxed a little, slumped like hard snow turning to slush.

"Toktar," she said, a little louder. "I'm here."

Dulat looked up and beckoned to her. Aisulu glanced around at Abai, then climbed over the wall and crouched in front of her eagle.

He was looking right at her. Almost imperceptibly, he snaked his head from side to side. He was gauging distance.

"I'm close," she said. "I'm right here."

Tentatively, she reached out and stroked his head, his back. He made no sound. He did not stand. But after a moment he blinked slowly, and turned to let her run a thumb along the corners of his mouth.

"Take the heart," said Dulat.

Aisulu took the rabbit's heart. She nudged it toward

Toktar. He waited one beat, then two, and then he snatched it and sat up, all in one movement. The heart was gone in a gulp.

Dulat pulled the rest of the rabbit over.

For a moment Toktar looked wildly around at the whole strange world. He looked at Aisulu. Then he fell upon the rabbit. He mantled over it, making a tent of his back and wings, his glossy, growing feathers. He was not a wild eagle, but this was a wild thing, mantling. This was how an eagle should eat.

Abai, Aisulu, and Dulat held very still and listened to Toktar rip into the rabbit. And when he had had enough, he straightened, lifted his feathers into a mop of puff, then shivered to let them settle.

"There you are," said Dulat. "You are an eagle, and the sky is not going to kill you." He laid his gloved hand on the ground and whistled softly. Aisulu crouched behind him, watching.

Toktar gave the glove a skeptical look: *That thing, I mostly hate it.* He shuffled backward. And then, all at once, he changed. His eyes got bright. He stretched out low along the dusty ground like a cat stalking slowly through grass. His head weaved from side to side.

Aisulu kept still. She held her breath.

And Toktar struck. He flapped his stubby wings once,

swung his feet forward, and flashed right over the glove to land hard on Aisulu's bare wrist.

"Aisulu!" her father shouted, and Aisulu shouted too. The young eagle had struck with such force. It was like being rammed by a yak, pierced by a knife. Pain and wonder rushed through her. But the next instant she made herself calm. Toktar was hurting her, but Toktar had come to her. Had chosen.

Aisulu rose slowly to her feet. There was blood on her wrist, but there was also an eagle: bright-eyed, looking three miles into the distance, swaying to find his balance in the wind.

"Aish!" her father cried. Slowly, Aisulu glided around to face him, holding Toktar up. His talons had pierced her like nails, and her blood was running around her forearm and dripping onto the dusty ground. But she stood, looking at her father. Looking at her sky. Looking at her eagle.

"*Masha-Allah,*" breathed Dulat. He looked at Toktar, and he looked at Aisulu. "You have the heart for an eagle," he said softly. "You are a man of your people."

Abai bundled up his daughter and rushed her inside. Aisulu was bleeding. Toktar's talons had wrapped around her arm and gouged three pierced spots in the soft inside of her wrist and forearm, and a scratch across the pale golden skin of her palm.

The Fox Wife started up from her churning. "What happened?"

"She's a man of her people!" Dulat had followed them in. He was almost giggling.

The Fox Wife took a sharp breath, then looked across the ger to the reindeer skull. She met its empty eyes with what looked like exasperation. *"Kazakh,"* she huffed. "That she is a boy—is that the only way you can think of to say a girl has worth?" She muttered something that Aisulu suspected was a prayer or a curse in her own language. "Come here, child."

Aisulu went to her, holding her hurt arm bent up. Trickles of blood wrapped it and dripped from the point of her elbow.

"You don't understand," said Dulat. "The eagle flew to her. He flew straight to her, and he rode her wrist. He pointed himself into the wind."

The Fox Wife would not be diverted. She peered closely at Aisulu's arm and tutted over the gouges. "Only one looks deep, but that one . . ."

Abai hovered. "Is she all right?"

The Fox Wife looked up. "I'm sure one of you *men of your people* has a bottle of vodka."

"Yerzhan would." Dulat named Meiz's husband.

"Well. Go fetch it."

Dulat went. Kara-Kat-Kis guided Aisulu onto a stool and set a pot of water boiling. "Are you all right?" she asked. She glanced around at Abai and lowered her voice. "It is a good thing you are not a boy. A girl is used to bleeding."

Aisulu nodded, though her arm did hurt. Thorns of pain stabbed all the way through it, hot and twitchy. And yet. "Toktar flew to me," she whispered.

Hopped and flapped. But it had felt like flight. It had felt like being chosen. Her father was twisting his hat in his hands, but Aisulu's pain was mostly drowned in her wonder.

The Fox Wife dumped some rags into the boiling water, stirred them with a knife, and lifted them out, draped over the point and dripping. She was using a hot rag to wipe the wounds clean when Dulat returned with a bottle of vodka. The Fox Wife seized it, muttered something over it, and then pinioned Aisulu's wrist and dripped the alcohol into the deepest puncture wound.

It was as if she'd poured fire. Aisulu yipped in pain, tears springing to her eyes. She yanked air in and blew the pain away, then gulped air again, one two three. Through all of it she did not move her arm. The Fox Wife's bony fingers loosened but stayed wrapped around her arm like a bracelet.

Aisulu felt distant and giddy. She fingered the Fox Wife's joints as if they were prayer beads.

"Toktar flew to me," she said under her breath.

Dulat looked down at them, nodding. "See. She does not even flinch. She is —"

"Do not call her a boy and mean it a compliment, Husband."

"She has the heart for an eagle," Aisulu whispered. It was what Dulat had said to her. And it was what her grandfather had said to Dulat himself, when he had become an eagle hunter, a true burkitshi, passing the test of cold and fear and distance.

Dulat nodded. His hands were empty, but they did not look angry. "You do. Aisulu. You have the heart for an eagle."

Her father had come and put a hand on each of her shoulders. She felt the heavy pride in them, the squeeze. But the Fox Wife shook her head. "The eagle is your heart. You put your heart outside your body." She gave Aisulu's wrist a rattle. "You've left it there long enough."

Aisulu blinked at her.

The Fox Wife again turned to meet the empty eyes of the reindeer, sad beneath the blue straps of its bridle. She got up and crossed to the dresser, touching each of the things on the mirror — the glasses, the tassels, the wolf bone

—before opening the drawer and pulling out a clean scarf to use as a bandage.

Aisulu sat on her stool and the Fox Wife knelt before her. "Where is your heart?"

With her hurt hand, Aisulu pushed her fingers into the soft place above her heart. But she froze: she could not feel it beating. Through her brother's black shapan, she could feel nothing.

"Can you feel it?" asked the Fox Wife.

Aisulu shook her head, silent, horrified. She could feel the weight of her family in her father's hands, the thorn pain of her wound, the wetness drying on the inside of her mouth. But not her heart. Not in her fingers, not in her eardrums, not in her throat.

All those times she had said *stop* to her breath, to her words, to her thoughts. Had she stopped her own heart?

"Give me your arm," said the Fox Wife.

Aisulu straightened her hurt arm, and the Fox Wife wrapped the scarf around it. She held Aisulu's arm, and with the other hand she tapped the back of Aisulu's hand. Slowly. Rhythmically. As it were a drum. *Tap. Dum. Tap. Dum.*

She began to speak. And though her words were ordinary, they had the same beat as her fingers.

"Aisulu." *Lub dub dub.*

"You will heal." *Lub dub dub.* "You are safe." *Lub dub dub.*

"You are safe, so feel your fear. You are safe, so loose your tears. Aisulu. Aisulu."

Aisulu suddenly remembered climbing the shale crag to rescue Toktar from his nest. She had climbed twenty, thirty, forty feet into the air. That far up, she'd been frightened but not struck with fear. It was not safe to be struck. The fear did not strike her until she had her feet back on the ground. Only when she was safe had her knees rattled, her hands shook.

She had not felt fear until she was safe.

And now she was safe.

And so she felt . . . she felt . . .

"Ake, you left me!" she wailed, twisting around, the words tearing out of her throat. "And, Eej—Mother—you didn't say goodbye! You didn't even send word! And Serik—he's damaged, he's— We have to leave here and— I want my brother!"

She gave a raw scream and started to weep.

There are men who are brave in the face of anything but tears.

Aisulu crumpled and cried, and the Fox Wife caught her, drumming the heartbeat on her back. Above them Dulat and Abai stood perfectly useless. "I . . ." said one, and the other: "Um . . ."

"My brother," sobbed Aisulu. "*Toktar.* He will live. He will live."

The Fox Wife kept tapping a heartbeat on her back. Aisulu could feel the *lub dub* of it, in time with her own heartbeat pounding in her hurt arm. She had put her heart into Toktar for weeks, and in those weeks she had not felt anything. It hurt so much to put her heart back in her body.

"He will," said Aisulu. "He will. He will live."

"He will," said Dulat, awkward. "Your eagle is strong."

The Fox Wife huffed sharply. "You have two degrees in aeronautical engineering. Can you not at least make us tea?"

"*Tsai oh, tsai oh,*" said Aisulu nonsensically, the way a baby might say *mama, mama.*

"Yes," said Abai. "We'll drink tea."

There was a long pause.

Then Dulat said: "I do not know how to make tea."

Aisulu folded forward, caught between tears and laughter. She let both out, in weird hiccups.

The Fox Wife sighed and stood up. "I have failed as a Kazakh wife and a woman. I have kept my husband waiting for tea."

"Now there." Dulat caught her around the waist. "You are the best of wives, and your grades were better than mine. Show me tea."

So Abai sat on the stool and wrapped up Aisulu, and

Dulat watched while the Fox Wife made a show of tea. She showed where the block of compressed tea leaves was kept, in a cloth bag under the bed, and where the hammer was kept to knock off a few chunks. She showed how to boil milk and water together. She showed how much tea to add and how much salt. The chunks of tea swirled apart into leaves. The milky water turned amber. Kara-Kat-Kis poured the pan of tea into the kettle without spilling a drop.

Dulat did manage to get out the tea bowls, all on his own. He handed the green and pink one to Aisulu, and for an instant he pressed his hands over hers, so that two layers of hands were holding that empty bowl.

Aisulu stood up, to free her father, but he kept his arm around her. "Aisulu. The disease your brother had is dangerous. But it was in his leg and they cut the leg off. He will be all right. *You* saved him."

"He begged me not to tell," she whispered.

"But you did. And that saved him."

"I don't want to go to Ulaanbaatar," she said. "Serik — he said you'd send him away. He said he'd lose everything."

They were going to lose *everything*.

"Abai." Dulat had stood up abruptly, frowning so hard that his mustache bristled. He dropped into grand pronouncement mode: "Come with me. Everyone. Come with me."

Dulat strode out of the ger and they all blinked at each other. Aisulu was the first to follow him. Her tears blurred the aul and made it more beautiful. Even the gray canvas of gers was golden in the evening light. Her home. Serik's home. Their everything. Dulat led the three of them over to the eagle pen.

"This is the age to take an eagle." Dulat's hands gripped the top of the new stone wall. "Old enough to survive without its parents, but too young to fly away. This is how I first saw Crooked Claw. My father showed me how to do it. We took Crooked Claw from her nest and we put her in a box that swung. We swung the box on a rope for three days, so that she could not rest. I stayed awake and I kept her awake. When she came out she was ready to be mine."

Aisulu could not even look at him. She looked at his hands instead. They were very big, very strong. He wore a ring of heavy silver set with a blue stone. These hands had put an eagle in a box.

"We broke her heart to make her mine," he said. "That's how it's done."

Toktar, full of rabbit, had come hopping over to them. Aisulu's pulse beat under her bandages.

"Abai," said Dulat. "It was on the radio, so perhaps you heard—the Eagle Festival has sponsorship this year. Some foreigners are making a television. Some football people, I think."

Abai's eyebrows folded up. "Yes? So?"

"I'm thinking of the money. They are giving prize money, to make our festival a game."

Toktar did not *ker-honk* at them. He was so full of rabbit that his crop stuck out, raising a patch of white down from among his dark shaggy feathers. He wobbled playfully from foot to foot.

"I know you must go to Ulaanbaatar," said Dulat. "The foreign prize money would take you there. If you don't have to sell your ger and your herd, then you could come back."

Aisulu looked up. Hope flooded into her. And then horror. They felt the same. "You're going to fly Toktar," she said.

"No," said Dulat. "*You're* going to fly him."

"What?" said Aisulu.

"To fly an eagle, you need the heart for an eagle," said Dulat. "And to win at the festival, you must have your eagle's heart. I can fly an eagle, but I can't fly Toktar. He is yours. It can only be you."

There was a space so long that Curious Yak came wandering over to fill it. Abai scratched the beast's back with a stick. For a long time the three of them were silent.

"Toktar's yours," said Dulat. "You've had enough heart-breaking."

Aisulu sucked in a breath that wobbled in her chest.

Her father looked down at her, and seemed at once to be trying not to smile and trying not to cry. "But—there's never been a girl, Dulat. Not in a thousand years. Girls don't become eagle hunters."

"That's not true," said the Fox Wife. "There have been women with eagles since ancient days. In Mongolia, in Kazakhstan, in Kyrgyzstan, in China, in Russia. Wherever the eagles fly and our peoples live sky-close to them, for thousands of years, there have been women."

"Though it's true there have not been many in Olgii City," said Dulat, taking his wife's hand.

"Well," said Abai. "Well, then."

"Things change sometimes," said Aisulu. She was not really thinking, but she heard herself speaking, heard the words fall from her lips like gold coins. The grief and the new hope, pulling her shoulders back. Her chest felt open, and her breath felt deep. Her heart was beating. "Sometimes things change."

Abai was silent a long time. Finally, he said: "My fox kit—do you remember your first horse race? You were so small. Do you even remember?"

"I remember." She had been seven, and slight for seven,

hollow-boned like a bird. Her father had helped her practice, across the tussocks of their winter camp in the valley, beside the sweeping curve of the cold Hvod River. She had started in the spring, when the river was jammed with broken towers of ice, great slabs of it tilted and streaked green as stained glass, green as emeralds.

Even now she could see the strange ice. She could remember learning the feel of a horse, learning how to ride with her thighs, moving so closely with her mount that she barely touched the saddle. She started fast, and she learned to go faster, sure-footed in the swerve so that no stone or hollow could slow her. She could remember outracing the eddying streamers of snow. They had trailed behind her like banners.

"I remember," she said.

"That first Naadam festival: You were little among all those horses, all those people. Those wrestlers—it seemed like you hardly came up to their knees. Do you remember what I told you?"

"No one thinks you can do this," said Aisulu. *"So let's give them a surprise."*

She was not quite sure what "football people" were. But she was sure she could surprise them.

Dulat barked a laugh. "And they say mares don't win medals."

"Aisulu did." Abai put his hand on her head, warm as a cuddle, heavy as a crown.

"And girls don't fly eagles, but Aisulu can," said Dulat. "We can teach her. And if she can win, you can come back from Ulanbaataar."

"'Burkit makes burkitshi: the eagle makes the eagle hunter,'" said Abai, quoting absently. He shook himself. "This is too much weight to put on a little girl."

"Oh, not so little." Dulat turned and leaned his back on Toktar's wall, looking down across the aul: the three gers, the sheds, the platforms for drying the cheese, the grazing yaks, the empty night pens for the baby goats. He was the oldest son, and this was life he had been summoned back to upon the death of his father. His eyes were distant, as if he were thinking of life he'd left behind. "My old company —my old friends—someone might have an apartment for you, or a ger. Don't sell your herd, Brother. Not yet. The world is a big place. Don't get trapped in a part of it that's wrong for you."

"Like you?" said Aisulu.

"Oh," said Dulat, and put the whole weight of the world of gers into the one word. "Who needs wind turbines anyway? It is perfect here."

And here is something that is hard but true: a place can be perfect, and still not be enough.

• • •

Great decisions made among the Kazakh people are to be chewed over with bread and butter, above a bowl of tea. So they went back inside.

Aisulu had watched her father walk when he'd come off the motorcycle, those weeks ago, with the news still inside him. He'd been ghost-riddled, dust-covered, stiff-legged and weary. He moved better now. There was hope in him.

Inside the ger, Dulat slid into his place on the futon without hesitating, the master of the ger. His brother should have claimed the seat next to him, but Abai wavered, and finally perched on the other end of the futon and pulled Aisulu down to rest on his knee, as if she were six years old. They spooned butter into their cooling tea and chewed the fresh squeaky cheese for a long moment before anyone dared to speak.

Finally Dulat stroked his mustache. "It's like this." He pulled his notebook from its place under the futon cushion, flipped to the first blank page, and drew three little lines at the top of the paper. "There are three pieces to the Eagle Festival. First there is a parade. You must ride before the judges with your eagle. They will judge the beauty of your eagle, and your riding, and the look of the gear you wear."

"I don't have any gear," said Aisulu. The embroidered shapan, the embroidered pants, the eagle hunter's hat—she had none of these things, and no way to get them. She had not thought of it before, but a lack of costume alone would be enough to disqualify her.

Dulat raised a hand and pushed her worries aside as if they were nothing. "Second," he said, ticking the second mark with a pencil. "You must release your eagle to strike a moving target. They use a rabbit on a rope."

"A live rabbit?" said Aisulu.

"Not for long," murmured the Fox Wife. She had finished setting out the tea foods, and she now crouched across from them, hunkering down like a cat by the stovepipe.

"A dead rabbit," said Abai. "A lure, stuffed with straw. They pull it along behind a horse." He squeezed Aisulu against his body, as if he thought a stuffed rabbit would bother her. He clearly didn't know she'd been the doom of all mice.

"Third," said Dulat. "You must call your eagle to you. I will climb the eagle hunter's mountain and release him, and you must call."

"Dulat, wait," said Abai. "She cannot fly a male eagle."

Dulat flipped backward in the notebook, to the incomprehensible chart he had shown Aisulu once before—and then tapped it as if it proved a point. "Since there was only one chick and we do not know the age, we can't be sure yet.

But the important thing is the size, the look of the bird. The big ones are always female, and every eagle we fly, we call she. And Toktar is big."

"*She,*" said Aisulu. Trying it out. It felt wrong.

"Call her female," said the Fox Wife, "for you will be asking everything of her."

Aisulu shook her head, trying to keep track. "You'll release Toktar," she said, "and I'll call."

"You must ride and call. You must catch Toktar at full gallop." Dulat pushed his lips together. "There are many people at the festival, and many other birds. It's too much for most eagles. They do not come to the call."

"Toktar will," said Aisulu.

"Yes," said Dulat. "This is what I thought. Toktar will."

Abai put his hand on top of Aisulu's head. She rose into him the way Toktar did when he wanted to be loved.

And then something strange happened. Dulat took Aisulu's arm and pulled her off her father's knee, until she was sitting on the futon between the two brothers, in the place of the most honored guest. A man's place. She had lived in gers all her life, and she had never once even thought to sit there.

In front of her the notebook was like an artifact from another world. It was a student's notebook, Dulat's student notebook, the facing page full of sketches of turbine blades and smudged columns of calculations in which letters and numbers were mixed together.

"It's like this." Dulat looked at her with his eyebrows drawn down and mustache wrinkled, as if making those calculations in his head. "The judges might favor you because you are a girl. Or because you are a girl they might give you no chance at all. There is nothing you can do about either. But if Toktar comes to you, if the eagle comes to you hard as a thunderbolt . . . if Toktar comes to you as I think he will . . ." He put his hand over hers. "They will have stopwatches. They will have eyes. This is why I think you can win."

Chapter Ten

FOR THE FIRST TIME IN HER LIFE, Aisulu stood at the center of her family.

Her father, Abai, rode up over the mountain, and when he returned, dust-stained in the twilight, his horse was dragging the branching trunk of a cedar tree. He put it in the eagle's pen, one end propped high, so that Toktar could learn to lean into the wind.

Her uncle Dulat went over and over the festival rules until Aisulu knew them by heart. She noticed he kept his notebook out, filled it with scribbles, with smudgy sketches of something that looked like the arc of a feather, or part of a wing.

Her twin boy cousins, Temir and Balta, set traps for rabbits and marmots to feed the eagle. They even helped (when Meiz made them) with the hauling of the water.

Her girl cousin, Enlik, continued her rodent reign of terror.

Her other uncle, Yerzhan, the quiet one, the one who

drank sometimes, put his dombra into tune and began to play music. Between the twilight prayer and the night prayer, he played songs that started slowly, with one plucked note and then another, with the snap of his fingernails against the wood of the sounding board—songs that grew and built, and built and grew until the little fiddle with its two strings sounded like a dozen horses pounding. The family sat by Dulat's stove to listen. Men stomped their boots until tiny bricks of mud fell on the floor, and the women churned to the beat.

The Fox Wife watched it all, her smile like the lip of a well whose cover had been nudged aside: sliver small, but deep and promising.

As for Toktar, he spent his days in his new pen, being admired by the family and by Curious Yak, and his nights in the big ger, near the rugs where Aisulu still slept. He perched on his stand, alternately drowsing, screaming for mice, and tending to his new feathers.

Aisulu and her father continued to stay in the big ger with the blue door. Four was a good number of people for a ger at night. Aisulu lay on her rugs. The band was tucked around the base of the walls. The flap was closed over the crown. The ger was warm, and smelled of the dung fire —grassy, dusty, spicy—and of tea and milk and people. The fire sounded crinkly and the metal stove clinked and dinged. Shifting blankets and snores blended into each other, and sometimes in the night the whole ger seemed to be breathing.

In the music and in the rustling nights, Aisulu felt the great love of her family and the deep roots of her people. But she had put her heart back in her body, and now she also knew that she was afraid.

The Eagle Festival was the first week of October, only eight weeks away. It was her chance to save her brother, but it was also her chance to fail him. To fail her family. There was so much to do, and every day that passed was one day less.

Toktar could not even fly yet, and he would need to learn to strike on her command and come to her call. Moon Spot had never worn a saddle, and she would have to learn to carry an eagle.

And then there was the matter of her gear.

Aisulu lacked all the things she needed to look like an eagle hunter: the traditional hat, the embroidered shapan and pants, the fine belt and boots, the pouch for carrying meat. Though her father and her uncle did not worry, her aunties did. They knew that embroidery was the work of a million stitches, a hundred evenings. A big piece of embroidery could take a whole winter, and winters were long. In the summer, with the churning and the milking—even with the bright evenings of the northern August, there was not enough time.

Aisulu thought that the judges would take one look at her—small, poor, and female—and fail her from the festival.

She needed an eagle hunter's outfit the way a knight needed armor. But she could think of no way to get one.

Toktar needed time to grow his wings, and the problem of embroidery seemed unsolvable, so the only thing that Aisulu could work on was getting a saddle onto her horse.

Moon Spot had been captured from a herd of wild horses when she was just a yearling. She'd been run down by horsemen with lassos, barely tamed, kept for her milk. But Aisulu had chosen her from among the milk horses. She'd named her because she named everything. She'd brought her treats, she'd stroked her nose. She'd leaned against Moon Spot's mottled side until the horse had let her mount. She'd leaned across her neck until the horse had learned to run. And all without a saddle.

But an eagle hunter's horse needs a saddle. And in eight weeks, Moon Spot would have to pass as an eagle hunter's horse. So Aisulu borrowed her father's saddle and set it gently on Moon's back.

It did not go well. Moon Spot spread her legs and made

them stiff, like a cat being stuffed into a box. *I have roots*, the horse's body seemed to say. *I have roots and there is something weird on me.* Her skin shivered as if flies were swarming her.

"My beautiful horse," said Aisulu. "My moonlight horse, there you are, easy there. It won't hurt you, take it easy."

Moon Spot snorted skeptically. She lifted one rear foot and it trembled, as if she would strike out with it.

Aisulu tugged her bridle.

The horse put the foot back down.

"It will be a long way to Oglii City if you won't take one step," said Aisulu.

The horse gave her that look peculiar to horses, the one that said: *I have gone with you 402 times but time 403 is scary.*

"I know moon horse, sky horse, I know, take it easy." Aisulu was crooning under her breath, pure nonsense peppered with words. The horse's ears were loosening up, beginning to tilt around to find Aisulu's voice.

"Now easy, you're acting like Strong Wind, take it easy."

Moon Spot decided to risk one step. The saddle did not attack her.

In the space of a tea brew, Aisulu got her horse to take five steps. In the space of butter churning, she'd led her once around the ger. By the second day she had the saddle strapped on. And by the third day she was riding.

On the fifth day they added the eagle.

Aisulu put Toktar on her glove before she swung into the saddle. On Dulat's advice she added the hood, too. But even with the hood to keep him calm, Toktar was uneasy. He spread his wings all the way out as she mounted, his weight shifting, and his talons clamped around her arm. She was sure he did not mean to hurt her, but his grip started tight and only got tighter. Every time the horse shifted or whuffled, Toktar's talons spasmed.

Dulat stood at her side, holding Moon Spot's bridle.

Mounted, Aisulu stroked her bird's back and Toktar leaned into her. But still she could feel the points of his claws, chiseling through the thick leather glove. "He's holding on so hard," she whispered.

"Your eagle must get used to this," said Dulat. "And your horse must. You all must."

Toktar's blind head whipped to the sound of Dulat's voice, and then wove a figure eight through the air, trying to find him. All the time his talons stabbed into Aisulu's arm as if to kill. Aisulu had heard of eagles breaking men's arms —it was easily possible. Moon Spot snorted. The mare's ears were twisted and pinned back against her head.

Aisulu felt caught between her two creatures. She felt bad for both of them, but she knew she must keep her heart quiet and strong. She stayed strong and quiet until Moon Spot let her ears soften and Toktar began to let go.

For that day's ride, Dulat had switched her father's saddle with his own. It had a forked branch attached to the front: a prop with a padded leather place for her to set her wrist. She did that.

Dulat let go of Moon Spot's bridle. "You have him?"

"He's not heavy." She could feel Toktar's beautiful, shifting balance. It was so perfect that it was as if the eagle were holding up some of his own weight. As if he were hooked into the sky.

Dulat took a step back and looked her over, stroking his mustache. "Have you ever held a weight for a long time?"

"Have you ever carried a pail of water up a mountain?" she shot back. Toktar might weigh ten pounds. A water bucket could weigh twenty, and she carried two of them.

Dulat shrugged and mounted. "Well, little strongman. Your shoulder will get tired. Keep it soft. Let the stick do the work."

Dulat's horse had an unusual straw-gold mane, and Aisulu had named him Fox Tail. Fox Tail was an evil beast: the kind of horse that held its breath when saddled so it could shake off saddle and rider later. Moon Spot side-eyed him. She seemed to think the whole project was a terrible mistake. But Aisulu kept her body steady and her reins soft, and sent a stream of gentle words into the horse's mane. And when Fox Tail started forward, Moon Spot did too.

It was awful.

Moon Spot was nervous, which made her steps stiff and jarring. The angle at which the prop kept Aisulu's shoulder was strange. Toktar's grip throbbed and stabbed. The strangeness of the saddle, the stick, the eagle—it all began to build up into pain. Aisulu lived in a world where she did the same thing over and over. She did not remember the last time she'd tried something she was not good at. It made her want to scream.

"A break," said Dulat, at last. He dismounted, and Fox Tail stepped sideways as he did it, to send Dulat staggering and then sprawling in the dirt. Aisulu got down, and felt good about not falling herself. She was stiff all over.

They were in the place where their mountain rubbed shoulders with the next mountain. The high point of the pass was marked by a heap of stones and silk-wrapped poles: the shrine to the sky. It was in this place that she and her brother had huddled together through the summer blizzard. In this place, she had felt the sickness deep inside him. She had named it.

She had set it free.

It felt as if—she knew it wasn't true—but it felt as if this were the place where she'd doomed her brother. And now it was the place where she was failing him. The eagle on her wrist was so heavy that she could barely hold him. Her arm was shaking.

Dulat was sitting in the grass, where his horse had dumped him. Reluctantly, Aisulu sat down beside him. At least that way she could rest her glove on her knee.

"I can't do this," she whispered.

"You must," said her uncle.

"Is *must* the only word you know?" Aisulu snapped.

"The things I have done," said her uncle, plucking a stem of grass to chew, "because of *must*."

Aisulu looked back up at the sky shrine. After a long time Dulat took Toktar from her — making the bird freeze and tighten his feathers — and carried him home.

A second day of riding. Little better than the first. Dulat and Aisulu traced the goat trails up the mountain. Toktar was stiff feathered. Moon Spot's every hoof fall was hard, as if the horse were walking on ice.

When they reached the sky shrine, Aisulu was glad to stop. Glad to sit on a stone in the sun, because at least the sun wasn't depending on her for anything.

They sat in silence awhile, while the horses pulled up hanks of grass.

"Does your shoulder hurt?" Dulat asked.

It did. It was a ball of aching, deep as a bruise. She wanted to curl up.

She didn't.

They were looking down into the thistle meadow where once she and Serik had found his stupid, straying horse. The meadow was grazed short now. "Have some," said Dulat, and handed her a lump of the bone-hard dry cheese that fueled men through their day of herding. She sucked on it. Toktar turned his blind head toward her to see if sucking meant food for him too.

Inside the heavy glove, her hand felt small and sweaty. A seam was rubbing a blister into the base of her thumb.

"I was thirteen when I captured Crooked Claw," said Dulat, at length.

"You've said," she grumbled.

"Most burkitshi begin training at thirteen. Your age."

"I'm twelve."

"Thirteen next month," he said, and she was touched that he knew. "You are of age, and your eagle is of age. Most new eagles are balapan: first-year eagles. A few will be older, wild caught, but most are a few months old, just fledged. They will not have more practice than you."

"They won't be girls."

"So they won't be girls," he said. He seemed to be trying to be kind. He was not especially good at it. "But they won't have your heart. They won't have an eagle that loves them. They will not have your need, your brother."

The sun shifted, and suddenly the thistledown meadow before them was gleaming silver, bright as water. Behind them the blue silk sang around the poles of the sky. Aisulu looked for a moment at her beautiful world.

"Serik and me—after the blizzard. We saw an eagle, right here. Toktar's eagle mother. She was eating songbirds."

Dulat gave her listening silence.

"Serik wanted to capture her. We had this stupid fight —I saw that he was limping, and I said he should tell our father. But he didn't . . . he wanted . . ."

"He wanted to be an eagle hunter," said Dulat, as if that made sense to him. "He was afraid of what he would lose, and he wanted everything."

Toktar, on her lap, leaned into her stroking hands. He was everything. Her eagle. She had everything. She was so close to having everything. And her brother . . .

There was a young man who lived near her school who had lost a foot to frostbite. He'd been a nomad, once, but now he drank too much and lived in the town. Now he begged in the street.

"How can Serik come back here? They . . . they cut off his leg."

"It depends on how high the amputation is, how good

he is with the prosthesis . . ." Dulat shrugged, sucking on cheese. "My thesis supervisor had one arm, and he could have been a blacksmith, I swear. He liked to do handstands in Suhkbaatar Square. In the city, Serik could get a good leg. You could go to school."

"I already go to school." She went in the winter, like all the nomad children. She lived in the dormitories in the town. "I like school."

"But you want more." He wasn't looking at her. He pushed himself to his feet and handed her a canteen. "Here, finish this. Then we'll head home."

Aisulu tipped a mouthful of water down her throat. It was warm and good. She poured the rest down Toktar's back. It ran off his feathers in beads. The eagle rustled himself happily. She stroked him smooth and he leaned into her like a kitten. Her eagle. Her everything.

But again it was Dulat who carried him home.

A third day. Moon Spot looked at Aisulu and sighed, but made no fuss as she mounted. The horse, at least, was getting better at this.

"Let me help you with your arm this time," said Dulat. "Little miss strongman."

He put his hand under her elbow, adjusting the set of her arm and shoulder, then stepped back and considered her. Then he stepped in and moved her arm again. He was trying to fix her, but she didn't feel fixed. She felt weird. She felt awkward. Toktar shifted from foot to foot. Moon Spot took a couple of steps forward and started to browse.

Aisulu leaned forward to scratch her horse's neck and get her attention back. And as she did it, her arm slipped into place. It was weird, it was awkward — and then, all of a sudden, it was right. She'd found the right place, and it was like that moment when she'd learned to see mouse holes. In an instant, everything changed. The prop held up her wrist as if she were hanging from the sky.

She grinned at Dulat, purely delighted. "Like this?"

"Like that!" he said — and Fox Tail took advantage of the moment to step on Dulat's foot. Her uncle grimaced and hopped, but he was grinning back at her. "We've been lazing along, these two days. I've heard that you can go a little faster."

"Ha! I'll show you fast," she said, and leaned forward, her face brushing the eagle, her knees digging in. Moon Spot stamped twice and then took off at a run. Aisulu settled her toes into her stirrups and rose out of her saddle, floating above her horse. With her arm supported, Toktar seemed to weigh nothing. He was hoodless. He was all hollow bones and bright eyes. He stiffened his neck and leaned the arrow of his head into the wind of their speed. His wings opened for balance. They were shaggy and the feathers under his chin were as scraggly as a boy's first beard, but his face was pointed toward the far horizon.

Feeling Toktar ride the wave of balance on her arm, Aisulu knew deep down in her bones that this eagle — who had her heart and was her heart — this eagle was a thing that was meant to fly.

That was Toktar's first taste of wind.

After that, Aisulu took her eagle riding every day. Moon Spot grew used to Toktar, and stopped tightening her ears and stiffening her legs. Aisulu's shoulder slowly stopped aching as she learned to find the point of balance on her arm support. And Toktar learned to love the wind.

Dulat propped one end of his log perch far up, and Toktar would jump onto that, flapping like a pigeon, and then sidestep his way to the highest point. There he would sit in his white boots, preening his new feathers and tearing up the cedar bark. Aisulu would see him as she flattened the yak poop with a shovel and spread it out to dry. She would see him when she milked the skittish horses. When she climbed back into the camp with her pails of water, she would see him silhouetted, a dark gloss against the brilliant sky.

Always he sat facing the wind. And then one evening,

ten weeks after she had taken him from the nest, he opened his wings.

Aisulu was out milking the yaks. She stopped milking and stood up.

The evening wind was blowing cold down from the top of the mountain. Toktar opened his wings. The wind caught them. Lifted them. Toktar was rocked backward and his talons clamped into the wood. She could hear it, the high shredding sound.

Gusts pushed Toktar's wings up and down. For a moment he twisted like Curious Yak, tipping his head to watch his own wings. He fiddled them. He shifted his feathers.

And then, with his talons tight, his wings spread, Toktar pointed his head like an arrow. He leaned into the wind.

Soon, thought Aisulu.

There were seven weeks until the festival.

Her hand clamped tight on the milk bucket. Her heart filled up with sky.

The last week in August came, with fine weather—winds and piercing sun. Toktar sat on his perch in the sunshine like the khan of the mountain. There was something new in his eyes.

The men came back with the herds—Dulat with a rifle

slung across his back—and brought with them three marmots: two for the stew pot and one for Toktar. Aisulu did the milking and the water carrying, and by the time she was ready to feed Toktar, the light was growing long.

Toktar saw her coming and began to cheep like a nestling. But once she'd climbed over the wall, he fell silent.

That silence nudged against her.

She looked up at Toktar.

He was looking three miles deep again. But not at her. At the marmot in her hand. She put it on the ground, at the other end of the long pen from the eagle. She stepped away.

Toktar kept his eyes hooked into the still fur. His head weaved from side to side. He leaned forward. He raised his tail and poop went shooting backward. And then, that much lighter, he opened his wings.

Aisulu held her breath.

Toktar bunched up like a snow leopard about to spring, then shoved his body forward, into the air, and he sailed.

The next instant, he had slammed into the marmot and was back on the ground, skidding gracelessly to a stop. But there had been a moment like a skipped heartbeat, a moment when he was in the air. "Toktar," said Aisulu. "You can fly! *Masha-Allah! You flew!*"

Toktar wasn't listening. He squeezed the marmot in pure predator delight, then folded forward over it. The smooth top edges of his wings—the ones that split the wind—were stretched out and down, sweeping curves as fine as holy calligraphy. The little gold feathers of his head and collar ruffled in the wind.

"Dulat! Ake!" Aisulu shouted to the men who were running over. "He flew! He flew!"

Her father seized her from behind and hugged her like a bear, pulling her up off her feet and into the endless sky.

Chapter Eleven

So Aisulu learned to ride with a saddle and an eagle, and Moon Spot learned to run with a saddle and an eagle, and Toktar learned the textures of the wind.

But that still left the problem of Aisulu's gear. By now they had tried several things. Her uncle had offered his own eagle hunter's outfit, which featured a thick coat of fox fur —corsac fox, red and blond and dappled black. She'd tried it on and little Enlik had burst into laughter. "You look like a bunny!" And it was true: the giant coat made little Aisulu into a puffball atop a pair of legs.

"You look . . ." She could see her father trying to be kind. "You look fluffy."

Dulat stopped mid-mustache-stroke, cupping his mouth with his hand.

Aisulu took the coat off.

After that, Abai had gone riding to talk to the old eagle hunters, to see if any had gear to spare. Aisulu thought this might work. Abai was big and warm and thoughtful. Everyone liked him, and everyone knew him. Before Dulat had returned to the aul, Abai had managed the trades of animals—borrowing the visit of a bull yak in the yak-breeding season, swapping cows in the late summer to keep the health of the herd. He was a man who always had a whetstone for your hay scythe, a scrap of tin to fix your still. And Kazakhs helped each other. The country was wild and hard. When a family moved and began to set up their gers in a new camp, every neighbor in sight would hurry over, bringing a thermos jug of tea, a bag of baursak bread, or a bottle of vodka.

But trip after trip, Abai returned empty-handed.

At first he tried to smile. But on the fifth trip he sat down to tea so hard that the table rattled.

"Jok," he said. *"Jok, jok, jok,"* they say. "They say I should not do this—should not give up my ger, my herd, my place here. For one child, for a son who will always be lame—*Jok,* they say. No, they say, it is a ridiculous plan: no girl can win at the Eagle Festival."

Abai was not a man to bang his fist into things. He closed it softly and tapped it against the table. "No girl can save me, they say," he said, softer. "No girl can do that."

Aisulu felt the table shudder under her hands. The tea bowls rattled. Her heart rattled. *No girl can save her family.* For the very first time, she thought: *I should have been a boy.*

Aisulu had wished for a bigger world. She had wished for a bigger life. But she had never, ever wanted to be something besides what she was. And now she did. It made her stomach sour, her heart twist. It was a terrible, terrible thing.

"If I were a boy," she said. Her voice broke. "If I were a boy I could save my brother."

"Don't you dare," said Abai. "You are a girl. You are my girl, and you have an eagle. These are just the facts. Do you understand me?"

Aisulu tucked her head. There were tears beaded up in her eyes and scorching in the back of her throat. "Yes, Ake."

Her father bumped her chin up with his soft fist.

"I will see you dressed as an eagle hunter, Aisulu. Even if I have to pick up a needle myself." He swept one hand over the bowls of cheese and butter, looking at Meiz and Kara-Kat-Kis like a king about to command the sea. "Begin the embroidery!"

Her aunties looked at each other. There were only six weeks until the festival. When it came to embroidery, that was too late to begin.

But meanwhile, Toktar flew. He flew that day, and he flew the next. His first attempts were labored and his first landings were worse. He pitched face first into things. The white underside of his wings and tails flashed like ruffly underwear, but Aisulu didn't care. No one cared. She had taken an orphaned eagle chick as small as a newborn puppy, as helpless as that, and now he had seven-foot wings. Now he could fly. Toktar: he lived.

"Well," said Dulat, watching the eagle's great surging wings, the trailing ends of his jesses skimming the grass. "Now we can begin to work."

Aisulu was carrying water again: she had just walked up a mountain with a bucket in each hand. "Oh, good," she said, putting them down. "I have had nothing to do until now."

But in fact, the work was hard. For the next week she practiced putting the hood on Toktar until she could do it with a flick, then learned to unhood him and thrust him into the air in one motion, practicing so many times her arm muscles grew lean and strong, so many times that the eagle glove rubbed a deep blister at the meaty root of her thumb.

Preparations are under way in Olgii City for the great Eagle Festival, which is now only five weeks away, said the tinny and calm voice of the radio one night. *We are expecting about seventy eagle hunters, and many tourists and special guests who will come to see the glory of the Kazakh culture. Radio listeners, there is special news: one of the eagle hunters will be a young girl.*

Aisulu tucked her blistered hand against her lips, sucking away the pain. She tried to remember what her father had said: *You are a girl, and you have an eagle. Those are just the facts.*

But they didn't feel like facts. They felt like something heavy to carry, like two pails of water.

And now everyone knew.

A few days later, Dulat announced that it was time to move.

The high bowl of the mountains had been a good camp, letting them reach the mountain meadows that were greenest in high summer. Now summer was turning—the iris blooms were gone, and the mayflies danced above the river. It was time to move the gers to the lowlands, to cut the hay and fatten the herds on the last good grass.

Toktar sat quiet and hooded on his perch as trunks and rugs were carried out of the gers. He kept sitting as the gers came down.

Aisulu and her father worked together on their own little ger. They unwrapped the outer skin of canvas, and the inner skin of gray felt. They took down the embroidery. They rolled up the reed mats that made the wall beneath. They untied the red-painted willow poles that were the roof staves and one by one tugged them free of the holes of the ger crown. They folded the lattice and unlashed it from the door. In an hour the aul and everything in it was piled in the back of the hay truck.

Aisulu's family did this every year at this time, as regular as the mayflies, as regular as the swans that moved with the seasons, as regular as the meteors that fell when the nights were warmest. But this time Aisulu looked at the camp and it seemed like a ruin. Even her eagle was something that blazed through her like a meteor. Something that was bright, and beautiful, but falling.

Serik needed saving, and she was not sure she could save him.

This camp was the last place she had seen him. She did not want to leave it behind.

Her hand was sore from the glove blister, and it hurt her as she worked. It throbbed as she scrambled up the back of the hay truck, perching with the Fox Wife and Meiz's children, fifteen feet up, on top of the heap of everything they owned.

Yerzhan climbed up into the driver's seat. Meiz swung her huge pregnant belly up and into the passenger seat.

Dulat passed Toktar up to her, still hooded, upside down on the end of a rope, his wings flapping wildly. Aisulu caught him by the rope, hauled him up, and wrapped him in her arms. She could feel his heartbeat vibrate through his body.

The truck was an ancient thing, left by the Russian soldiers when they finally let Mongolia go in the 1990s. Maybe older than that, even. Abai and Dulat had to work together to turn its stiff, big crank. The men cursed and grunted. The engine wheezed and sputtered. It caught. The truck shuddered. Toktar's beak fell open with fear while Aisulu murmured to him. Her hand hurt.

Her heart hurt.

They left.

Aisulu's family usually made fall camp near a bend on the river. It was a good place. The grass was thicker than in other places. There was water nearby. There was a power line that sometimes brought them electricity—more electricity than their solar panels could generate. There was reception for Dulat's cell phone, which their summer camp did not have.

They struck out toward that place. The big truck bumped and swayed its way slowly down the mountain.

Dulat and Abai followed on horseback, driving the herd, the cows and yaks and milk horses. Soon the truck had left the riders behind. And therefore they were away from the older men's protection when it happened.

The truck was growling along the skirts of the foothills. The road there was just a groove in the dirt, scattered with new falls of loose sharp shale. The truck sent up a giant plume of dust, and for a long time they were alone on the empty road, as if they were the only people in the whole country.

And then: They were in sight of their usual fall camp when two horsemen swept down upon them. The men galloped down the slope above, their horses golden against the red and purple and brown of the foothills, their shapan coats dark and rich with gold embroidery. Hooves pounded and rattled. Manes and tails flew like banners.

The strangers rode out into the dust of the road and whirled the horses about. They stopped there like spearmen, poised to strike. Yerzhan slammed on the brakes. Aisulu lurched forward, pulling Toktar close. Kara-Kat-Kis tightened her grip on baby Naizabai with one hand, threw her other arm out to catch the twins. The twins toppled anyway. The truck skidded, then stopped, shuddering. The engine coughed twice and went still. Suddenly it was very quiet. Aisulu could hear the rustle of Toktar's feathers, and the tiny click of his inner eyelids blinking.

The truck swayed as Yerzhan climbed out of it, shouting. He went stalking toward the horsemen. The horsemen shouted back. Aisulu could not make out the words, but she could hear the angry voices. She could see Yerzhan stabbing his finger down toward their usual camp, the horsemen sweeping their arms as if they held swords. Shouts gusted and slapped around her. Yerzhan stripped off his shirt and threw it down behind him. His fists came up. One of the horsemen got down and took off his shirt: he was a young man, smoothly muscled. Yerzhan lunged at him. The stranger grabbed Yerzhan by the shoulders — they grappled, growling, snarling in each other's faces, trying to twist each other to the ground.

The other horseman leaned forward, his face angry. He put hand inside his coat, as if he might have a weapon there. The dust from the truck was settling slowly, and now Aisulu could see that in the place where they always put their gers, strange gers were already set up: four of them. From that strange aul, someone was coming on foot.

Yerzhan and the smooth-muscled stranger were grunting and wrenching, knees striking out. But the other horseman shouted and pointed. The two fighters looked. They stumbled apart, panting. For a moment everyone watched the person coming toward them.

It was an ancient woman. She tottered slowly forward on a cane, so bent over that her bright blue headscarf nodded like a mountain poppy. The two interlopers watched her come. The one still on his horse started to blush like a scolded child. The one on the ground kicked at the dust once before he put his shirt back on.

They waited. Aisulu kept holding Toktar. Enlik kept

sleeping—she was sprawled on her back in a fold of a rug, her hand flung up above her head, her round tummy bare and breathing. Temir and Balta leaned together and whispered. The Fox Wife bobbled baby Naizabai on her knee and watched the old woman the way an eagle watches things. Silent and very still.

Finally the old woman reached the three men on the road. Aisulu recognized her: Beskempir, a famous local widow and matchmaker, which is to say, a busybody, but an honored one. Earlier that summer, she'd brought the news that Serik had been moved to Olgii City. On the road now, her voice rang high and squawky, like a frog's chirrup. Aisulu couldn't hear what she said. Yerzhan and the two strange men pulled close to her and they all talked. The horseman pushed one hand up the back of his head, hackling his own hair, but he didn't raise his voice. The smooth-muscled fighter made that sword-sweep gesture at the truck and its load of gers—and then he was pointing, right at Aisulu. Looking at her, and at the eagle in her arm. Beskempir looked up at Aisulu too, and chirruped something. Then she bent over and drew something in the dust with the tip of her cane.

Aisulu came up on her knees so that she could see the drawing. It was a map: she knew the curve of the river. It marked their usual place, and another place farther on.

More talking. Yerzhan kicked the map away and the old woman stabbed down her cane and backhanded his bare arm. She redrew the map and Yerzhan put his shirt on, sulking.

A few more moments and the whole thing was over. Yerzhan got back in the truck and the strange men helped turn the crank and start the engine. The Fox Wife wiped a snot bubble from Naizabai's nose. And they went on driving, leaving their usual spot behind them.

After some searching they found a new site for the aul, a bend where the river widened around two willow-drifted islands. Wild horses were grazing there, and they looked up like deer as the truck rumbled in, then splashed through the river and away. The sky was a high clear blue, chased with horse-tail clouds.

It was a gentle, wild place, a good place — though the power lines had not reached it. Aisulu's family got down from the big hay truck and began to unload: roof staves and ger crowns, rugs and stovepipes, folded lattice walls and wobbling tables.

Aisulu set Toktar on his perch, near the river. He turned his blind head this way and that, listening to the unfamiliar water sounds. After a while, he pulled one foot up against his belly, which meant he was content and comfortable. The wind ruffled over him and carried away tiny tufts of the baby down that was still caught under his feathers. He was a fully fledged eagle now, and sometimes it was hard for Aisulu to believe he was only thirteen weeks old.

She missed her brother.

After some hours, the herd caught up with them. Abai shrugged philosophically over the tale of Beskempir and the two strange horsemen. Dulat was angry. He snapped his notebook down on the table. "This whole bare country!" His arm swung out. "This huge and empty country. Surely there is enough space that they don't need to take ours."

"Space is one thing," said Yerzhan. "Grass is another. That was good grazing they took."

"It's been our place for twenty years."

"They say if you do not respect the traditions . . ." said Yerzhan.

"What does that mean?" snapped Dulat.

"You know what it means." Yerzhan was drinking watered vodka from a bowl. It was common to toast and celebrate the striking of a new camp, but it was usual to wait until the walls were up. "You know what it means," he said again.

His gaze slapped Aisulu.

Was he right? Had the horsemen taken their usual camp because she was a girl training with an eagle? Would their herd go hungry? Would her family go hungry? Was it her fault?

Her hand throbbed and her heart pounded as they put the gers up, lashing the lattice to the doors, raising the crowns, setting the roofs staves in their holes. Her blister seemed to catch on every rope.

No one part of a ger was strong. It was made strong by the way it was all tied together, each piece pulling on each other piece. What if the Kazakh people were like that too? She was stepping out of her place as a girl. What if that tipped over other things? What if it brought everything crashing down?

She'd known that a girl training an eagle was unusual. But now, for the first time, she wondered if it was dangerous.

Chapter Twelve

In THE NEW PLACE to which her family had been exiled, Aisulu taught Toktar.

He was a baby whose food had always come to him on the end of a matchstick. Now he had to learn to hunt.

Kara-Kat-Kis showed Aisulu how to squeeze and prod Toktar's legs and the muscles along his keel, learning to judge how much to feed him so that he was strong and healthy, but light enough to fly. She showed her how to wash his meat free of blood to keep him hungry enough to use his three-mile eyes. She helped Aisulu stuff a rabbit skin with straw to make a lure. They tied it to a rope, and while the men were away with the herds, they took turns running with it.

Aisulu held Toktar and watched Kara-Kat-Kis run sure-footed across the tussocks and hummocks of the flat land by the river. Behind her, the lure bumped wildly, catching with a tug between two stones and then jouncing up into the air, almost as if it were alive. Toktar watched it.

Aisulu could feel his talons tighten in excitement, his balance snake as he leaned forward. Suddenly he launched himself with the strength of a yak kicking. He shot toward the lure, swung his talons forward, and landed on top of the skin as if claiming a kingdom. Kara-Kat-Kis gave him a rabbit leg, cooing to the eagle as he ripped meat from bone.

They did this over and over, and Toktar quickly learned to hunt. It was what he was built for. What he was meant to do. There is no joy like the fierce joy of doing what you are meant to do. Toktar felt it.

Aisulu felt it too. In the new camp by the river, she ran, and Kara-Kat-Kis ran, and they were both fast and strong. The ground was hummocked: rises of strappy iris leaves and dips of bare earth the color of dirty salt. To run on it without twisting an ankle took a kind of sixth sense, a way of feeling the land through the bottom of her boots. Kara-Kat-Kis had it, and as Aisulu learned it, she had this thought: the Fox Wife was not what they called her, not a witch or a trickster, but a woman whose boots knew hummocks and whose eyes knew faces and whose heart knew hearts. She was different because she had made different choices.

As Aisulu was making. Running the lure, flying her eagle, day after day, Aisulu began to find a joy to go with her fear, her fear of failing her brother, of failing her family, of being the broken rope that brought down a whole ger.

On Monday mornings, she would see the children walking alone in the distance, heading to the village to spend the week in the school, in the dormitory. She should have been with them—she and Serik, hand in hand. But it was as if the breaking of his leg had paused the world, and she had stepped outside it. Outside her routine, outside her family, and into a world with eagles in it.

That Friday evening, after the great prayers, she took off Toktar's hood and sat with him by the river, the glove resting on her knee. He was fearsomely quiet, gazing at the bright water, his eyes piercing every ripple, every mayfly. Sometimes he would preen Aisulu's hair, drawing strands of it through his beak as if arranging her flight feathers.

After a long while, his head nodded forward and his wings softened and slumped. He ruffled and settled his feathers and tucked up one foot. Soon he was asleep, leaning softly against her. The other children were coming back from school. She watched them, the eagle asleep on her arm.

She felt herself quiet. She felt herself lost. Both things.

The joy that goes with fear is sometimes called faith.

By the time the new camp had been in place for a week, things had settled into a routine. Each day after the morning milking had been done and the herds had been driven ploshing through the cold shallow water to the green islands, Aisulu and her family taught the eagle.

Aisulu could already flick Toktar's hood off so quickly that it was as easy as breathing. Now, with her uncle dragging the lure, she learned to flick Toktar's hood off, thrust him into the air on the end of her arm, and give the strike shout, all in one moment. Before she could even breathe back in, Toktar would lock on to the bouncing skin and launch. Three strong thrusts of his white-flashed wings, a swinging out of his striking talons, and he was on the rabbit skin, squeezing to kill it even as the rope made him bump along. Aisulu laughed in delight as his hackles came up and he balanced with his wings, bewildered by the way his catch kept running.

The eagle was a deadly thing, but a sweet thing. She could hold him cradled like a baby, and he gazed into her eyes. If he was tired, he liked to have his belly rubbed, from the corners of his mouth to the feathers of his boots, from the strong center of his breastbone to the warm creases under his wings. He lay back in her arms with his huge curved talons fisted at the sky and made *ker-honk* noises.

He could break her hand without trying. And she loved him.

Finally they were ready to fly him as he should be flown —from mountaintops. Aisulu would go with Kara-Kat-Kis during the day, or with Dulat in the evening. They would climb into the foothills, the scorched red and purple places. Amid the humped hills of dust and sharp ones of shale, they taught Toktar to dive. He was fast, and he was getting faster.

He had already learned to come to the lure, and then to get meat from the hand. Next they taught him to come to the hand directly. He learned quickly that Aisulu's shout meant go, and Dulat's shout meant come — quickly learned to spot the rabbit leg clamped between Dulat's thumb and glove.

Once Toktar knew his part, Dulat declared Aisulu ready for the hardest task in eagle hunting: not to launch Toktar, but to catch him.

Toktar had grown huge. He was more than twelve pounds now, and his curving black talons were as long as pocketknives. His level flight was faster than a racehorse's gallop, and his dive was like an arrow: 120, 150 miles an hour. Standing in front of him was like standing in front of a lightning strike. It took pure faith, and pure nerve.

At the foot of the shale hill, Aisulu stood. She watched her uncle climbing up with Toktar on his fist, his high black boots sending blocks of shale scattering. She remembered that sound: like bones breaking.

Her heart beat in her throat. She could smell the blood of the rabbit leg she held clamped in her gloved hand. She knew Toktar would come to her. Or she thought he would. He had learned to come to Dulat. He was a smart creature, at least when it came to raw meat. He trusted her. And she trusted him.

She watched her uncle climb and the world dialed in, like the world through binoculars. Her vision was narrow and sharp. She was seeing nothing but Dulat standing on the outcrop, dark against the bright sky, the eagle ready on his glove. She was hearing nothing but the wind thumping in her ears.

She took a deep breath and listened to her own strong heart. Then she thrust up her gloved fist and gave the eagle hunter's shout. In the same second, Dulat flicked the hood off Toktar and launched him into the air.

The eagle stroked twice against the hard bright air, his wings and body undulating, his head like an arrow pointed straight at her face. Then he was diving for her, his legs slung back under his tail, invisible, only his jesses trailing. His wings were arched and still, perfect as scythe blades, and he came at her fast. He was coming. He was almost on her. His feet swung forward, his wings flared out, flashing white, flashing silver, and just then, someone spoke.

"Careful," said a voice. "An eagle can break your arm."

Aisulu flinched.

It was the wrong moment to flinch. Toktar struck her

glove with a blow like a gong striking in her ear. The force spun her around. But she had begun spinning too soon, and one of the eagle's talons had also snagged in her flying braid. The next second Toktar was hanging upside down from her hair as if from a rope, and flapping wildly. Aisulu shouted, almost screamed—half her head seemed to be on fire. She couldn't even hear herself over the rush of wings and the pounding of her heart in her ear. She spun and Toktar spun on the end of her braid. She seized him. Her scalp felt torn, but she set Toktar upright on her glove. Even then he was still caught in her hair. She had to hold him up next to her ear.

Toktar fell upon the rabbit leg she was holding, snapping, tearing. The sound was huge. He was tangled too close for her to see all of him, but she twisted her gaze to look. From this angle his eyes were clear domes, like drops of glass, with the disk of the iris flat in the back. The hairlike feathers between his beak and his eyes were thick with blood. He looked snakelike, alien, and for a moment Aisulu was terrified.

"Did I distract you?" said the voice.

Shuffling her feet, trying not to stumble or tug, she turned. Behind her, watching her, was a man on horseback. He was close, not a ger's width away. Aisulu recognized him as one of the horsemen who had swooped down on them the day they'd moved the gers—the one who had stripped off his shirt and squared off with her uncle Yerzhan. He was wearing an eagle hunter's red hat, but no shapan, just a cowboy shirt with snaps instead of buttons. He was young, and he had the kind of muscles of which some young men are so proud.

There was a smirk on his face, and a hooded eagle on his arm.

"Eagle hunting is not a game," he said. "I've really heard about one breaking the arm of an inexperienced man. You should be more careful."

There was a little flare of his nose on the word "man."

Distantly, she could hear Dulat shouting.

"You should know better than to bother an eagle in its training." Her voice was gulping but her words were calm words. She was proud of that.

The young man shrugged. "You're going to have to cut off that braid."

"What are you doing!" Dulat was storming up to them, outraged as a bull yak. "What do you think you're doing!"

"Seeing if the little girl needs help," said the young man. "It's neighborly."

"I see exactly what you're doing," said Dulat. "Go away."

"Are you sure?" The young man leaned forward. The

eagle on his arm shifted and spread its wings. "You haven't seen how tangled they are."

Dulat's eyes flashed to Aisulu. His face was flushed and tight. She could not turn to look at Toktar, but she could watch Dulat look. His face frightened her: it was hard and empty.

"I'll hold her," said young man, "and you cut her hair."

"*Ket*," said Dulat. It meant "go away," but it was a word only used for dogs. "*Ket*. Go."

Aisulu refused to look at the stranger, but she could hear the hoof beats as his horse shifted and then left.

She raised her free hand between her face and her eagle, to hide herself from what was happening.

"Aisulu," said Dulat. "That wasn't — this isn't your fault. You did well."

She felt his hand on her arm, his fingers in her hair. Toktar shifted from foot to foot, and the entangled braid yanked on her scalp. It was being pulled so hard that her scalp felt hot.

"Not one man in a hundred can catch an eagle out of a dive," said Dulat. "And you caught yours."

But no man in a hundred would wear his hair in two long braids. Girls did that. *Little* girls.

Dulat was close to her. She felt him pick up Toktar's

entangled foot. There were more yanks and flares of pain as he tried to work the talons free of her braid. Tears smarted in her eyes. "Unbraid it!" she said. "Unbraid it, try that!"

He did, but still Toktar was snarled. The eagle flapped to keep his balance, wings whapping Aisulu in the head. Dulat fussed—so close to her that she could hear his fingers.

Finally he said, "Aisulu, we have to cut it off."

She swallowed and said: "Cut it off."

She thought he would be bad at the cutting, forgetting that he was a man who had shorn a thousand sheep. She felt the pinch on the root of her hair, and heard the rasp of his pocketknife. But it didn't hurt. He spared her that.

Finally the eagle was free. Aisulu twisted her face away and saw the black hair blowing and snagging in the yarrow around them, lifting and whipping back and forth like prayer flags.

With her eagle on her wrist, Aisulu looked at her hair, blowing away. She touched the place on her scalp and the top of her ear where the wind was suddenly cold. Her mother's voice was in her head: *Now you look like a fine girl.*

"Let us ..." Dulat shifted from boot to boot, like a scolded child. "We can wait until tomorrow before we do this again."

• • •

Aisulu gazed into the dressing mirror, trying to avoid the reindeer's eyes. With one braid partway cut off she looked . . .

Young. Sick. Injured.

Like a girl, but in a new way, a way that made her feel sticky and sick with shame. She felt the way she had when thinking *if I were a boy I could save my brother.*

Dulat was holding court at the table, telling the others the tale. Aisulu wasn't listening. Or she was trying not to listen. Toktar sat on his perch by the fire and cheeped as if he'd learned nothing.

"It was one of Zhambyl's sons," said Dulat. "They're the ones who claimed our grazing places. I don't know his name, but he's an eagle hunter. Or at least, he had an eagle. Not everyone who carries an eagle around is an eagle hunter."

The young man hadn't bothered to introduce himself, so Aisulu, in her head, named him as she might name an animal: Sneering Muscles. Just thinking about his face made her feel sick.

Her fingers fumbled with the rubber band that fastened her remaining braid. She twisted it free and then unplaited her hair. It was long—unbraided, it fell over the mosquito -bite places where she was beginning to get breasts. It came almost to the bottom of her ribs. It held the memory of the braid in twists of shine.

There was a hairbrush on the dressing table, an ordinary thing under the reindeer skull and blind eyeglasses, among the strange stones and the dice cup full of anklebones. She picked it up. The tug of it through her hair made her think of her mother—so suddenly and so strongly that it was as if a ghost had risen beside her.

Her mother always helped her brush her hair.

Always, except on that last morning, when she'd gone out to milk with her hair wind-snarled and sleep-matted. That day, her mother had not even scolded her. Who cares about a daughter's hair when a son was hurt?

When Toktar was smaller he used to prance about on the dresser when Aisulu did her hair. She didn't even want to look at him now. She picked up the brush. The cut braid was not all gone. There were long strands left. Yes, there were hacked pieces that curled up, blunt ends amid the shine. But brushed out . . .

It wouldn't look too bad. She would still look—she looked like a girl. She did not look like an eagle hunter.

Jok, a girl could not be an eagle hunter—that was what her father had said. *Jok, jok, jok.* He could not find gear for her. The embroidered collar for her shapan, which he had commanded the women to make, was still stretched on its frame, the patterns drawn in milk fat, the stitching only four inches long. It could never be finished in time. She would go before the judges at the Eagle Festival in worn-out old boots and her brother's plain shapan, faded gray with embroidery fraying. Her uncle had given her what he could, of his, of his grandfather's. He'd given the hood and the jesses, the glove and the saddle, the little pouch with its pink and lime embroidery that held the meat for the eagle. But she would go before the judges with her hair hacked off and her shabby secondhand clothes, and it wouldn't matter what happened next; that would be the end of it.

She would call her eagle to her hand and he would come and hit her like a spear. Like a spear that would end her. She could never catch him. She was not strong enough. She was going to fail. She was going to fail her brother.

She had gone too far, too fast, and she had been hurt. She was going to break like a rope. Her whole ger was going to fall down.

They went out again the next day.

It was a cloudy day, swept with cold winds and spits of rain. The newly exposed tip of Aisulu's ear seemed to glow with the cold. Her mouth tasted strange, and she'd lost that hooked-from-the-sky sense of balance. Toktar was heavy on her arm, and Moon Spot's every bounce was jarring.

Dulat held his reins in one hand, and he kept looking over at her, a sideways look that made his mustache bristle.

"You must understand," he said. "To catch an eagle from a dive . . . it is very hard. You did well, for a first try. You did very well."

When they came to the foothills he took Toktar from her, then looked her up and down.

"You must forget about yesterday," he said.

But how could she, with the glow in her ear and the clench in her throat and the brace in her body that added up to one thing: shame.

And when Toktar dove to her he looked like a blow coming. She didn't duck, but she tensed, and when he hit her glove it was like getting yak-kicked in winter: the hit seemed to rattle right through her bones. She could feel it in her teeth.

Toktar tore into the rabbit leg and Aisulu sat down in the dust and sobbed.

The next day they did it again.

And the next.

She did not fail to catch Toktar. He did not fail to come. But there was nothing easy about it—no point of perfect balance, no moment when it shifted like the mouse holes and came into view. She learned to stand there with her arm out and her teeth set together.

On her feet or from the back of her shuddering, shivering horse she could catch Toktar, not every time, but often. But even so, even when she did catch him, it was hard, every time.

Even so, she was frightened, and ashamed.

Chapter Thirteen

It was only three weeks to the Eagle Festival. Three weeks until Aisulu would go to Olgii City and see her brother. Three weeks before she would stand in front of hundreds of people and fly her eagle.

Day after day, out in the foothills, Aisulu caught Toktar. She could do it: not the first time, or the second, but soon after that. Soon she missed him only rarely, even on horseback, even at a gallop. And yet every catch was a blow. Every catch was something broken, sheared off like her hair.

Every time, after the catch, Toktar would tear into the rabbit meat and she would feel fury and loss, and fight the urge to fling him to the ground. Fight the urge to cry. Great eagle hunters, she was sure, did not cry.

And then, a week in, Aisulu and Dulat returned from the foothills and found an unfamiliar motorcycle leaning against the cheese-drying stand.

Visitors.

Visitors were not unusual, especially in the riverside

camps, which were closer together than the ones in the mountains. People popped in, they shared tea, they brought packets of Choco-Pies as a kind of social currency. So the visitor could be anyone. But when she saw the motorcycle, with the brilliant rug tied over the seat and the puff of owl feathers hanging from the handlebars, Aisulu's first thought was: *Sneering Muscles.*

She did not want to see him.

She looked around. Far out across the flat steppe, she could see her father and her uncle Yerzhan talking with a stranger. She was too distant to see who the stranger was, but all three had their arms crossed, spikey anger flaring between them. Dulat's eyebrows and mustache bristled. He leaned toward the knot of men, glanced at Aisulu, and then rode in that direction without a word.

Aisulu lurked outside the big ger for a moment but heard only the voices of women. She braced herself, then ducked through the door.

And froze.

The ger was transformed.

Before the big ger had belonged to Dulat and the Fox Wife, it had belonged to Dulat's parents, Aisulu's grandparents, Pazylbek and Gulsara. They had been married for thirty-seven years, and every winter Gulsara had stitched. She had cut the patterns in the felt rugs. She appliquéd the bright blue scallops to the canvas band that tucked in the ger. She had made her husband an eagle hunter's shapan that he wore for the festivals and embroidered the round skullcaps he had worn every day of his life. Most important, she had hung the walls with embroidered hangings, big as tablecloths: nine of them. Circles full of flowers. Diamonds full of curls.

Kara-Kat-Kis had taken the wall hangings all down. She was standing in the middle of all those stitches. The hangings covered the table, the beds. They covered every inch of the floor, except its center, where a beam of sun encircled an old black sewing machine, and an ancient woman sitting on the floor in front of it. A very familiar ancient woman. It was Beskempir, the woman who had stopped the fight on the road. The mother of Zhambyl, whose family had taken their grazing grounds. The grandmother of Sneering Muscles.

"*Tsai oh*, Aisulu?" the Fox Wife offered. "*Tsai oh*, Beskempir?"

Tsai oh, let's have tea. *Tsai oh*, let's make an alliance.

"Tea!" the old woman cheeped.

Beskempir, the settler of disputes. Beskempir, the matchmaker. Beskempir, the most powerful woman in a hundred-mile radius. She sat on the floor like a one-woman parliament. Kara-Kat-Kis handed her a bowl of tea.

Aisulu glanced at the futon, where honored guests (if they were male) were usually seated, and saw, instead of a guest, a wedding dress. It was not a white frothy American dress, as many people were starting to wear, but a traditional dress, made of purple brocade.

"Aisulu," said Kara-Kat-Kis, picking up the wedding dress. "I have decided that there must be changes."

"As long as I don't have to get married," Aisulu said.

Meiz laughed.

"It is my dress," said the Fox Wife. "And it does not come with a boy in it."

"Aish, we need your clothes," declared Meiz, still laughing.

"What?"

Of all the people in Aisulu's family, Meiz was the best at catching a sheep for shearing. Before Aisulu knew it, her auntie had headlocked and manhandled her up onto a suitcase that served as a little stage. Meiz stripped off Aisulu's shapan and wrapped her up in measuring tapes.

Aisulu pressed one hand over her T-shirt and the other over the damaged spot in her hair. "What's happening?"

Beskempir was still sitting on the floor by the sewing machine. One leg, in a dark green stocking, stuck straight out. The other was tucked up behind her. She was wearing an orange skirt and a blue blouse with polka dots, and her headscarf was hot pink. She spoke so fast, and so mushily without her teeth, that Aisulu could barely understand her: "My son, he says you are going to fly an eagle at the festival. My grandson, he says no woman can be an eagle hunter. But what do men know about what women can do? I had twelve children and I buried three of them, and I buried my husband. He's been buried thirty years — thirty years and I'm still kicking. My son, he says I'll bury him yet, and I might, girl, I might."

She looked at Aisulu, twinkling: "My grandson, now, my grandson I might have to *kill* and bury."

Sneering Muscles. Apparently, his stunt had not gone down well with his fearsome grandmother. Aisulu felt the smile creep over her face.

"I paid a visit to our neighbors yesterday," said Kara-Kat-Kis. "To tell Beskempir how things were, with your festival gear."

Something inside Aisulu was thawing.

"Thank you," she mouthed.

"I make half the wedding matches in the district and I go to all the funerals," said Beskempir. "And I sew. I will sew something for you, girl. I can and I will."

The Fox Wife swept toward Aisulu, holding the dress high on one arm. The dress was so stiff that it looked as if it were moving by itself, like a specter. It was not quite a

Kazakh dress. It was cut differently, embellished differently. It was brightly colored — fuchsia purple, with a stomach piece of cobalt blue and sleeve bands of orange and yellow.

"My mother's dress," said the Fox Wife. "And my grandmother's before her." The dress seemed to rustle as if with their spirits. The Fox Wife spoke mildly. "They were important women. It is a very good dress."

Beskempir clapped her hands together. "And we are going to cut it up!"

"Oh," said Aisulu, looking at the beautiful dress. "But you can't—"

"Of course I can," said Kara-Kat-Kis. "It is my dress. And you are my daughter. I give it to you."

Aisulu was too bare. Standing on the suitcase beside the stovepipe, half her skin was glowing hot; the other half was shivering cold. "I'm not—"

"You are the daughter of my heart. And more. You are the only daughter I will ever have." She hung the dress from a roof stave and spoke from behind it. Aisulu could not see her face. "Your brother will never have a cousin. This will be his aul one day. His herd. His people. He will inherit." She stepped around the dress. It hung behind her like a shadow. "My daughter, do you understand me?"

"I understand you."

"Your brother belongs here," said the Fox Wife. "And

you belong in the sky." She put an arm around Aisulu, pulled her in, and kissed the top of her hair. Once, their hug together had been rigid as a camel skeleton. Now it was rich as warm butter.

The Fox Wife stepped away and became all sharp business. "The silk is old, and stiff. Not warm enough. We will use your shapan for the pattern and the lining, my husband's foxes for the collar and the trim."

"It's—it was Serik's shapan." Aisulu glanced at Beskempir. "My brother's."

"Even better," said the old woman. She had a face like a two-winter apple, and bright, bright eyes.

"And the hangings?" said Aisulu. "My grandmother's . . . ?"

"Well," said the Fox Wife. "You can't look like a *man of your people* without a little gold thread."

Meiz snorted.

"True," said Beskempir. She turned the hand crank of the sewing machine and it made a flapping whir, as if applauding. "True true true! The boys love to be pretty!"

Her brother's shapan, her uncle's foxes, her grandmother's stitching, and the magic dress from a distant land. Aisulu understood: if there were men who would not make a space for her, there were women who could. They would make it, and she would claim it.

"Leave this to us, Aisulu." Meiz snapped the cloth tape measure against Aisulu's shoulder like a goat flail. "Go teach your eagle. Go milk something."

Aisulu stepped down from the suitcase but didn't get far. Beskempir grabbed her, and Aisulu found her hand trapped between the old woman's hands. She crouched down to where the matchmaker was sitting. The warm sun laid its hand on the back of her neck. Beskempir patted her hands around Aisulu's. Aisulu could feel the hardness of silver rings sunk between knobby knuckles, but the hands were soft as dust, and the nails were model-perfect, pale smooth ovals.

"You go," Beskempir whispered to her, like a blessing. "Fly, fly, fly. We will make you something beautiful."

That night, Aisulu slept badly.

Before her life had changed, she had never slept badly. She worked hard and ran far in the clear air, and she slept deep. But since the day Toktar had gotten tangled in her hair, her sleep had filled with dreams she couldn't remember, dreams that left her jolting and cold with failure and fear. And now she was filled also with hope: hope like sunshine on a sewing machine, hope like bright silk.

She tossed and turned, slept and woke. Finally, dawn came. The shape of the door began to show, and light came skimming under it to wash the linoleum, seeping up to pick out the first colors in the red and green embroidered band that marked the bottom of the sloping roof. The walls looked strange, in the strange light, with the hangings down. Aisulu could hear the goats wandering right outside—one was actually banging at the door. She hoped it was latched.

There was another sound too, something less familiar than goats. A tiny *tick-tick-tick-tick* and *zip*, like a mouse nibbling on stiff straw.

Aisulu's eyes warmed up to the dimness, and she spotted the source of the sound: Toktar, awake, and preening his flight feathers. He had chosen one from his left wing and was working it through his beak like a woman repairing a zipper, hooking together each tiny vein and barb. The feather was lifted from the wing and into a sweeping curve, and everything about it said *flight*.

Aisulu watched as he finished the feather and let go of its tip. It snapped into place, and Toktar selected the next one, carefully, his head tipped to one side.

When she'd rescued him, he'd been a tiny ball of murderous fluff. But now: The feathers on his head were dark brown at the roots and gold at the tips. They were soft and dense, pointed like iris leaves, arranged in layers like the scales of a dragon. His eyes arched across the top and straight across the bottom, just like hers, just like Serik's.

They had the brightness of sun through a dust beam, just like hers, just like Serik's. Only the freckles of white down poking through his glossy breast feathers said he was still a baby.

"Toktar?" she whispered, not knowing what she was asking him.

He turned his head toward her and *kree*d softly. Whatever she'd asked, his answer was yes. However he'd hurt her, she forgave him. She rolled onto her side and watched him tend to his wings until the light came up and Kara-Kat-Kïs awoke and they went out into the dawn light to milk the cows and yaks.

After that, Aisulu untucked the ger, and swept the floor, and drew buckets of water from the river, and then, as she had every day, she went out to the foothills again, to learn to catch her eagle.

That day, she caught him every time. And when she did, the tears that came to her eyes were tears of joy.

Fly, fly, fly.

In the evenings, her aunties stitched the embroidered panels into pants. Her uncle Yerzhan played music, or drank, or both. Her uncle Dulat sketched. He opened his notebook, flipping through old smudged pages and finding soft new ones. In the secret spaces he shared with his wife, they used secret words: words like *aerodynamic*. Words like *lift* and *drag*.

And out in the rocky foothills, Toktar and Aisulu flew and flew.

Aisulu was painfully aware that though it took only weeks to train an eagle, it took years to become a master eagle hunter. She was only beginning. The only thing she had that was special was Toktar's heart.

But maybe that was enough.

If she dragged the lure behind her horse, or if she held the meat in her hand, Toktar could lock on and launch in a single heartbeat.

She threw her shouts out hard: "Toktar! Here! Here!" This became her favorite sound, ringing across the rocks like Serik's name.

Serik, get down from there, her mother had shouted. *Serik, come back here!* And that was what Aisulu was shouting now, calling her eagle down from the mountainside. *My heart, my heart, come here.*

Toktar, Toktar, Toktar.

The pants were almost finished.

Her uncle was drawing windmills: Blades and shafts. Math and notes and the arrows of the wind.

The Eagle Festival was ten days away, and then a week,

and then it was time for them to go. But by then, they were ready.

Beskempir, the matchmaker, the mastermind, the master stitcher, showed up the day before Aisulu and Dulat needed to set out for Olgii City and the festival. The tiny woman was perched on the back of a motorcycle.

Driving the motorcycle was none other than Sneering Muscles.

Dulat bristled and glared at Sneering Muscles for a moment, then invited them both in for tea.

Beskempir didn't bother to retrieve her cane from the back of the motorcycle. Instead, she leaned on her grandson's elbow—and steered him by grabbing him by the ear. She walked him clockwise around the stove, as respectful visitors should walk. She sat him on the stool instead of in the place of honor behind the table. Dulat and Abai sat across from him, folded their arms, and donned identical glares.

Sneering Muscles put two rug-wrapped bundles on the table.

Beskempir pushed one toward Aisulu. "Open it, girl. Open it!"

Aisulu didn't want anything that came from the hand

of Sneering Muscles. But Beskempir was almost bobbing up and down—as Serik used to—and that made painful hope flare in Aisulu. She undid the knots. She unwrapped the rug.

The sky was inside it.

A coat.

They had cut her brother's shapan apart, to be pattern and padding. For both the outer coat and the inner lining, they had used the silk of Kara-Kat-Kis's wedding dress. It was a purple so bright it was almost pink, a blazing dawn color, and the brocade was of knots and feathers. A yellow-orange piping made the color look brighter still. Not a piece of it was blue, but it was a sky thing: a sunrise, a high cloud catching fire.

An eagle hunter's hat was usually red, but no one in the family had enough red silk, and so they had used the orange and purple there, too, and lined it with the best of her uncle's furs. They were corsac fox furs: a pale red-gold, thick as snowflakes, soft as feathers.

"Oh," said Aisulu. "Oh." She could not make a word as big as *thank you.*

"*Try it, try it!*" Beskempir sang.

So Aisulu pulled on the purple shapan, and put the hat over her damaged hair.

"Oh!" said every woman in the ger.

Even her uncle, in his big-man place behind the table, grinned like a child. Tears sprang into her father's eyes.

The shapan fit her better than her brother's had: it did not gape around her little waist, or fall halfway over her hands. She looked down at her wrists in wonder. She reached up and touched the thick fur over her ears.

"Look!" said Beskempir. She took Aisulu by the shoulders and spun her toward the mirror.

Aisulu saw herself. The fox fur, the sky silk: they lit her. Her cheeks were wind-raw and as bright as Serik's. Her eyes were welling, and bright as Toktar's. She did not look like an eagle hunter, in a dark thing with bright stitches. She did not look like a poor girl, with a small frame and chopped hair. She looked like something brand new.

She looked like a hero. She looked as if she could stand on the sky.

Meiz gleefully held the finished pants in front of her own swelling belly, then in front of Aisulu. They were eagle hunter's gear, to be pulled on over her own pants to add warmth. They were made of her grandmother's embroidered panels, gold and pink on black, the work of love and pride and winters.

"Chudruk," said Beskempir sharply, and slapped Sneering Muscles on the shoulder as if he were a yak.

Sneering Muscles glowered and pushed the other bundle

across the table to Aisulu. Chudruk must be his real name, but Aisulu didn't care. She was remembering his voice, sneering and certain. That certainty had planted doubt in her — doubt that had sent tangled roots into her gut. So it gave her great delight to see him look at the floor and mumble, "This is for you."

Aisulu opened the bundle. Inside was a black belt with silver ornaments, and boots: knee-high, leather, and shiny.

"They were mine," muttered Sneering Muscles. "I out-grew them." He rubbed one ear with the flat of his hand, as if remembering how hard he'd been pinched there. "I want you to take them."

Beskempir patted him on the head as if he were a horse.

Aisulu picked up the glossy boots. *"Köp rahkmet,"* she said formally. "Thank you very much." She smiled down at him, dangerous as weather, and gave him a Choco-Pie.

The next day, they set out before the sun was quite up.

Tourists say that Mongolia has four seasons: July, August, September, and winter. It was the end of September now, and in the predawn chill, Aisulu could see her breath. In the aul around her, two gers were sleeping, shadowy purple in the dimness, amid the goats. One ger was awake: gold light spilled from the open doorway. The tack made crisp, sharp sounds as they saddled their horses. Humans and horses breathed out little puffs of white. Curious Yak lowed once, deep as an ice age.

The festival was the next week, in Olgii City, seventy miles away. It had been decided that Dulat and Aisulu would ride there, as Aisulu would need her horse. Abai would follow in the borrowed blue truck that had once hauled away Serik. With the truck, he could bring the smallest ger, Aisulu's old home ger with the yellow door. They could put the ger up at the festival: a place to live during that week. Later, they could sell it, if they had to, to fly the family to Ulaanbaatar.

To Aisulu, it seemed like forever until they were ready to go.

Then, when the time came to go, it seemed too soon.

She stood beside the ger door in her sky-purple shapan over her old pants and boots—it was, after all, the only coat she owned. She felt different in it. She felt tiny and she felt huge.

She felt ready.

Her father stood in front of her and fastened her belt, and straightened the eagle hunter's pouch that hung from it, which had been his own father's. He smoothed his hands down the silk of her arms. With his eyes, he pronounced her beautiful. But he did not seem able to speak.

Kara-Kat-Kis was holding the horses' bridles. She was

standing very still, as if she had thrown roots into the earth. Her blackberry hair was uncovered. Dulat was still packing the saddlebags, but he paused to take the bridles from her. For a moment their hands were stacked on the rawhide ropes, their fingers touching.

"Do you want to give her . . . ?" he asked.

She nodded, slipped her hand from his, and came over to Aisulu.

Aisulu watched. Kara-Kat-Kis moved like a child: like little Enlik striding around without a hint of self-consciousness. That was the only thing strange about her, Aisulu thought: that she moved as her heart moved her, and did not care what people thought.

"Let me do your hair?" she said.

Aisulu's breath caught. She turned around and stood looking at the river, at her own shadow coming into being as the light rose slowly. She felt the Fox Wife's cool fingers on the nape of her neck. She felt a tug on her hair.

Aisulu had pulled her hair into a ponytail and doubled it up under the rubber band to make a rough knot. Even so, the blunt ends stuck out above one ear, swept around under her chin.

Kara-Kat-Kis took her hair down and began to brush it. The sound was entirely familiar, but powerful as the crackle of lightning, and the tug tug tug of the brush went straight into Aisulu's heart. Tears rose to her eyes. Kara-Kat-Kis brushed and brushed and brushed: a hundred strokes. Then Aisulu felt her hair lifted and twisted, plaited into a long single braid that spilled down her spine.

"Perfect," whispered Kara-Kat-Kis. "Beautiful." And— and it was so different, so different than needing to *manage*, needing to tighten and neaten her heart to become a *fine girl*. She didn't need to change into a fine young woman. She didn't change anything. She was beautiful. She was perfect.

The tug left her hair and she turned around. Kara-Kat-Kis tucked the chopped end of her hair behind her ear and then fastened it there with a new hair clip. The clip bore a rosette of blue ribbon, bright as the banners at the shrine of the sky.

Aisulu gulped down happy tears and pushed herself against her aunt, against the woman who had chosen to be her mother, as blind and happy and wanting as a baby horse against its mother's side. The Fox Wife held her the same way—completely.

Aisulu could feel the warmth of her aunt's body and the tight thrum of her heart and muscles, of her power.

"My daughter," whispered Kara-Kat-Kis. "Fly."

Chapter Fourteen

AISULU AND HER UNCLE RODE for three days, up into the roll of the mountains. The grass, where there was grass, was scorched, stunted, grazed short. The mountains were dappled red and gold and gray like fox fur. The sky had pulled up and hardened. The wind was strong and endless. Toktar rested on Aisulu's hand.

There were clusters of gers here and there, moved down into sheltered places, and a few places where families had already moved into the mud-brick cabins some used in winters.

They could stop in any aul or cabin and have a meal of tea and baursak, butter and cheese. They were always welcome, always given the best: fresh kumiss ladled generously into bowls, hard candies set on silver dishes, Choco-Pies in crinkling red wrappers, and once, astonishingly, a plate of sliced cucumbers, cool and crisp and tasting of greenness.

It was always the same. They rode into a whirl of barking dogs and happy children. They rode into women who stopped what they were doing—the milking, the churning, the cheese making—and made them tea. They rode into men who gave them meat, if there was any meat. Once, a man honored them by slaughtering a goat, though Aisulu saw with her sharp heart that the goat was already lame.

This was what it meant to be Kazakh: to welcome, and to be welcomed, unconditionally.

There were a few strange moments. The little boy who saw her take off her hat—her single braid swinging down—and bleated: "You're a *girl*!" The woman who nearly wept over Aisulu, exclaiming, "But you're so small!" But most looked at Aisulu—a slight girl holding a great eagle—and though their eyes were full of stories, they told no stories. They asked no questions.

In this way Aisulu and her uncle made their way over the mountains. It was a dry place, and they rested wherever they crossed water, letting the horses drink deeply, then easing the bits from their mouths so that they could browse, and slipping the felt pads from beneath their saddles to cool their backs.

They rested by one such stream, the wind ruffling over them. Dulat let his hand ride in it, tilting it back and forth like a burkitshi training an eagle to balance. Like an engineer designing a wing. Toktar, unhooded, waded out into the inch-deep current at the edge of a rushing stream. He marched like a man wearing big boots, and looked like one too, with his wings lifted and his long, feathery pants exposed. For a moment he stood, staring down at water that covered his toes.

Aisulu put her chin on her knees and watched Toktar sink his butt into the water. He spread his tail feathers and wiggled, flapping his wings and dipping his head. He tossed the water so that it ran down his back, and twisted to wet each wing in turn. Soon the most magnificent bird in the Altai was flapping like a deranged chicken.

Aisulu laughed at him and flopped back into dry, prickling grass. She watched the endless sky and thought: *No matter what happens* . . .

It was a thought with no ending. She thought: *Fly.*

Olgii City, and the Eagle Festival.

Olgii City, and the hospital.

The hospital, and Serik.

She would see him. He would forgive her and he would love her. Or not.

And then she would fly her eagle and she would save him. Or not.

It was a lot to ride with. But water ran off Toktar in shining beads and he was beautiful.

On the last night of their journey, as the sun sank, they found themselves riding into a new aul, a cluster of six gers that glowed smoky gray against the dark gold of their hollow, like white stones at the bottom of a tea-dark stream.

"This aul belongs to Nursultan," said Dulat. "He is the legend. The oldest living eagle hunter."

Aisulu's stomach twisted, and she raised her free hand to press the cold place where her hair no longer covered her ear. Toktar picked up her unease and shifted on her arm.

"We cannot pass by without a visit," said Dulat. "Don't worry. If he does not like that you are a girl—well, he does not like it. If he does, that could help you."

He was saying she had nothing to lose. She could almost hear the Fox Wife in her head: *What do men know of what women have to lose?*

Then again, what did men know of a girl's way of being brave? She shifted her arm in its prop and straightened her spine, then rode down into the strange camp as if into glory.

Nursultan's family came pouring out to meet them, as every family did. They met great hunter's oldest son and youngest son, his grandchildren, his flock of great-grandchildren. It was a rich aul, clearly: six gers, all with decorative banding, a thousand head of goats and sheep, a whole bank of solar panels twinkling like a night sky.

Dulat and Aisulu were ushered in to meet the great burkitshi.

Nursultan sat behind the table like a khan on his throne. His white hair was wiry as goat's, thick tufts of bristles at each corner of his mouth and in the center of his chin. He had only one eye, but that eye was keen. It glittered at Aisulu from deep in his wrinkled face.

Eagle on her arm, she made a little bow.

"Asalaam Aleykum," said Dulat formally. "How are your herds fattening?"

Nursultan seemed to consider it. "Well," he rasped at last. "They fatten well. It was a good season. We will slaughter many when the cold comes, and we will eat like kings."

A woman—a granddaughter, perhaps—was ladling kumiss into bowls. She said nothing. The bowls clinked onto the table.

Toktar was dozing on Aisulu's arm. His wings drooped and rested against her glove. His shoulders softened.

"Your eagle is comfortable," proclaimed Nursultan.

"He's sleepy," she answered.

"Eh," said Nursultan. "If she's sleepy then she's comfortable."

The pronoun *she* hit Aisulu's heart all wrong. But she said nothing about it. Dulat gestured at her. "This is Abai's daughter. Pazylbek's granddaughter."

"The girl who got lost in the blizzard."

Aisulu had forgotten that everyone in reach of the summer camp had been called to search for her and Serik in the spring blizzard. Word would have spread.

"I was saving my brother," she said.

Toktar's head wobbled into sleep like a spinning plate rattling into stillness. His beak settled into his breast feathers. Nursultan watched him, frowning. "I heard of an eagle girl. I did not know it was the same girl."

Aisulu lifted her chin. "I saved the eagle, too."

"Eh," said Nursultan, as if entirely unimpressed by all this saving of things. "And are you a burkitshi, girl?"

"Not yet."

"Not yet. That's right. At least you know that. Men who dress up and hold eagles. Men in fur and hats. Men who bundle an eagle onto the back of their motorcycle and make money along the road, taking pictures with tourists. There will always be plenty of those. But they are not burkitshi. There are no new burkitshi."

"There are some," said Dulat.

Nursultan snorted. The kumiss still bubbled in its green and golden bowls, untouched. Aisulu stroked the back of Toktar's nodding head and said nothing.

"I remember Pazylbek," Nursultan said. "He was burkitshi. And I think I remember you, too, lad. Did you not hunt with eagles?"

"I've had two eagles," said Dulat. "One for five years, one for seven, before I gave them their freedom. I've caught foxes and hare in the mountains. A wolf, once."

"Ah," said Nursultan. "That's right. I remember the wolf."

"I'll never forget the wolf," said Dulat.

"But now you have no eagle," Nursultan sighed. "And I have no eagle. I am too old now. I am too blind. I have had seventeen eagles. Just last year I went to the mountains to let my last eagle go. I brought her a lamb as a last offering, and I slaughtered it there on the mountaintop. She, now. She caught five wolves. I dream about her."

Dulat nodded.

"If she is safe. If she can find a mate, make a nest. If she can catch her wolves without me. I think about these things, and I dream about her."

"I dream of my eagles," said Dulat. "Seven years gone."

"You're going to the festival?"

"Yes," said Aisulu. Nursultan was talking mostly to her uncle, but she was determined not to be silent.

"Eh," said Nursultan. "You will fly this eagle, girl child?"

"Yes," said Aisulu.

"Show me, then," said Nursultan. He got up with a heavy wheeze and shuffled around the table. He pointed idly and one of the silent women passed him his cane. In another moment he was in front of Aisulu—close in front, peering at her through that one fierce eye. "What do you think of her weight?"

In his first months, Aisulu had simply let Toktar eat and eat and eat, turning meat into poop and into eagle. Now she fed him carefully, enough to keep him bright-eyed and fit, but not so much that he lost his keen, fierce edge. Keeping him at the right weight for flying was a tricky thing, a fine skill, and she knew she did not yet have it mastered.

Nevertheless, she squeezed each of Toktar's legs, pinched her hand up his breastbone, and stroked the muscles over his ribs and under his wings. The sleepy eagle lifted his head and honked a complaint.

She chirred back to him, rocking her hand, and then tipped him backward so that he lay in the crook of her arm like a baby.

"She lets you do that?" said Nursultan. For the first time his voice was soft for her. It was like that moment when her arm had settled into the prop, and all the weight had vanished.

"He loves me," she said.

"Eh," said Nursultan. "Why 'he'? This eagle is unquestionably female."

"Yes," Aisulu said. Over the weeks since Dulat had made his little chart, it had become clear, from Toktar's great size and the slower speed at which the feathers had come in. "He is female. But also, he is my brother."

"Ah," said Nursultan. He looked at her, and he was shining. She had won the old man's heart. Somehow, holding her eagle belly up in a way no wild eagle would ever let itself be held, assigning it the wrong sex—somehow, in doing everything wrong, she'd done something right.

"Toktar is my brother," she repeated.

"The brother you saved?" said Nursultan.

"I'm still . . ." Aisulu paused to put Toktar back on her wrist. "The one I'm still saving.

"Her brother lost a leg," Dulat explained. "He needs to go to Ulaanbaatar to get an artificial one, and to learn to use it. If Aisulu can win a prize at the festival, it will pay for the travel."

"And if not?" rumbled Nursultan.

"My father will sell our ger," said Aisulu. "Our herd."

"And," said Nursultan, "you will lose your eagle."

She knew that. Of course she knew that, though she fought not to think about it. A city girl who lived in Ulaanbaatar could not also be an eagle hunter. She *knew* that.

But it surprised her—surprised her like an arrow to the heart. Shock shot through her body. Her arm trembled, suddenly, under the weight of her eagle. She wanted to sit down on a stool and wedge her arm against the table. But she dared not, not while Nursultan was standing in front of her. She stood still and tried to keep living.

Dulat, meanwhile, was stroking his mustache. "I fear my brother's family will be trapped in Ulaanbaatar."

"Eh," said Nursultan, as if he'd had quite enough of distant national capitals. "I heard there was a prize this year. I did not know the prize was freedom."

"Money is freedom," said Dulat, but he looked as if the words tasted sour. "Money is one kind of freedom."

"Eh," said Nursultan, as if he had enough money—and of course, he did. "Eh." He coughed sharply, until he had to spit into his sleeve. "An eagle is freedom. Say instead: poverty is a chain."

"Yes," said Dulat. "Say that instead."

"I will go, then," said Nursultan. "I will go one last time, to see the festival." He snorted phlegmily. "All those boys in hats and furs. I have no time for them. But I would like to see the awarding of such a prize."

"*Inshallah*," murmured Dulat, and Aisulu bowed her head. It was a moment before she found the courage to speak.

"Will you tell me what you think of my eagle's weight, grandfather?"

She called Nursultan grandfather as a term of respect, but also of closeness. It was a risk. If he rejected her calling him that, it would be a wall between them. She held her breath, and held out her arm.

Nursultan snorted roughly. The hands he used to examine her eagle were gnarled and tough as tree roots. But they were gentle as they felt Toktar's breastbone. "Eh. She — *he* — is good. Make her a little keener the day before she is to fly. Give her the lungs of a rabbit, not more than that. And tea with sugar."

Aisulu nodded.

Nursultan tilted his head to examine her out of his one shining eye. "What's your name, granddaughter?"

Dulat had named her Pazylbek's granddaughter, Abai's

daughter, Serik's sister. But her name was Aisulu, and she said it out loud. Aisulu, which means "the beauty of the moon."

Nursultan, the shining king, nodded, and answered: "Burkitshi."

Chapter Fifteen

OLGII CITY HUNKERED ALONG the river, windswept and squat. The outskirts were all gers and gas stations, but as Aisulu and Dulat rode in, the buildings changed: there was a ring of mud-brick cabins with fenced yards, and then a district of concrete. Aisulu nudged her horse closer to her uncle's. Buildings rose around them, a few stories high. They were white, or blue, or brightly colored. Their peaked roofs were lined with perched hawks.

Silently, they rode past a hotel, a bank, a telephone office with cardboard over one window. A concrete bridge that spanned a river where women were washing clothes and cows were wading. There was a courtyard where a pile of trash was smoldering.

It was her own country, but Aisulu felt foreign. Moon Spot's hooves clattered on the rough pavement, and the sound bounced back from the hard buildings. The horse's gait was stiff. A yak wandered by. Following the yak's path was a man in a suit and tie. Tourists—white people in North Face jackets—turned their hungry cameras on her.

She tried to keep her breathing soft, so as not to frighten Toktar. But that was difficult. Motorcycles whizzed past them, jeeps, a sputtering bus. The city smelled. It was loud. The air and the light were a different color than they were in the world of the gers. They passed a government building, white with big columns, and paved city square with an obelisk in the center.

And then they saw the hospital.

Somehow Aisulu had thought the hospital would be like her school. It wasn't. It was a big building—half a block long, three or four stories high—clad in yellow plaster. There were glass windows. A turquoise double door.

It was smaller than the government building, but when they stopped in front of it, Aisulu thought it was the biggest building she'd ever seen.

Dulat got down and tied Fox Tail to the solar panel beside the streetlight. He put a hand on Moon Spot's bridle so that Aisulu could get down too, but for a moment, she just sat there, staring at the hospital. How could she go and see her brother when she was dressed as an eagle hunter? How could she go see him dressed in purple silk and fox fur, when he would be sick and would only have one leg? How would they have dressed him? What did sick people wear?

When last she saw him, he'd been wearing a jean jacket. He'd been huddled under that jean jacket and tied to a drag sled, his eyes weird with pain. He'd begged her not to send him here. He'd said he would hate her forever.

He'd been trying to catch an eagle.

Aisulu got down from her horse, leaving Toktar perched on the saddle prop. Her uncle kept hold of Moon Spot's bridle. He nodded at her. She understood that he would take care of the horses, the eagle.

She looked again at the hospital. The plaster was cracking off—the bottom of the wall was so badly cracked that it was like the gap at bottom of the gers that kept the air fresh. Once upon a time, she and Serik had tucked their own ger in every evening, tugging the canvas between them. Aisulu straightened her shapan. She took off her magnificent hat. She pulled her braid out of her collar and let it swing between her shoulders. She refastened the blue clip that held the shorn hair behind her ear.

She would just have to see her brother dressed like this, that was all. She was not so grand that she had more than one coat. The concrete square was echoey and chill. She strode up the ramp, ignoring the stares of the strangers, and pushed open the turquoise door.

It was quiet inside. Almost empty. The floor was shiny yellow pine. The walls were robin's-egg blue on the bottom, white on the top. A hallway opened up in front of her, long and very tall to a girl from the gers. It was lanced with streaks of light. There was a sharp smell, almost like vodka, and underneath that the choking dust of the coal furnace.

She didn't see anyone at first. There was a cat there, an orange striped one that went slinking down the hallway. She followed it until she heard voices. Her boots echoed.

At the foot of a green staircase she found a woman in a white coat, talking to another woman dressed in pink scrubs. They both stopped talking and looked at her. Again —with her hat in her hand, and her beautiful purple shapan—Aisulu felt like an intruder. The doctor and the nurse both pursed their lips and looked her up and down.

"I'm—" she said. She would not let herself stutter. "*Asalaam Aleykum.* I came to see my brother."

The doctor smiled. She had very white straight teeth. "What's your brother's name, dear?"

"Serik?" It came out as a question. She could feel herself blushing, bright enough to match her coat.

"Oh," said the nurse. "The cancer child." She said it as if she were describing his hair color.

"He's my brother," said Aisulu. She was repeating herself. But she wouldn't let Serik be reduced to *the cancer child*.

"Pediatrics is on the third floor, dear," said the doctor.

"All the way to the top, and on your left." She raised a clip-board as if dismissing Aisulu from the world.

Aisulu began to climb.

She heard the children's ward before she saw it. The rush and pound of little feet. The high squeaking voices. She thought of the goat kids streaming down the mountains at the end of the day, running and crying out to be reunited with their mothers. Everything was busier on the third floor. There were distant voices, and people glimpsed through open doors. The bright varnish was worn to dullness in the center of the hallway. The fold-down wooden seats in the hall held people: a man twisting his head against a cell phone. A woman from the gers, in a dark coat and a red headscarf, bending forward as if struck by stones.

Following her ears, Aisulu found her way to the big room at the center of the children's ward, where three children were watching a small, boxy television. Two of them were sitting on the floor. The third was in a wheelchair.

The third: it was Serik.

She could only see the back of the chair and the back of the head, the line of the neck and shoulders. But she knew that line. She would have known the smallest part of him anywhere. For a second she stopped breathing. Something aching and solid formed inside her, flowing from the roof of her mouth to the pit of her stomach. What would his face look like when he turned? Would he still look like her brother? Would he hate her, for changing him? She wanted to shout his name, but the solid thing in her windpipe wouldn't let her.

Serik must have felt her gaze on him: his head twisted around.

Their eyes met.

She had to look down to meet his eyes.

She had to look down to meet the eyes of her brother, who had been tall and beautiful. Her brother. *Serken.* Her mouth shaped his name — his childhood name, though he'd surely grown out of it.

"Aish!" Serik cried, and his face opened like a flower. "Aisulu!" Beaming, he turned his chair around in a series of zigzags and rolled over to her. "Look at you!"

But she was looking at him. His nose had sharpened and his red round cheeks, twin to hers, had faded. His hair had changed. It was very short, and — bizarrely — glamorously curly. He had on a green T-shirt she did not recognize, and pants with one leg cut out of them.

Hanging out over the black leather edge of the wheelchair, one leg ended in a stump, above the knee. It was wrapped tight in stretchy bandages, layered and ridged like a turban.

The leg stuck out into the silence between them.

"If you say one word about being sorry," said Serik, "I will run over your toes."

"Okay," said Aisulu.

"I don't need you to be sorry for me."

She wasn't sorry *for* him—she was sorry for what she'd done *to* him. "You were right, though," she managed. Her voice in her rigid throat felt squeaky. "They did send you away."

"Only, it turns out, they came with me," he said. "It's *you* that got left."

"That's true," she said. Oddly enough, saying that made her voice thaw, her throat loosen up.

"Freeing you to turn into a purple goddess," he said, flicking his fingers at her shapan, the hat under her arm.

"Also true." She could move now. She twisted her hips to display her coat.

Serik popped his chair into a little wheelie.

"Showoff."

"Yeah, getting pretty good. Look." He held up his hands. Peeled, healed blisters were turning into thick calluses across his palms and the base of his fingers.

Aisulu flipped over her own hands, showing her tough palms. She'd earned them as nomad women did: with years of gripping churn dashes and shovel handles, years of hauling rough ropes and milking tough beasts. She also had the calluses particular to girls: the line across the top of palm where a bucket handle pressed. "Keep it up," she said, "and you'll be able to carry water."

"If only I'd known—could have practiced." Serik's hands rested on the tops of the wheels. He fidgeted the chair back and forth, bumping against the edge of Aisulu's boot.

"*Bold-da,*" she said, and nudged his knee with her knee.

He could never stand still. He used to bounce on his toes.

She had promised not to be sorry for him.

"Will you get a new leg?" she asked.

"When this heals some." Serik slapped a hand against one side of the bandage, as if trying to shift a stubborn yak. "I have to keep it wrapped so it will shrink to shape. Do you want to see?"

She did not really want to see. But if he wanted to show her, she could be brave for him. She shrugged.

"It's okay," said Serik. "You don't have to."

"I want to."

So Serik led her down a hall and around a corner. There was a little room there, with two cots in it. She recognized her family rug, serving as a mattress cover, and their mother's coat and spare headscarf, hung from pegs. There was a poster on the flaking whitewash that seemed to be promoting breastfeeding in Africa.

"Boobs," said Serik, flapping a hand at the poster woman. "At least there's that!"

"Serken!" Aisulu covered her mouth with the back of her hand. "That's awful."

"What can I say? There's not a lot to look at."

Serik threw a lever on his chair, then swung himself from chair to bed. That didn't look easy, but he did it easily. He flopped onto his back, pointing his knees at the ceiling, and began to unwrap his leg. There were new muscles in his arms, which had always been strong, but they were a man's muscles now. She could see the three points where they attached at the elbow. He'd lost weight, and lost his softness. But his flop into the bed was as young as a puppy's. She thought: *This is still my brother. He has changed, but he hasn't changed.* The bandage was the only thing that was a barrier between them.

Serik had unpinned the bandage, and had it half unwrapped. She grabbed hold of its trailing end and pulled it up. It came off in loops and spirals. It came off and off, long as a magic trick.

She pulled and pulled, and it became ridiculous.

She pulled and pulled, and it became hilarious. She started to giggle, and Serik laughed with her.

They were both hiccupping and flushed by the time his leg was bare.

They both looked at it.

It was pinkish, streaked with scars, tracked with stitches, shiny.

They looked some more.

"It's healing," said Aisulu, and at the same time Serik said: "It's going to heal, I think."

"It's going to heal," said Aisulu.

Then they were both very quiet.

Though they hiccupped occasionally.

Aisulu flopped down sideways on the bed, beside her brother. It was a little room, a plain room. There was not much to look at, besides the breastfeeding poster.

"I named her Monica," said Serik.

Aisulu hit him.

They were quiet awhile.

"O purple goddess," said Serik. "Favor me with your healing story."

"How do you get outside from here?" said Aisulu. "There's something I want to show you."

The hospital elevator looked as if it had been broken for fifteen years. They took the stairs instead: Serik kept his hands on the wheels, braking hard, and Aisulu dragged him down the stairs back first, bumping and lurching, moving fast because she was close to sliding entirely out of control. A pair of crutches rattled and slid in Serik's lap. They were both half laughing and swallowing the laughter, trying not to be caught by the ward matrons. Their little barks and gulps shot between the green iron railings. They did not get better as they went down, just faster and more full of breathless giggling. By the bottom floor, Aisulu was convinced that she was going to be buried in an avalanche of brother.

And she wanted to be.

But they were not killed, and they were not caught. The ground-floor hallway was still tomb empty—even the cat had gone. Serik swept along it, moving at such a clip that Aisulu had to trot beside him. With both hands he thrust the big blue doors open.

There was the ramp, and the sky, and bright air. In the doorway, Serik threw his head back, opening his face to the sun. Aisulu looked ahead. At the bottom of the ramp, on the saddle prop of a moon-gray horse tied to a lamppost, was her eagle.

"Serik," said Aisulu. She caught one of his hands. "Serik, look."

Serik looked.

His hand tightened on hers. Then he let go and took

hold of his wheels. He moved slowly. He seemed struck—by awe? by the sun? Slowly, braking with his newly toughed hands, he went down the ramp.

Aisulu followed. The chair had handles, but she did not take them. They stopped in front of Dulat and the horses. Their uncle had somehow developed the good sense not to say anything. Serik's eyes were only for Toktar.

Toktar was awake; his wings were folded, his hooded head held high. The sun struck him, too, and he shone: his hooked beak was blue steel, his feathers brass plates edged with new copper. He was more magnificent than any statue, but easy, too. White freckles of down sprinkled his curving breast. Pale fluff covered the base of his tail. As they watched, he turned his hooded head into the wind and a tiny piece of down, soft as a snowflake, rose from his shoulder and went spiraling away.

"Toktar," Aisulu whispered.

The eagle's head swung around to her and he *ker-honk*ed like a rusty bicycle. Aisulu laughed at him—he always knew how to undercut his own beauty. She lifted him from the prop and set him on her glove, pulling on his big yellow toes to settle him. She squatted down so that Serik could see. A scar slashed across her brother's eyebrow—the eagle-talon scar he'd gotten as a child, trying to hold one of Dulat's eagles. He was flushed, and that made the scar look white.

"Can you take off her hood?" Serik spoke softly. His scar glowed; his words glowed.

"Okay, but you're close." Aisulu shifted back on her toes. Toktar fanned his wings to balance. She tucked one wing behind her own shoulder.

"Move slowly," said Dulat. "Don't startle—"

Serik stuck out his tongue at his uncle. Aisulu flicked Toktar's hood away.

The eagle sharpened, feathers tightening, feet closing. He looked at Serik with his three-mile eyes.

Serik met the gaze. His body mirrored Toktar: stilled and brightened. "Wow."

"I know, right?" Aisulu said. "His name is Toktar."

"His?" said Serik, squinting.

"Don't worry, he's female."

"You are so weird," said Serik. "And Kazakhs don't name eagles."

That was true: even a nickname like Crooked Claw was fairly rare. And yet, she knew she was right, and she said: "Toktar is my brother."

"Well." For an instant, Serik flashed that bitterness he'd shown in the blizzard. "At least you'll have *one*."

But he couldn't hurt her like that, and she wouldn't let him hurt himself. She said: "Don't be stupid."

He snorted. Toktar tipped his head all the way over.

Aisulu laughed again: her slapstick rubber-necked eagle. "Can you ride a horse?" she asked. "Because we're going to the festival."

"Right now?" said Serik. "Jailbreak!"

"Don't be ridiculous," said Dulat. "Your father has the ger set up at the festival grounds, and he is coming with a truck." He waggled the cell phone in his hand, to show how he'd gotten the news. "You must wait for him."

"*Must* is his favorite word," Aisulu murmured to Serik, who grinned.

"You'll be there before us," said Dulat. "But we need to go."

"O purple goddess!" Serik clamped both hands over his heart. "I'll miss you."

"But you'll come?" Aisulu asked softly. Serik had wanted to capture an eagle — that had been his dream. Would it hurt him to see her living it?

But there was no hurt on his face. She had an eagle in one hand. Her brother took the other.

"I wouldn't miss it, Aish. Not even for Monica."

And so Aisulu left her brother behind. She had made no preparation for that, given it no thought. Certainly, she had not expected the way it scooped a hole out of her. She had not expected the sting of tears in her eyes. All summer, she had buried her longing for him and her fear of losing him. She had buried it deep. Seeing him and then leaving him had dug it up and laid it in the light.

But there was nothing to do but ride.

Sayat Tobi, the hunter's hill, dominated the dusty bowl outside Olgii City like the pyramids outside Cairo. Made of a single thrust of shale, the hill shone blackberry red as the sun struck it, and all the gray and gold land seemed to sweep toward it, even as the clouds banked behind darker, higher peaks in the distance.

Toward Sayat Tobi rode Aisulu and her eagle.

Aisulu kept her back straight and her body soft. She guided the horse with her knees and the reins in her left hand. With her right hand she carried her eagle down to be judged.

Dulat rode beside her. They left Olgii City behind, crossed the river and climbed a rise. Everything in front of them seemed small. One road crossed the bowl like a pale thread. One jeep left a plume of dust small as a down feather. They could see white gers scattered like pebbles at the base of Sayat Tobi. They could see the gathered trucks and horses there, like salt grains, like sand.

Aisulu blinked back her fear and her tears, and they started down.

The festival did not start until the next day, but people

were already gathering. Aisulu and Dulat rode in among boys on bicycles, horsemen in groups of three and five. Jeeps and trucks. Tourists with gear strapped to them. Camels hung with rugs and boxes. Eagles on the backs of motorcycles.

Through it all, they rode.

In an hour, they were among the eagle hunters.

There were others, of course. Aisulu saw troops of dancers in matching silks, archers in hats the shape of sprouting onions, city Kazakhs in their best furs, tourists in their puffy jackets. But Aisulu only had eyes for the burkitshi, and for their eagles.

The eagle men wore furs of many sorts. They wore shapan coats with gold embroidery. Their coats were dark: black, navy blue. Here and there was perhaps a wine red, a forest green. They wore red silk hats with fur lining — the richly striped red and black and tawny fur that was said to be made of thirty-six foxes. Each of the hats was high and peaked, with a little tuft of owl feathers on top. Each had earflaps that framed the men's faces like wings.

The men did not look like she looked.

The men were staring at her.

She heard their voices as she rode among them. They were not speaking to her, but they were speaking about her, some excited, some muttering. *A girl. The girl. Too small. A stunt.*

Suddenly the horsemen were parting around something, like a stream parting around a stone. She was near whatever it was, almost on top of it, before she saw it. It was a man—no, a woman—with a camera. It was not just a tourist camera, not just a big-eyed, handheld thing, but a giant movie camera that was strapped to the woman, a heavy black harness encircling her purple coat.

The camerawoman was running backward, and the camera floated in front of her, lifted by bending black metal arms. It had a big square hood sheltering a deep-set single eye. That eye was pointed at the riders. Then it was pointed at Aisulu.

It was staring at her. The woman was jogging and bobbling but the eye of the camera was steady, the way an eagle's head stays steady as it swoops toward you, its body and wings undulating.

It was uncanny. Aisulu found herself looking right at it, even as the riders' talk kept striking her ears. *A girl. That girl.* She looked at the camera; she passed the camera; she rode on and away.

There was a cluster of gers on the sunny side of Sayat Tobi that was not an aul and was not a town. It was a strange place. On foot amid eagle hunters and tourists, Aisulu and her uncle weaved among the gers. Toktar rode on her wrist.

Dulat led the horses. The brittle grass between the canvas walls was not yet trampled. It crunched under their boots.

Aisulu was aware of the eyes on her, and of the cameras. But she was looking only for the familiar little ger with the triangle of new canvas on the roof, the familiar yellow door with orange panels and turquoise flowers.

In the end, she did not see the patched roof. She did not see the yellow door.

She saw her mother.

Rizagul was outside the ger, draping laundry over a boulder. She was wearing her lavender headscarf with the little dark purple flowers. As if through binoculars Aisulu looked at the way the lace edges of the scarf lay intricately rumpled against her mother's hair.

"Mother?" she said.

A question, even though she was sure. The last time she had seen her mother she'd been driving away, bent over Serik in the streaking sunlight, the back of the truck. She had not said goodbye. She had not looked back. She had told Aisulu to manage the milking and grow into a fine young woman and Aisulu had done something completely different.

Toktar shifted on her arm.

"Mother," said Aisulu, a little louder, and her mother turned.

It had been fifteen weeks since they had seen each other.

For just an instant, Rizagul's hands came up to cover her mouth, as if holding in a thousand words. A wet pair of stockings fell from her hands into the grass. "What are you wearing?" she said. "What are you—"

Toktar was tight feathered with all the noise. His beak was cracked open. Aisulu could feel that he was nervous, that he was dangerous.

"Mother," said Aisulu. And then the child's word: "Eej."

Rizagul stooped and picked up the fallen stockings, draping them over the stone. Then she walked toward Aisulu, wiping her wet hands down her skirt. Aisulu knew those hands, that gesture. Her mother, completely familiar. Her mother, completely strange. In this new place. With her face marked with new lines, thinned with new sadness.

And still—*still* not proud of her.

She had rescued an eagle. She had done a great thing. But it was not the thing she was supposed to do.

Aisulu's heart cracked; her lungs twisted. Tears started in her eyes. Dulat put a hand on her shoulder.

And then, without warning, two things happened.

First, her father and Serik came out of the ger—Abai tilting back the wheelchair to clear the little lip at the bottom of the door. Second, the television crew came around the corner.

At first, Aisulu paid the cameras no attention, because suddenly her family was together. The four of them: man and woman, boy and girl, a picture-perfect little Kazakh family that made Rizagul warm and soften, as if she'd stepped into the story she wanted, the one where Serik was a strong young man and Aisulu was a fine young woman. All at once her mother was beaming at Aisulu, telling her news: how they had traveled from clinic to hospital, how they had missed her, how Serik's hair had fallen out and now it was back all curly.

All at once it was perfect. Aisulu knew it wasn't—not the way the Fox Wife had pronounced her perfect—but she still stood in the triangle of her family, and she wanted to spin around and around as if in the sun circle under the crown of a ger, as if on a dance floor.

But then Dulat spoke suddenly, sharply—and not to them.

It was five sounds, a foreign language. Aisulu and Serik had both studied English at school, but even so, it was not until Dulat repeated himself that they understood what he was saying.

"What are you doing?" he said, in English. He was facing down the television crew.

There were three of them: the white woman in the purple coat and camera harness, and two white men. The men wore identical dark puffy coats and black fleece beanies with a jumble of red foreign letters on the front: ESPN. One had a pointed little beard, and the other was wrangling a microphone on a pole, but otherwise they were hard to tell apart.

"Do you speak English?" said the bearded one.

"Enough to do asking," said Dulat stiffly.

The language was already leaving Aisulu behind.

The bearded man shot a look sideways, and the next time he spoke, a Kazakh woman to one side of him spoke almost on top of him, like an echo. A translator. She had gold earrings and bright pink lipstick.

"We're making a television show," said the white man with the beard, and the lipstick woman translated. "We do the weird sports, and we're doing an episode about the eagle games. I'm Gary. This is Alex, and Karl."

"You're filming us?" said Serik, taking half a roll forward.

The other man, Karl, spoke: "The color and—she's a girl. Good television, you know?"

"She's not a zoo animal," Serik snapped.

"It's all right," said Dulat, extending a hand in front of Serik. "We heard that television people were coming. We heard that you had provided prizes for the festival."

As the translator rendered his words, Dulat shot Aisulu a quick look, and she thought she understood. It was probably best to be nice to the people with the money.

"Word gets around," drawled Karl.

"We heard there was a girl," said Alex, the woman with the camera. She had a long auburn braid shot through with silver. "Is that you? Are you going to fly in the festival?"

"This is her," said Dulat. "And she will be flying her eagle tomorrow. But this family—they haven't seen each other in a long time. Turn your cameras off. Let me speak with you."

The three white people exchanged glances. Gary-with-a-beard shrugged. Dulat handed off the horses to Abai and stepped closer to the foreigners and their translator.

Aisulu's family drew together. It was meant to be a moment in which they might finish their reunion, but that was hard to do. They found themselves huddling like an opposing sports team.

"He's telling them about me and Toktar," said Aisulu, glancing over her shoulder. "He's telling them about you, Serik."

Serik grimaced. "Why me?"

"Because it's a good story, Serken," said Abai gently. "If Aisulu wins the festival, we can go to Ulaanbaatar. We can get you that new leg."

"From where?" snapped Serik. "The moon? Moscow? The land of miracles?"

"Serik, we talked about this," said Rizagul. "The doctor said prostheses and rehabilitation are available in the capital." She put the medical syllables together as if punching a needle through leather.

"When we talked, I said I didn't want you to give up the ger and the herd." Serik's face was fierce and pinched under the crown of his new curls.

"And if I win the festival, we don't have to," said Aisulu.

"Oh," said Serik. And then: "Oh!" She watched realization work its way across his face, rising like sunlight.

She became aware that she hadn't wanted to tell him all this. She hadn't wanted him to feel—hopeful? Fearful? Guilty? She'd been trying to spare him, as if he were a very young child. But he wasn't a child. Being sick did not make him a child. "I'm sorry. I should have told you."

"I'm still your brother," he said. "Your *older* brother. I'm just down a quarter."

"You're terrible." She nudged his wrapped leg with her knee. "And that's not more than an eighth."

"Right," he said. "So, my plan is to keep cheating off you at math tests."

Dulat, still bent in conference with the foreigners, was now beckoning her over.

Aisulu tried not to scrunch up her face. "I think I have to go talk to them."

"Nervous?" asked Serik. "I've read that when you're nervous Westerners want you to imagine that they're naked."

Aisulu sputtered. "Where did you read that?!"

"Around." He shrugged. "How about this? Imagine you are carrying a thirteen-pound killer eagle."

She glanced at the foreigners. The men were making squares with their hands, gesturing like men planning a hunt. The woman in the purple coat was offering her a smile.

"Two bags of rocks," whispered Aisulu. "And a thirteen-pound killer eagle."

She squared her shoulders and lifted Toktar like a serving tray, then strode on over.

Chapter Sixteen

AISULU WOKE.

The warmth of her brother's back was pushed into her back. They were lying together on a single stack of rugs, sharing a single quilt—curving away from each other, but still as close as two birch leaves coming out of the same bud. They were breathing in time. She knew, from years of sleeping just like this, that Serik was still asleep.

Her father, too, was snoring his big rumbly snore. Her uncle was carrying the high snore harmony. But her mother was up—early enough to do the milking, though there was nothing to milk. She was dressed for the day in her stockings and skirt, in her green cardigan sweater. She was doing up her hair. For a moment, Aisulu just watched her.

Rizagul was bent double, pouring her hair into her headscarf. Aisulu had never seen anyone else tie their headscarf like this. And no stranger had ever seen her mother do it. It was just between them. They had stood together in front of the mirror, every morning.

"Mother . . ." Aisulu whispered.

"Shhh . . ." Rizagul bent down, almost in passing, to brush her fingers across her daughter's cheek. "Don't wake your brother." Her skirt hem and the long belt of her cardigan swung across Aisulu's face as she went to stir up the fire.

Aisulu twisted her neck. Toktar was asleep on his perch at the head of the rugs. He had one foot tucked up.

It was the day of the festival.

It was time to begin.

Aisulu watched her mother fuss at the stove, which should have been the most homelike thing she'd ever seen. It should have made her feel complete, but it didn't. It made her feel hollow, and somehow it was Kara-Kat-Kis's face that came into her mind. Her lip-of-a-well smile, her blackberry hair.

Family—family are the people who choose you, no matter what. Her mother chosen Serik, and of course she had: he was her son, and he was sick. But the way she'd done it had laid bare something Aisulu had always known in her heart but kept wrapped away from her thoughts. It was not just that her mother had a son and a daughter, and chose her son. It was that her mother had a fine-girl daughter whom she imagined, and a sky-heart daughter who was Aisulu as she really was.

I was twins once, the Fox Wife had once said. And she

253

really had been, but also, this: Long ago, Rizagul had chosen. She had not chosen Aisulu, sky-hearted. She had not chosen Aisulu at all.

But Kara-Kat-Kis had.

Wordless, Aisulu got up and crossed to the mirror to brush out her hair.

Overnight, the festival grounds had transformed. There was a roped-off field of scrub and dust. Outside the rope were gathered the people. Outside the people were the gers and tents and trucks and camels. At one end of the field, a stage was set up on the back of a flatbed truck. At the other end was the purple and dusty face of Sayat Tobi, the hunter's hill.

The first and hardest thing Aisulu had to do was to walk in front of that crowd, climb up onto that stage, and register for the festival.

She had been to a city, but she had never seen a crowd.

She had grown up under an open sky, but she had never seen a stage.

She felt as if the eyes on her were like the cold needles of a blizzard. As if each one pierced her a little deeper. Her hands were numb by the time she reached the foot of the steps. She took off her hat—a mistake, because she could feel the moment her braid swung free, the moment the crowd noticed she was a girl. The vast muttering made a noise that was almost like the wind. Shivering, she climbed the wooden, wobbling steps. She was, for the first time, wearing her full costume: she had three pairs of socks inside her shining boots. She could hear the stitches of her embroidered pant legs brushing together.

On the stage, three judges sat behind a wooden table. They were all men, grandly dressed men who did not look as if they ran out of butter in the winter. They had velvet shapans. They had big rings. They had new skullcaps embroidered in bright colors. The one in the middle was holding the clipboard and the stack of paper.

As she walked up to him, the two on either side leaned in. The three of them muttered.

Aisulu glanced wildly around, like a hunted thing looking for a way out. Alex-in-purple was pointing a camera at her. Aisulu saw the camera flex its eye and lock on her as if she were a lure. She was not sure how she felt about that camera, but she liked Alex-in-purple. The first words Gary-with-the-beard had said to her were, "Tell us what's wrong with your brother." Alex had said, "Would you tell us about your eagle?"

They were part of a crew who did "the weird sports," they said, for an American TV channel. "The caber tossing in Scotland," Gary-with-the-beard had explained. "This ultraviolent capture-the-flag thing at the Japanese West Point, and the one in Indonesia where they set the soccer ball on fire." He'd named the three countries as if flying between them were nothing. Aisulu was not even sure she could take the last step across the empty boards of the stage. It was such a big world, and such a small one.

Alex-in-purple flashed her a thumbs-up. The three judges finished their conference. The one on the right was sitting rigidly and pulling down the corners of his mustache. The one with the clipboard grunted to her. "Name?"

"Aisulu, daughter of Abai." Her voice shook a little. She steadied it and told the judges what she'd told the camera the day before. "I am here to fly my eagle."

The clipboard judge held his pencil in his fist as if it were a chisel. He started scratching her name into the paper. Once he was finished, the three of them leaned together again and looked at it. They kept her standing there. They muttered. Aisulu began to hear her own name bouncing through the crowd behind her. She glanced back and saw her family—her brother in his wheelchair pressed against the rope, short because of the chair, among the littlest children.

Her brother needed her.

Aisulu turned back to face the judges. "Aisulu, daughter of Abai, granddaughter of Pazylbek. I have saved and trained an eagle."

The rigid judge grew even stiffer, and the clipboard one blew through his lips like a horse. What would she do if they did not accept her? She had no plan. She wished she had thought to carry Toktar. It was harder to deny she was an eagle hunter when she was carrying an eagle. She stood straight. Her hand sweated into the fur of her clutched hat. She mentally named the judges Clipboard and Stiff Face, as she had named the goat Next Week You're Lunch, as she had named Sneering Muscles. She tried to keep her eyes neutral.

Finally the third judge—the one who hadn't been harsh enough to earn a nickname—spoke. "We have put you in a riding group with Oraz, Chudruk, and Yrymbassar."

Clipboard tapped her name with the eraser end of his pencil. "*Asalaam Aleykum.* Welcome to the Eagle Festival." Aisulu did not exactly feel bathed in warm welcome. She pivoted on her heel and walked back down the bouncy steps, past the TV camera. She collected her horse and her eagle, and headed for the foot of Sayat Tobi. She tried not to look at her brother.

Aisulu walked Moon Spot toward the burkitshi clustered at the foot of the hunter's hill. Behind her the festival was unfolding. There were dancers and speeches, archers with their tight-banded sleeves shooting wicker balls, children racing atop fast horses, horsemen playing tug-of-war with a decapitated sheep.

But no one had come to see any of that, not even the part with the sheep.

This was the Eagle Festival.

Finally Aisulu reached the foot of Sayat Tobi. All around her, the burkitshi milled, trying to steady their animals. The eagles were making the horses skittish. The eagles were making each other skittish. The eagles were just plain skittish. Aisulu saw many an eagle panting or whirring with reptilian panic. They were, after all, solitary. It was not unknown for one to have a heart attack in a place as strange as this festival.

Aisulu knew how they felt. The day seemed tight and breathless. Moon Spot shifted under her, her ears swiveling, her lip curled as she blew at the other horses and eagles. Toktar swayed on her wrist. Off to one side, a portable building of white metal was marked with the logo of the American TV station. More foreigners stood there, watching. A generator fumed and roared.

The burkitshi blinked away camera flashes and drank water from plastic bottles. A festival marshal in a forest-green shapan and lavender-tinted sunglasses was sorting them into their riding groups for the parade. They would stay in those groups as they moved through the three events of the festival. Aisulu's only job right now was to wait for the marshal, ideally without dying.

It was a hard job. She could feel the eyes of the other riders on her — their horses and eagles that sometimes pressed too close. Some were curious, some were hostile, some were smiling — but there were so many of them. Added to them were tourists who were not giving the eagles proper space, the diesel reek of the generator, Alex-in-purple standing a little distance away and swinging her camera in slow loops, and somebody's idiot dog attacking every stirrup.

Aisulu felt awful.

Up by the stage, dancers were performing. Music crackled and gusted over the loudspeaker. There were speeches happening, but they were too far away to hear. She could no longer spot her family, just the bump of Serik's wheelchair.

Sweat trickled down the back of her neck. Her stomach churned. Then finally the marshal was at her side. "That girl, there. That girl, there. This way, come!"

"Aisulu," she corrected him, because she wasn't going to let herself be *that girl* any more than she would let Serik be *the cancer child*. The marshal reached for her bridle and she pulled Moon Spot's head up, out of his grip. The little gray horse jerked and whinnied. "This way," said the marshal, pointing. "Hurry. Come."

He led her over to her group of four, and named the other three quickly.

Oraz. He was older than her father. He had a face that had squinted into a thousand fox hunts: wrinkles that spoke of hard winds and bright snows and long smiles. His young eagle had a decorative plume of owl feathers tied to her shoulder, and she sat like a crown on his hand. A threadbare buttoned shirt poked out from under his dark shapan.

Yrymbassar. He was a young man in a pale suede coat —one of those men who had grown tall at the expense of growing wide. He had a narrow face with a pursed and pretty mouth, and when he looked at Aisulu, a furrow appeared between his eyebrows. It was so deep it looked as if an axe had struck him there.

But she had no eyes for either Oraz or Yrymbassar, because Chudruk—how she had forgotten?—Chudruk was Sneering Muscles.

He smiled at her, pure poison. "Nice boots, little girl."

"Thank you for them," she said. "They suit me."

But there was no time to squabble. The loudspeaker was booming welcomes, and the marshal was on a horse of his own, a light blue flag waving. Ahead of him a grandly draped camel was swaying forward, its rider holding the national flag, a splash of royal blue and red and yellow. Aisulu took in a gulp that tasted of dust and diesel. Toktar rocked and spread his wings.

The riders in front were beginning to move: she had a view of the backs of heads and the tails of horses, the bobbing undersides of eagles. And then it was time for her to go. With reins in one hand and eagle in the other, with horsemen pressed close all around, Aisulu rode down one side of the cheering crowd and passed before the stage. As they rode back up the other side, she could see her brother. He raised his hand and waved as if he were throwing a lasso.

In answer she raised hers, high above her head, full of flaring eagle.

Her heart cried out as if it were breaking, or as if it were a newborn. As if she had lost something, or as if something great was beginning.

Chapter Seventeen

AT LAST, THE TIME CAME for the Eagle Festival's first event. The eagle hunters on their horses made a line midfield. Alex-in-purple paced sideways in front of them, her camera holding her in its insect hug. They endured a speech of welcome, words about fine horses and fine eagles.

And then, one by one, the eagle hunters were called forward.

They rode to the stage, trotting or galloping, their eagles on their fists, their gear on display.

This was the event that Aisulu dreaded. It was about eyes, not about eagles. It was about who could look like an eagle hunter. Five official judges sat on the stage in their fine and spotless shapans—Clipboard, Stiff Face, the nice one, and two more. They had mustaches and big hands; they had skullcaps or the high peaked hats that Kazakh wore to weddings. They were all men. Behind them loomed the vinyl sign that was the stage backdrop. It said *Eagle Festival,* and it was printed with a photograph of burkitshi carrying their eagles. They were all men too.

All around her, boys and men.

Right beside her, Sneering Muscles. "Did anyone bring scissors?" he asked the riders around them. "This one sometimes gets things caught in her hair." Aisulu twisted away and considered pretending that she had not heard, even though she knew that did not work on bullies. On her other side, Yrymbassar's considering furrow grew so deep that she mentally dubbed him Axe Thinker. Sneering Muscles persisted, even if he did have to speak to the back of her hat. "Who told you you could be here?"

"Well . . ." She turned back to him, touching the front of her purple shapan. "Your grandmother, for one."

He did not flush, as she'd thought he would. Instead, he grew still, and his face paled. He looked as if he would like to hurt her. She kept herself steady, but she must have been sending fear through the reins: Moon Spot shivered and pinned an ear.

"My eagle belongs here," she said. "And I belong with my eagle."

"Yes," said Oraz. "The eagle makes the eagle hunter. Burkit makes burkitshi." He pushed his horse between Aisulu and Sneering Muscles. He was craggy as a cliff face. The argument was over.

The judges kept calling the eagle hunters forward. Alex-in-purple darted in and out with her camera. Kazakh names rolled and rattled: Kenjahan, Holegar, Tenti . . . As they were called, the men rode. The judges gave points for outfits and riding style, for horses and for gear. They were taking points from anyone whose ride was stiff and awkward, from anyone whose eagle tilted off the glove or stayed too tight with fear. They were taking points from poor men whose boots were old, whose shapans were threadbare.

As Aisulu watched, they called a young man who had come all the way from the northernmost mountains, where the wind blew and the borders tangled. His eagle spread her wings grandly, and he rode as if he were one of the five thousand falconers of Genghis Khan. But his fur coat was so old that it looked like bad taxidermy, and his boots were laced with broken strings.

The judges lifted yellow boards with red stenciled numbers. The young man from the north got a five, a seven, then two sixes and a nine. It was respectable. But Aisulu knew it would not be good enough. Even if his eagle later came to his hand in a lightning flash, it would not be enough to overcome that score. The best riders were getting eights and nines, even strings of pretty tens. The young northerner had ridden flawlessly. He was not like the men who lost control of eagle and horse, earning twos and threes. But he was not the face of the burkitshi that these judges wanted to display to the world. The butter-fed men would not let his worn coat and hungry frame be the face of their pride.

How had she ever thought they might pick a girl?

But she did not need to win this event. She just needed to do well enough that she would not be desperately far behind.

One after another the eagle hunters were called forward. Menke. Merim-Khan. Bash-Baatar. They were old men and young men, and many boys her own age. They wore furs and embroidery. Some of the young men were simply men carrying eagles. But the old men: they were burkitshi.

"So the first event," Gary-with-a-beard had said the previous day, "the ride. That's, like, the swimsuit competition." Aisulu and her uncle had blinked at that, and the translator had blushed to match her lipstick as she struggled to explain. By the time Aisulu understood, she was half convinced that Serik had been right: Westerners really did want you to think about them naked.

"He means," said the translator, "I think he means it is only about beauty."

Dulat had agreed cautiously: the ride was about beauty.

But he'd been wrong, Aisulu thought, watching the line in front of her group dwindle to ten men, to five, to three. The ride was about finding the true burkitshi.

"Let Oraz come forward."

Aisulu's heart gave a lurch, but beside her the craggy man clicked his tongue as if doing no more than riding out after the herd. His horse tossed its head once and pranced willingly forward, then headed for the judges at a trot. "Oraz," said the marshal, "our famous hunter of the Altai. He took fifty foxes last season!" It was a good ride, quick and bouncing, showing both speed and the rider's ability to be smooth atop a rattling horse. Oraz's eagle inched open her wings and leaned into the wind, steady as if she were the knot from which the whole thing hung. The judges held up their yellow scores: eight, seven, ten, nine, and nine.

Aisulu did the math in her head. A good score, though not exceptional. A full ten points more than the poor northerner.

It was almost her turn. The judge Stiff Face seemed to be looking at her. The marshal fiddled with his lavender sunglasses and picked up the bullhorn. "Let Yrymbassar come forward."

Yrymbassar, the Axe Thinker, straightened his hat. He smoothed his hand down the front of his pale coat. He lifted his chin. His horse eased forward.

"Yrymbassar," said the marshal, "a new hunter from right here in Olgii!" As the words squawked around him, the Axe Thinker put his reins in his teeth and slapped his horse with a crop. The horse exploded into a gallop—a streaking toward the stage, fast as a racehorse. The horse was black and Yrymbassar's coat was cream suede fringed with white fur. His black belt and boots shone like oil. His velvet trousers were embroidered in silver. He was rich and tall and stunningly, strikingly beautiful.

Then he dropped his eagle.

What happened was that his horse missed a step and bounced, and he lurched forward, and the eagle swung around his glove and spent three hoof beats hanging by her leash and flapping wildly. Yrymbassar scooped her back up, but too late: there were boos and laughter. The axe wound was back in his forehead and his pinched little cheeks were flushing cherry.

Six, read the first scorecard, and Aisulu was surprised. But then: two, two, three, four. A truly terrible score.

The crowd was still laughing happily, because everyone likes to see a rich twit fail. One of the judges was shaking his red two and giving some kind of lecture. But the marshal was finished penciling down the score.

Aisulu watched the marshal, and her world seemed to narrow and then to stop. Her hair felt damp under her fox fur. Her shapan was stiff and hot. Tight-feathered, that was what she was. Toktar's talons curled in, putting pressure through her glove.

"Aisulu, come forward."

For just an instant she could not move. And then she was moving.

Aisulu rode. The loudspeaker was saying something about her. *Girl* was in there. And *young*. But she was young, and she was a girl, and she was wearing her aunt's silks and her uncle's furs, her elders' blessings and her brother's hopes. And she was carrying her heart in her hand.

For a moment she felt every hoof beat of her horse, but then she rose to float above the saddle, and everything turned fluid. She rode as if suspended from the sky. She rode as if lifted by the earth. Galloping in front of all those eyes, she lifted Toktar high on one fist. He flared his wings and tail. White flashed in the corner of her eyes and she felt the backward shove and upward pull as the great eagle caught the air. But his talons were tight and her arm was strong. In that moment, all she could think was: *Toktar!*

And then it was over.

Oraz was smiling. Aisulu's eyes were stinging, blurred with wind-drawn tears. She turned to face the yellow plastic, the red numbers.

Eight, nine, ten, ten.

Then on the end, Stiff Face held up his three.

Sneering Muscles, beside her, barked a laugh, and on her

other side, Oraz snorted like an angry horse. Overwhelmed, Moon Spot pranced and trotted in a little circle.

Aisulu missed it when Sneering Muscles was called forward. Suddenly his big horse and his white leer were just gone.

"Chudruk, son of our esteemed judge Zhambyl." The judge Stiff Face nodded solemnly. Aisulu realized: the judge who had given her the three was the father of Sneering Muscles.

"Pfff," snorted Oraz. Aisulu was so furious that her teeth clicked together. But there was nothing she could do.

It was worse because Sneering Muscles was good. Not extraordinary, but good. His shapan was dark and his hat was bright and his eagle's hood had a crest of leather tassels. He rode fast and smooth. He showed the bird well. He looked like his father, now that Aisulu knew to look for the resemblance. He looked like an eagle hunter should.

The numbers flashed: eight, seven, eight, seven, nine.

By the time he was back to the line, she had her horse soothed and the math done. It was a good score, though not an outstanding one. Four less than Oraz.

And one less than her.

There was music, then, gentle dombras amplified until they rattled the loudspeakers. There were speeches. There was a race in which the galloping riders had to lean out and snatch a marmot skin clean off the ground. Aisulu had been good at that race, once. It was her kind of quickness: a quickness that could reach and swerve and bend.

As the young riders competed, the eagle hunters and their helpers climbed the hunter's hill. It was time to release the eagles from the heights and have them strike the lures. Aisulu went with Dulat. Horse hooves clattered on shale in the shadow of Sayat Tobi. In the hand of the festival marshal was a bleeping walkie-talkie.

The judges were setting up along the sidelines now. Aisulu could not resist a look at Stiff Face, who she now knew to be Zhambyl, the father of Sneering Muscles, the head of the family who had stolen the place for her family's gers. He was Beskempir's son, too, and she wished the old seamstress were there to grab him by the ear. She wished she herself could grab him. She wished—

She wished for exactly what she was seeing: Nursultan. The oldest living eagle hunter, the one who had called her burkitshi, whom she had called grandfather. Nursultan, the legend, was leaning over the judge's table and shaking his cane at Stiff Face like a grumpy schoolmaster. From her perch near the hill, Aisulu could not hear what was happening. But no one looked happy.

"Maybe Nursultan will take the place of Zhambyl."

Oraz scratched his beard wistfully. He had taken to Dulat at once: with one soft, double-handed handshake and a shared sense of grievance, they were long-lost brothers. "There is no one more esteemed."

Aisulu's heart hoped for a moment, but Dulat was already shaking his head. "He's missing an eye. He cannot see well enough to judge for us."

"Pfff," huffed Oraz. "He sees well enough to spot what's going on."

"He does," Aisulu said—and found herself grinning as Sneering Muscles turned to glare at her. "He does, doesn't he?"

Nursultan pulled up a stool close behind the judges and perched there with his boot heels up on the stool rung. Aisulu's fist around the reins felt happy. With Nursultan sitting there, there would be no more threes.

Besides: This event wasn't about boys and girls, about costume and pageantry. This was talent and training. This was bond and skill.

She knew she'd been cheated by Stiff Face's three in the first competition—she knew that her score was good where it should have been great. She would have to make up ground here. But she was not like the northerner in the threadbare coat, not like Yrymbassar the Axe Thinker, who sat pouting on a rock, resplendent in his cream and silver. She was not out of the running.

And she remembered day after day after day when she and Kara-Kat-Kis had run with the land in their boots, had launched Toktar at the lure. Toktar had learned to come far and come fast. He had learned to rise to the sound of her call as if he were the note rising into the air. Now, her uncle would release him from the mountain, and she would drag the lure behind her horse until it looked like a fox dashing, and then Toktar would strike it like thunder. Aisulu was sure.

Then the other eagle hunters started their attempts, and the sureness started to leak out of her.

There was a hunter whose eagle launched, veered sideways, and landed on someone else's arm. There was a hunter whose horse suddenly objected to being dive-bombed by a hundred-mile-per-hour eagle and took off into the crowd. And there were many—most—whose eagles hesitated before they launched, or struck behind the lure, or overshot and swooped upward, past the rider, into the air. The golden eagles of the Altai had great wings and great hearts, but their eyes weighed more than their brains. To bring an eagle among the knotted crowds and horses, among the bright snapping flags and the red bobbing hats—it was a lot to ask.

She had not realized, until she sat on her own horse at the bottom of Sayat Tobi, how much she was asking of Toktar. And she had not realized how little her practice in the empty foothills would have prepared him for the crowds.

"It's time," said Dulat as hunter after hunter flew their eagle, as hunter after hunter failed. "You must give him to me."

Aisulu lifted her wrist from the saddle's prop and brought Toktar close to her face. She breathed him in: dust and blood, and a strange smell that was like the smell of heat, like a pan heated empty. "Trust me," she whispered. She stroked the smooth feathers over his breastbone, and he fluffed up and lifted his wings so that she could scritch her fingers through the down of his armpits. "That's right. Trust me. Come to me." She leaned so close that she had to tuck her shoulder under one of his wings. She felt the pulse thunder through his body. "You are my heart, Toktar. Just come to me."

"Pretty speech," said Sneering Muscles, but Aisulu was beyond caring. She passed Toktar down to her uncle. Her hand felt too light without him. She turned her back because it felt like a loss. It felt final.

As Dulat threaded his way up the face of the shale, Aisulu rode off a few paces, away from the ESPN trailer. She was careful to stay in reach of the marshal's voice, of his squawking walkie-talkie. As long as it didn't come at the start of her group, her turn would not surprise her. Moon Spot liked being a little farther from the crowd, the eagles. Her ears hung softly to the sides, like hands opening in prayer.

Aisulu watched the poor northerner in his taxidermy coat land his eagle as if he'd done it ten thousand times. She watched a burkitshi in a wine-red shapan land his eagle on top of the lure, but then drag the skin over a stone so fast it bounced both bird and lure high into the air. The northerner had eights and nines and tens. The wine-red man had sevens and nines.

To catch up she would need to do as well as the northerner, who had been perfect. To stay in the running, she would need to do as well as the wine-red man. But most eagles were not doing as well as either.

She heard the walkie-talkie call for Chudruk.

Sneering Muscles flashed her that awful perfect smile as he rode by her. His horse was a bay with white speckles. A stallion, of course. She wondered who would launch his eagle for him, since his father was busy judging.

Up on the stage, Stiff Face sat, sneaking looks at Nursultan like a boy trying to sneak an extra Choco-Pie.

A flag dropped. Sneering Muscles rode fast, and then faster, the bay horse kicking up dust and the rabbit skin lure skipping over stones. Soon he was at a gallop. He passed the marker flags and called out for his eagle. Aisulu twisted around in the saddle.

As much as she wanted to smack Sneering Muscles in the teeth with a rancid dishtowel, she had to admit that his eagle was beautiful. The eagle took two strong beats to rise high into the air, clearing the side of Sayat Tobi and banking to catch the wind. She rose, her wings curved and motionless. She stayed up in the sky one beat, two beats, three—too long, Aisulu thought—and then she was diving. Aisulu barely had time to twist around to see her strike.

The lure skipped up over a stone and the eagle's talons swung around and struck down two inches behind it. In a blur of dust the eagle rushed after the lure, one huge wingtip catching the earth and pushing off, like a man grabbing a pole to take a corner. In a blink the eagle was on the lure, squeezing it even as she skidded forward.

A great strike. But not a perfect one.

Aisulu felt her heart pounding inside her purple shapan. Sneering Muscles slowed his horse, stopped his horse, and reeled in his eagle.

In the distance, the yellow pine of the judges' table shone like a dust beam. Yellow cards lifted red numbers. Nine, eight, eight, nine. Stiff Face hesitated over his score and even glanced backward at Nursultan before lifting a seven. Two nines, two eights, and a seven made forty-one. A very fine score.

Aisulu particularly liked the seven.

She nudged Moon Spot back toward the mountain. It

could be her turn at any moment. She was ready. She was so ready that her teeth hurt.

Only an unlucky hop of lure over stone had separated Sneering Muscles from perfect. One unlucky hop had laid him open to the judges.

Inshallah, she prayed, inside her heart, but did not know what to ask for. Above on the mountain, the walkie-talkie made a noise like a crow and said Oraz's name.

The craggy eagle hunter moved calmly to the first flags, threw down his lure, tightened his knees, and burst into speed. Aisulu pushed her fingers over her heart, and the silk there felt slick as ice.

It was over in ten heartbeats. Oraz's eagle came in fast —faster than Chudruk's—too fast. She overshot the lure, snatched downward with one powerful leg and grabbed a rabbit ear. But it was not enough. The lure got away from her and she banked upward, following the lure line, past Oraz, up into the sky.

And just like that, for Oraz, the competition was over. Two, flashed the red and yellow. Five, three, three, four. That afternoon Oraz could call his eagle all he wanted. But no matter his speed in the next event, there was no winning with that score.

Oraz rode back to Aisulu, and seemed to take in the wide-eyed horror on her face. He smiled like a mountain smiling: craggy and calm and slow. "She took fifty foxes last winter," he told Aisulu, stroking his eagle's back. "And she missed at twice that many. They all do. Don't let it bother you."

All, thought Aisulu. *They all miss; they all do.* She wished Toktar were on her hand. Moon Spot was standing very still, and her eyelids were crinkled—picking up Aisulu's tension. Aisulu scratched her horse's neck and tried to breathe easy.

The true burkitshi did not live for festival scores—they lived for fox hunts. They lived for cold days with new snow, for long nights full of meteors. But no other contestant had a brother whose hope was tied to a score.

Aisulu and Oraz watched side by side as Yrymbassar the Axe Thinker rode out in cream and silver and called to his eagle as if he were a god calling lightning. He certainly looked the part. It was only sad that his eagle did not think so. She never tried for the lure at all. His score was dismal.

Then it was time for her, for her and for Toktar.

Moon Spot pranced out to the yellow flag. Aisulu paused there. She could hear the creak of the saddle leather as the horse shifted. The click of a hoof on a stone. The voices of the crowd, which were like one voice, like the wind speaking through many grasses. She could feel the horse shift and bunch under her. The sun-dazzled and stony field stretched away in front of her. The flat rawhide of the lure rope was dusty in her fingers. The fox fur was soft against her face.

Aisulu cast the lure out behind her. She took one more deep breath. And then she shot into action so fast that it took her stomach a moment to catch up.

The horse leapt forward. Aisulu dug her heels in hard. The reins were thrumming in her left hand. The lure jerked and tugged in her right. Her eagle's name rose from the bottom of her ribs: she shouted it before she even knew she was shouting. "Toktar! Toktar!"

As if she had left her heart in Toktar's body, she felt him lift.

Aisulu squeezed her knees in tight and stretched her front over Moon's gray back. As she did it, her whole body remembered racing down the side of the mountain after the blizzard, chasing her brother, who was chasing the feasting eagle. In front of her she glimpsed Serik sitting in his wheelchair behind the rope at the edge of the field. He was just a flash of details: the sunburst spokes of a wheel, the knots of his hands as he held the rope.

The image stayed in her eyes even as she twisted in her saddle. Again she had only a glimpse: Toktar hanging dark against the sky. Wind rushed over her ears.

She looked ahead of her, and every stone loomed and shone.

She looked back and Toktar was diving. He was heading right for her.

She looked forward to pick a smooth path.

She looked behind and Toktar was right there—and he flashed into her eyes as his wings opened, and she felt the yank as he struck the lure. The rope jerked in her hands and it jerked in her heart, strong and hard and true.

In the privacy of the center of the field, she found happy tears springing into her eyes. She could hardly see the red numbers of her score: nine, nine, eight, seven, nine.

That made forty-two.

It was one more than Sneering Muscles, and she thought that was beautiful.

The festival paused for lunch. Aisulu and Serik made their way back to their ger, him in his chair and her on her horse, both of them trying to ignore the cameras. In the familiar shelter of their ger, their mother was already rolling dough and cutting it into fingers.

"Oh!" Rizagul jumped up as they came in. "I couldn't bear to watch, how did you—"

Dulat came in behind them, declaiming: "What an eagle—what a fine eagle. Toktar flew well!"

"Because Aisulu flew him," said Abai.

"Stop, Ake, you'll make her insufferable," said Serik.

"Too late!" exclaimed Aisulu, and raised Toktar over her head.

"A good score," said Dulat, stroking his mustache. "A fine score."

Aisulu and Serik looked at each other. A good score, but good enough?

Their mother managed to click her tongue and play the role of responsible parent. "Put that bird down and eat your dinner." Then she gave up and grinned helplessly, even as she tossed the dough strips into the sizzling butterfat.

"Well done, Aisulu," said Abai. "Well done!"

Aisulu put Toktar on his perch by the door. They ate the baursak hot enough to singe their fingers. They ate spiced and dried horse meat. They ate Choco-Pies and dipped hard cheese in tea.

And then, as the adults murmured over watered vodka, Aisulu and Serik settled onto the pile of felt rugs. They bent their heads together and did the calculations. Oraz was out of the running, and Yrymbassar had never really been in it. Sneering Muscles had a total score of eighty. Hers was eighty-two.

She led him—just barely.

"Have you been keeping track of the others?" Aisulu asked.

"You're the one who's good at math."

"I'm also the one who's *busy!*" She scribbled on a bit of scratch paper. She knew the top scores from the "swimsuit competition," and from the lure race—she just could not quite remember which hunters had done very well at both. She sucked on the tinny end of her pencil. "I think the best score must be between eighty-five and ninety."

Serik squeezed a hand around the bandaged end of his thigh. "So . . . you're not winning?"

"Have some faith, boy," said a voice in the doorway.

"Nursultan!" Aisulu cried. The three adults scrambled to their feet like schoolchildren.

The ancient burkitshi was tottering on a carved black cane, but he entered easily, certain of his welcome. He began to circle clockwise, like a guest, but Aisulu seized his arm eagerly and drew him counterclockwise over to Serik, and to her eagle. "Nursultan! This is Serik—this is my brother."

"Your *other* brother?" The old man smiled, and Aisulu remembered that she'd told Nursultan that Toktar was her brother.

"My other brother," she said happily.

"Eh," said the old man, as if he'd had enough of metaphors. "This one's got fewer feathers."

"I used to be the pretty one." Despite his quick words, Serik had his chin tucked and was tracing a knuckle along the edge of the one of the rug's bright pink scallops. Aisulu realized that he was pinned there, sitting on the floor without his chair or crutches in reach. She reached out and dragged the chair closer, but Serik ignored it.

Nursultan pointed at a stool, a command both thoughtless and certain. Aisulu's mother brought it over.

"Nursultan..." Aisulu was thinking of the three she'd received from Stiff Face in the first event, and the nine in the second. "You talked to ... I saw you talking ... Thank you!"

Nursultan sank onto the stool, spent a moment arranging his shapan and cane, and then smiled at her, prim as a schoolgirl. "Thank me? Eh? What for?" Then he began to cackle. Aisulu looked at Serik, and their faces cracked into identical grins.

"*Tsai oh*, Nursultan?" asked Rizagul, hovering.

The old man held out a hand and accepted their best bowl, then slurped politely. "I came to be sure that your eagle had tea."

"Tea? For an eagle?" said Serik.

"An old trick. Not so many of these feather boys know it. Tea for an eagle." Nursultan glanced over his shoulder at Aisulu's mother. "Black tea with sugar."

It was an eccentric request, in a land where tea was brewed in watered milk and drunk with salt and butter. But Rizagul did no more than frown a little as she poured water from bucket to kettle, and fetched the precious bowl of lumpy white sugar.

"Now, young man," said Nursultan, wiggling his cane head at Serik. "You must have some faith in your sister. And her brother female eagle."

"I already told her how weird that was."

"Did you?" said Nursultan. He looked innocent a moment, then broke—again—into a happy cackle. Serik flushed, but Nursultan went on. "The afternoon event is calling the eagles to the glove. It is the only one that puts fire in the heart of a true burkitshi. It is the most important event. If Toktar is the fastest there, your sister will win the festival."

Aisulu's heart caught on Toktar's name. She was absurdly pleased that Nursultan had remembered it. That he was not angry with her for doing that strange thing: giving a name to an eagle.

"The tea is ready." Rizagul took Nursultan's empty bowl from him and handed him one that was full and steaming. He accepted it as if he were a khan on a throne and she were a minor courtier: he was that certain in himself, and he had that little interest in her. And yet his single eye shone down on Aisulu like a star.

Nursultan swirled the bowl in his hand, dissolving the little mountain range of sugar. Then, from his pocket, he pulled a length of clear plastic tubing. "This is from my great-granddaughter. She steals gasoline." He coughed, as if he'd had enough of law abiding. "She's a hustler," he added fondly. His gaze fell again on Aisulu. "Little burkitshi, cradle your eagle."

Thus it was that Aisulu ended up holding Toktar in her lap, a leg in each hand, as the oldest living burkitshi used plastic tubing to spit tea down her eagle's throat. Amazingly, Toktar didn't seem to mind. After a few moments she released him. Toktar hacked up a little tea, and a lump of fat and fur. Then he raised and ruffled his feathers as if he were the happiest bird in the world.

"A little lighter, see," said Nursultan. "And the sugar will make him a little keener. A second here, a second there."

The world is strange, she thought. *Strange as a wheelchair in a ger.*

"Drink the rest, granddaughter." Nursultan passed her the bowl. The tea was hot and sweet. The ancient hunter rested his great hard hand over her hair and she cupped her hands to hold his blessing, then rubbed it over her face like water.

The world is strange, she thought. *The world is strange and old and new and beautiful.*

And then, and at last, Aisulu climbed into the sky.

The eagle hunters perched with their birds and horses

on the shale sides of Sayat Tobi. The afternoon was bright —the sun strong, the crowd below stretched and tiny.

There are moments on which your whole life turns. Sometimes you see them coming, and sometimes you don't.

In her fur and silk, on the side of the ancient hunter's hill, Aisulu tried to imagine Ulaanbaatar. A city of more than a million people. A city more than a thousand miles away. A city of universities and discos, a city of coal plants and bus routes and department stores. They spoke a different language there. They did not milk things.

They did not keep eagles.

She had never let herself think that. But of course it was true. They did not keep eagles.

Serik needed to go to Ulaanbaatar. In Ulaanbaatar, he would get a good leg, and the help he needed to learn to walk, to run, to turn handstands in Suhkbaatar Square. One way or another, he would do that. She knew it. She could feel it. She could see it.

If Toktar was the fastest, then Serik could go, and also come back again. He could be the shining prince of the gers, and someday, if he wanted, the king. If Toktar was the fastest, her father could go, and then come back. Her father would not spend his life as a slaughterhouse janitor, as a uranium miner. He would come back to his herd and his ger and his family and his sky. Her whole family could go, and then come back.

If Toktar was the fastest, she could go, and then come back.

But Toktar could not go.

I will release him on a mountaintop, she thought. *I will slaughter a lamb for him and I will give him a white ribbon.*

She tried to convince herself it was a happy ending. Once upon a time there was a girl who saved an eagle. Once upon a time there was an eagle who saved a girl.

There would be a day, and very soon, when she would never see him again.

All summer long she had not let herself think it. But the moments in your life that change you, change you—even if you don't let yourself see them coming.

Her shapan was beautiful and her fur hat was beautiful. There was a fresh rabbit leg in the pouch that hung from her belt. The eagle on her arm was calm and keen and fast as lightning. He was her whole heart. He would come to her.

Of that part, she was not even afraid.

The event stretched out through the afternoon. Aisulu watched the eagles that struck well, and the ones that lazed about in the sky. The top score started at thirty seconds, fell to twenty-seven, and then to seventeen. But many eagles were nowhere near that. She watched the eagle that flew sideways and entangled itself in another eagle, and the tight moment when the two handlers worked to unwind the knot of yellow feet and black talons. She watched one eagle soar off Sayat Tobi, land on a smaller outcropping, and peep down at her hunter in the field, as if to say *No thank you.*

"Fed her too much," she said, to the others, to no one. She could feel the bright and empty calories of the sugar tea. It buzzed through her—and through Toktar. She could feel it in his feet, in his heart, as if they had one heart.

She leaned her face against his wing, smelling him. Dulat was threading his way up the shale toward her. Soon it would be her turn. He would take Toktar, to launch him. She would find her horse, and her voice, to call.

"Will you sell her?" asked Yrymbassar.

"What?" Aisulu's eyes snapped away from her uncle.

"She is a splendid eagle," said Yrymbassar, the Axe Thinker. "She is very tame also. That's good for the tourists. Will you sell her?"

She imagined Toktar in the picture Nursultan had painted of the false burkitshi. Toktar wrapped in a rug and hauled around on the back of a motorcycle. The Axe Thinker in his splendid costume, parked at the crossroads, charging foreigners money to hold Toktar, to snap his picture. Toktar surrounded by dust and diesel.

"Eagle hunters do not sell eagles," growled Oraz. "Eagles are not *sold*."

"I heard she needs the money," said Sneering Muscles.

"She will not sell her eagle." Oraz sounded certain.

"She hasn't heard a price yet," said the Axe Thinker.

"She won't," said Oraz.

Aisulu nodded sharply, once. But what she was really thinking was: *Even if it could save my brother?* The thought tangled in her hair.

The "weird sports" foreigners and their prize money. Swimsuit competitions. The burkitshi becoming tourist attractions. Would they still ride out in the winter, when the snow was new and the fox fur was thick and the fox tracks were blazing? Would they still stop the hunts in the spring, when the tourists came but the foxes were busy with their kits? Would they still release their eagles, as her grandfather had, as her uncle had? Would they still tie their yellow legs with white ribbon, a mark that meant they should never be captured again?

Next week she would go to Ulaanbaatar. She would never see Toktar again. Did it matter if she sold him, if that would save Serik?

And then she thought, with a huge and sudden certainty: Yes. It mattered. Of course it mattered.

Her uncle climbed up to her, smiling, puffing slightly, and she rose. Toktar on her arm rocked back and forth, his claws east, his wings just open. In this strange place, in this moment on which everything depended, Toktar was calm. And Aisulu felt calm. The calm was improbable, crisp but soft, like a flight feather.

That Toktar had lived was a miracle. That she could hold him was a miracle. That she could trust him was a miracle.

She was going to catch him, now. She was going to catch him at full gallop, and no doubt would tangle her, and she would not be afraid.

"Masha-Allah," she said under her breath, and handed over her eagle.

She straightened her shoulders and retied the little bow under her chin. The last thing she needed was to lose her hat. "I'm not going to sell him," she said. "I'm going to win."

Finally it came to this: Aisulu riding Moon Spot in the long slant of the afternoon sun, with the eagle behind her and the crowd in front of her. She drew level with the starting flags and pulled up. Moon Spot, excited, pranced on the spot.

Aisulu wiped sweat from her eyes and peered down

the field. She was watching for the moment when the field marshal would drop his sky-blue flag, when the stopwatches would click on, when time would both stop and begin.

There are moments on which a whole life turns. The sweeping wall of a blizzard. The crack of a leg bone. The climb of a cliff. The three-mile gaze of a young eagle. They ticked by like seconds.

The flag dropped.

Everything inside Aisulu opened.

It would be right to say she exploded into motion, the horse surging into a gallop, her voice rising and ringing. She was that fast. But to her, it felt more like a blossoming. The meat was in her glove and she twisted in the saddle, calling for Toktar, and calling for her brother.

Toktar was flying.

He cleared the rock and caught the wind. Up he sailed, like a stringless kite, one hundred feet. Two hundred, and then he curled his wings and fell. So fast. His wings didn't beat; they were curved and still and powerful, like an archer's bow. He swooped right at her, faster, and then faster, and then faster. She could see everything about him, his shine and his power. He was close, he was on her. His wings flared and his tail flared and his claws swung forward.

"Serik!" she shouted. "Serik!"

Her brother eagle hit her glove at a hundred miles an hour.

Aisulu felt the hit, like the blow to the chest to start the heart beating. She let it spin and raise her arm, as if she were waving a flag. Toktar stayed strong atop her, his wings white flashing.

And the crowd began cheering.

High-stepping with horsey pride, Moon Spot bounced forward.

They were calling her name on the loudspeaker. They were saying words and numbers. But she could not hear them, over the crowd, and over the one voice she needed, calling for her: "Aisulu! Aisulu!"

Serik. Her eyes sought him and found him, standing—standing!—at the edge of the field, a crutch wedged in each armpit. He was cheering for her, shouting her name.

She got down off the horse and ran to him, and they threw themselves into a hug, a messy thing of rope and crutches and eagle. Aisulu thrust her arm clear and Toktar flared his wings.

"You did it," Serik was shouting. "You are so crazy! You did it!"

"Did you hear the time?" she panted. "Did you hear the score?"

"Seven seconds!" he shouted. Yes, that was the number the loudspeaker had said, that the crowd had repeated. But she could hear it when Serik said it. It was as if in all the crowd, only he and she shared a language. "Seven! They think it's a record!"

It wasn't. She'd studied, and she knew: the record was five.

But seven was perfect. Seven was Ulaanbaatar and Serik's leg.

Seven was leaving Toktar.

If you take an axe and break through the ice to the river, the water can shoot upward, can gush and bubble. That is how you gather water in the winter. That is success.

Aisulu felt as if an axe blow had broken through her. She burst into tears.

Chapter Eighteen

"HERE ARE THE EAGLE HUNTERS who have made us known to the world," squawked the loudspeaker. "They are the ones who have cared for the traditions passed down to us from our great ancestors. Join me in cheering all these honored men!"

All these honored men, and one honored girl.

The ceremony went in a blur, and Aisulu remembered little of it. The jostle of the horses. The grins of the highly honored men—the men among whom her place was certain. The songs, the jokes from the judge. A flash of Nursultan's bright eye catching her through a gap in the horsemen. A man dancing with his eagle on his arm.

She heard the name Chudruk: Sneering Muscles had come third, and she was so happy and so sad that it did not bother her. The man in the wine-red shapan came second, tucking his head so that they could drape his neck with a medal.

The other burkitshi were nudging her to the front of the

group; they were laughing and slapping her shoulder. Oraz reached out and stole her hat. "Our winner today," cried the festival marshal, "is Aisulu!"

They draped her in a medal that snagged on her hair ribbon and hung crookedly from one ear, as Toktar had once hung. She had been so alone in that moment, when the eagle had hung from her hair, but in this moment the other eagle hunters laughed and reached to tug and straighten. Kara-Kat-Kis and her sewing and her strength, Dulat and his *musts* and his teaching — they had made her a place, and she had proved she could stand in it. And she was welcomed. To be Kazakh is to welcome. Hands brushed her hair, her face. Hands brushed her hands. They gave her a scroll, which she thrust at Dulat. They gave her a trophy, a gold cup on a wooden stand.

Alex-in-purple was there, behind her camera, steady, crying. Nursultan was there, pushing Serik's wheelchair. Her father, her mother weeping on his shoulder. Her uncle Dulat thrusting a hand into the air as if he held an eagle. Flashbulbs, stomping, music. "Aisulu, Aisulu," said the loud-speaker. "May our sons be like her!"

"Sons and daughters!" shouted Abai.

Aisulu lifted the eagle and he flared his wings like the sun.

The crowd cheered and cheered.

. . .

And then it was over.

It was sudden as falling onto a stone.

It knocked the breath from her belly.

It was over. She had done it. She had saved her family. She had proved her place. She had flown her heart. She had won.

Sometimes she grinned and sometimes she cried, and sometimes she helped her mother make tea for everyone.

The TV people showed up at the ger, or some of them: Gary-with-a-beard and Alex-in-purple.

Gary-with-a-beard grinned at her and handed over a white envelope. She frowned at him and ripped it open: it contained a money order for more tugreg than she had ever considered in her life. There was a letter about the ESPN company, about the "model release," about the how the Mongolian tugreg translated into in American dollars, and even that number had four zeros. Aisulu blinked over it.

Alex-in-purple glanced at the translator and smiled at Aisulu, almost shyly: "Is it enough?" She asked, in Kazakh, then switched to English: "Is it enough to save your brother?"

Dulat gave her a stormy frown, but softened when he saw that she wasn't pointing her camera. She was just asking. "It's enough," he said gruffly.

"Save some if you can," said Alex-in-purple, and Dulat

translated for her. The English was just out of Aisulu's reach. "For school. For college — university."

Aisulu rocked back. "I'm thirteen years old."

"Well, kiddo," said Gary-with-a-beard. "You make good television."

"That's Gary's way of saying *thank you*," said Alex. Like a woman who had never lived someplace cold, she added softly: "Just remember. It doesn't hurt to leave a door open."

Days passed. The TV crew hung around, and Aisulu learned the English word *B-roll*. Gary-with-a-beard managed to actually say "thank you." Alex hugged her. Karl-with-the-microphone said they might come back after the fire soccer, and Aisulu felt her heart stop, because she did not know how they would find her. She did not tell them she was about to be lost. She just let them go, and one day they were gone.

Almost everyone was gone. Aisulu's family left their ger in place even as the other gers were taken down, even as the air filled with dust and the fumes of trucks and motorcycles.

Abai rode Dulat's horse into town, to see about the money order and the plane tickets and all those other bizarrely foreign things. But Aisulu stuck close to the ger with the yellow door, as if it were the one still place in a world that was whirling. She had taken off her purple sha-pan, donned her mother's green sweater. There were those who passed her with a cheer and a handshake, and those who saw only the rolled-up sleeves of a child and the long single braid of a young woman.

On the second day, when the encampment was almost empty, Nursultan showed up between the sunset prayer and the evening meal.

They ushered him in and gave him their best, though the meal was a little strange: they had city luxuries like pota-toes and spiced sausage, but traveling away from their herds, they had run out of milk. The ancient burkitshi dug through the great pockets of his swinging black coat and produced a packet of hard candy, two tomatoes, and a half-dozen tiny vodka bottles with little foil tops.

They drank the tea black with sugar and the vodka only lightly watered, and Nursultan himself sliced the sausages, passing around his favor on the point of a knife.

"So," he said. "You will go? Eh?"

"As soon as we can get tickets," said Abai. "Next week, perhaps?"

"Soon," said Rizagul. "The children should be in school."

Abai managed a move that was both a shrug and a nod. "The tourists are going home; the planes are filled this week. It is complicated."

"But you will be back?" Nursultan looked at Aisulu, his eye glittering.

"Yes," she said. She could feel the sugar tea inside her again, like warmth, like certainty. "We will be back."

"What of your herd?" said Nursultan. "How many have you?"

"About a hundred," said Abai. "Forty sheep and sixty goats. Twenty-seven in milk."

"I will care for them," said Nursultan. "Unless your aul can work them without you?"

Dulat and Abai looked at each other. "It will be a stretch," her uncle admitted. Aisulu had seen them doing the figures and calculations, adding cryptic lines of dash marks next to Dulat's sketches of wind power generators. Suddenly she understood what they'd been deciding.

"I will take them, then," said Nursultan. "My aul can absorb such work easily. I will do the slaughtering when it turns cold, sell the meat, and wire you the money. I have a wholesaler in China. There is always demand."

"Nursultan, that is too generous," said Abai. "I—"

"And in the summer, I will send the cashmere fleece money. But the felt money I will keep. Felting is hard on these old shoulders."

"Nursultan," said Abai, again.

"Eh," said Nursultan, as if he'd had enough of interruptions. "I want this young burkitshi back in her mountains, is all. I want to see her prosper. You can reclaim your animals and their offspring when you return."

He turned to Aisulu, his one eye gleaming. "What about it, burkitshi?"

Aisulu raised her chin. "Thank you, grandfather. Your gift will bless my family."

"*Inshallah,*" he muttered, then coughed sharply. "I think," he said to her, as if it were private, as if it were a whisper, "before you go, there is a thing to do."

"There is," she said. Suddenly she was blinking back tears. Toktar. She must set Toktar free. "But I don't know—" She swallowed. "How?"

Nursultan sipped slowly at his bowl of vodka, then put it down with a clink. He squared his hands on the head of his cane. "I have white ribbon," he said. "And a good mountain. Before you must go to Ulaanbaatar, why don't you and your brothers come home with me?"

He thrust the head of his cane at Serik. "You, Pretty One. Do you ride a horse?"

Serik returned the thrust with the head of one of his crutches. "Only since I was two." He made a face. "I think so. A little way."

• • •

Two days later, they took the blue truck up the mountain. Abai drove. Serik and Aisulu rode in the open back, with the wheelchair and the crutches, with the eagle and a dozen felt rugs.

The ride was bumpy and dusty and freezing, so Aisulu and Serik made a nest of the rugs. They tucked them underneath their bodies and piled them over and around their knees. They stretched one rug around both their backs, and the thickness of it kept it upright, its slight sag making a dome above them, so that their space was dusty, dim, almost holy. Apart from the potholes. Their bodies pressed together, warm and jostling. Toktar rode on his perch at their feet.

"Was it pretty bad, the hospital?" asked Aisulu.

"It was pretty boring," Serik huffed. "But, bonus, I learned all about breastfeeding."

"You are awful."

"And you love me."

"Yeah," she said. "So. Pretty bad, the hospital?"

He paused. "At first. Right after—" The empty leg of his jeans was rolled up and pinned together at the knee. He made a chopping motion that bounced off there—the exact motion their father had once made, though of course he could not know that. "And then they gave me all this medicine that made me sick. My leg hurt, and it hurt worst where it was gone. At first. Pretty bad." He looked over to where the wheels of his chair—which was upturned and lashed down—spun like frost whorls in the fall sun. Above them the sky was hard as enamel.

Serik shrugged, his shoulder nudging against the blanket and letting a bit of cold into their pocket of warm. "After I started to get better, I was mostly just . . ."

"Bored?" Aisulu guessed.

"Frightened."

She let him say that. She heard the word, and held it.

"I hated you for a while," he said. "Then I realized you actually saved my life. So naturally I hated you for that. And then I loved you."

"That's a real camel ride you took there," she said, and let the next bump sway them from side to side, a little more than it had to.

"Yeah. But through the whole thing, I missed you. I missed everything. I thought—I thought it was forever."

"We can come back," she said.

"Maybe."

"We can."

Serik was silent. They had left the valley around Olgii City and were climbing into the mountains. There were no roads, just a swath of tracks, several hundred yards wide, braiding in and out of each other. The big truck growled into a lower gear. Between their knees, Toktar stirred and spread his wings to balance.

"Will he let me hold him?" Serik asked.

"I think so." Aisulu made coaxing, clucking noises as she reached out and stroked Toktar. The eagle ruffled his feathers and *kurr*ed. "You put on the glove, and I'll lift him." She unpeeled Toktar's claws and guided him onto Serik's arm. She popped off his hood.

The eagle went tight feathered, but just for an instant. He stared at Serik, and then at Aisulu, weaving his head curiously from side to side.

"We look alike," said Aisulu. "Do you think he sees it?"

Serik didn't answer. He was entranced, enraptured. "Hello there," he whispered. "Hello."

Toktar tipped his head and kept tipping it, until he was holding it upside down. Serik laughed—but softly, gently, so as not to startle the eagle. Aisulu felt love rush through her. "I am sorry we can't take him," said Serik. "Ake says Dulat has a friend who has a friend who found a high-rise apartment for us. So I guess that won't work—keeping the eagle on the balcony or whatever. But I'm sorry."

Under them the truck lurched and grumbled.

Aisulu reached out and scratched under Toktar's upturned chin. The eagle's head slowly swiveled upright. He stroked the sides of his beak against the edge of her fingers.

"He's heavier than I thought he'd be," said Serik.

"This is his flying weight. He can get heavier yet."

"You must be strong," said Serik. "I mean, I know you're strong. Here, take him back." He hooked the perch closer with his one remaining foot and lowered Toktar toward it. The eagle deigned to step onto the perch, arranged his feathers like a fine shapan, and then lifted his tail and shot poop toward the wheelchair. It splattered across the leather seat.

Serik laughed. "Seconded, feathery brother." He passed Aisulu her glove. "I guess what I wanted to say was thank you. To you. To your eagle. Will you tell him?"

Aisulu put on her glove and let Toktar step up onto it. She brought him close to her face. And then something astonishing happened. The eagle stretched out his wings and mantled them forward, one against each of her cheeks, against each of her ears. She could see nothing but feathers, but she could feel the soft strength of the wings and hear the crisp rustle. She could smell Toktar. She could feel his heart.

"Tell him thank you," said Serik's voice. "And tell him I'll always be the pretty one."

Aisulu closed her eyes and mouthed it: "Toktar. Thank you."

It was not easy to get Serik onto a horse. It required a milk stool, their father's strong shoulders, and a desperate grab and drag at the saddle. The horse they'd borrowed from Nursultan — a brown with two black stockings — paced sideways and snorted in disgust. Even once in the saddle, Serik had to wiggle and rock. But Aisulu could see the moment when he found the right way to use his new body — like the moment when she had found the point of balance in her saddle prop and the weight of Toktar dragging on her shoulder had vanished.

Toktar.

She sat on a strange black horse, with her wrist in a strange old saddle prop — an ancient one carved with wings and animals. Toktar rested calmly on her arm.

Calmly, and for the last time. The sun struck him and made him glow like a brass dome. He was so, so beautiful.

Nursultan also creaked and groaned his way onto his horse, but once up he sat tall in the saddle, commanding and craggy as an old glacier. "See, Pretty One," he said to Serik. "A horse is better than a chair."

"Not arguing!" said Serik. Aisulu was glad they'd had the days by Sayat Tobi to practice; she didn't need to worry about whether Serik could ride for a few hours.

"Are you sure you do not want me . . ." said Abai.

"I—" She fought down the urge to apologize. She needed Nursultan, to show her how to release an eagle. She needed her brother—her brothers.

But she needed to be alone.

"I understand, kitten," said her father. "I'm so, so proud of you."

They rode.

The October day was kind to them, bright and crisp, with a fresh and swirling wind. A wild day, a clear day, but not too cold. Aisulu was snug under her shapan and her fur hat. Serik had a new skullcap, to replace the one the eagle poop had ruined. She'd bought it for him. She was rich now, though there was nothing she wanted.

They rode through the lion-colored grass and into the stony parts of the mountains, up and up. Hooves clicked and clattered. No one spoke. Nursultan had a lamb tied to the back of his saddle and it bleated occasionally, in a *well, this is odd* kind of way. Toktar rode hoodless, watching the wind.

They went up, and up. An hour, and then two.

Finally they reached the crest of Nursultan's mountain.

It was a small mountain: large ones rose farther on, and larger ones behind that, rank after rank, shining dark and snowcapped, all the way back into the distance.

"When you free your next eagle," said Nursultan, "you must take her farther. Far from your home, to a wild place an eagle might like, so that she will not dream her way back to you. This is not Toktar's home. But it's what the Pretty One can manage."

Serik snorted like a horse, but did not argue. There were tears in his eyes.

"So come now," said Nursultan. "We will walk a little way. To the top of the rocks." He got down and pulled his cane from where it was slung across his back like a rifle. He stuffed the hogtied lamb under one arm.

Aisulu got down, Toktar on her arm. The ground seemed strange to her, as if the world were tilted. She staggered, and had to put her hand on the black horse's saddle.

"It's all right," said Nursultan. "We're all a little broken. We'll only go a short way."

"I'll be right here," said Serik. "I'll be waiting for you."

She knew he was trapped on the horse. She wanted him —she did not want him—

"Go ahead, Aish," he said.

She went.

The eagle on her arm had never felt as heavy. The scent

of him blurred around her. The stones clattered under her boots. There was the smell of yarrow. Toktar had hatched in slate, in yarrow. Maybe he would like this. Maybe he'd remember.

They reached the top of the rock. The other side of the mountain dropped away in front of them, sweeping red and purple and golden, vast and wild. Nursultan handed her a white ribbon. He held out his hand again, and in it was a knife. She took the blade in her hand. It was cold, and heavy. She tucked her chin for a moment and then cut the ribbon in half—half for her, half for Toktar. As if she were cutting apart her heart. Then she passed the knife back.

"Will you?" she asked. "Will you slaughter? I've never done it. I don't know the prayer."

Slaughtering was a man's business. And she could learn it. She would learn it. But right then she did not want to put the eagle down.

Nursultan looked at her a long moment, his face craggy and still. Then he nodded and creaked down to his knees. He crouched there a moment, murmuring *"Bismillah,"* his hands cupped in prayer. Then he washed the blessing over his face and without further fuss cut the lamb's throat. It wiggled once, and was dead in seconds. Nursultan opened it.

"Eh," he said, as if he'd had enough of heartbreak. "Come on, then. Come."

Shaking, Aisulu knelt beside the lamb. She took off Toktar's hood. The eagle instantly zeroed in on the meat, hopping onto the woolly body and plunging in his sharp beak.

"Undo his ankles," coaxed Nursultan softly.

Toktar didn't look up as she undid the buckles and pulled off the ancient leather jesses, the new Astroturf padding. His claws tightened and bit deep into the lamb, dragonlike, powerful.

"Now the ribbon," said Nursultan.

She took a little strip of snow-white ribbon. She ran it between her fingers, once, twice, three times. And then she tied it to Toktar's leg,

"You have to tell him what you're doing," said Nursultan. "All the eagles, and all the eagle hunters, for all these years. If you tell him, he will understand."

"Toktar?" she said, and her voice cracked. The eagle was busy. He fluffed his feathers, but he did not look up. "Toktar. This is our last meat together. You'll have to catch your own now. I know you can. Your wings are quick. Your eyes are golden. And you've been a good friend, Toktar. You've been a good brother."

She swallowed. "I love you, Toktar. I'll love you forever."

Then she got up and ran down the mountain, crashed

into Serik's knee, and wept until there could be no more weeping.

They rode down.

Aisulu felt emptied, as if she'd been scoured like a pot, as if she'd had everything scooped out of her. Her head was light and her hands were shaking. It was hard to keep her eyes off the empty prop of her saddle: the ancient carvings fascinated. Men and creatures. Wings and wings.

They rode down, and down. An hour. Two hours.

"It was well done," said Nursultan finally, his voice creaking into the silence like an old saddle. "That is the hardest thing a burkitshi can do. I have done it seventeen times, and each time was the worst time. It is like the end of the world."

"Yes," said Aisulu. The slashing scar through Serik's eyebrow shone.

Two hours. The sky was bright and high. A beautiful afternoon.

"Stop here," said Nursultan. "I'm an old man. I need some bushes. There's cheese in your saddlebag."

Shaking, Aisulu dismounted, turned her back discreetly, and went poking for cheese. She found some, and a thermos of tea. She slugged some down, and passed it the thermos to Serik. "Are you doing okay?" she asked.

He shifted uncomfortably. "I have blisters in places I am not allowed to mention."

She huffed half a laugh. "You're strong, though," she said. "I know you're strong."

Serik squeezed the end of his knee and shrugged. She could see the lump inside his cheek where he was sucking on the dried cheese.

Nursultan came wobble-striding back to them. He rummaged through his saddlebag and produced Choco-Pies in red wrappers. He handed one to Serik, began to hand one to Aisulu, then stopped.

"Eh," he said. "Little burkitshi. I think you had better put your glove back on."

"What?" said Aisulu. Nursultan was looking past her, so she turned.

Like an ink-brush stroke on the blue glass sky, the distant form of an eagle. It was flying toward them. Gaining fast.

Aisulu dashed to her saddle and thrust her hand into her glove. She did not know what to do. She just stood there while Serik watched, his hand full of Choco-Pie, his mouth open.

The eagle was closer. It had white flares under its wings and tail. It was wearing a new white ribbon.

"Toktar!" Aisulu shouted, and threw her arm into the air.

The eagle dove toward her. Its diving back was black against the sky. Its shape was the shape a child draws to mean *heart*. Then its talons swung forward and its wings untucked and it hit her glove so hard she spun in place, around and around and around, shouting: "Toktar! Toktar! Toktar!"

Ker-honk, ker-honk, ker-honk, Toktar scolded. Gripping her glove, he bobbed up and down like a goose.

"You can't be hungry," she said, because that was his *I need something* noise.

"No," said Nursultan. "Just angry. Just happy."

The joy was draining out of Aisulu. "But. What do I do?"

"Burkit makes burkitshi," said Nursultan. "Didn't you know? You don't choose an eagle. An eagle chooses you."

She stood there, with her heart in her hand, looking at him.

"You keep him, kid," said Nursultan. "That's what you do."

"I—" she said. "But . . . I . . ."

"I could use a hand with those extra goats of yours I'm

taking in." He winked at her, and cocked his head like a raven. "And I can teach you."

"What?" she said. The ability to make whole sentences had been knocked right out of her. But her eagle preened on her arm.

"You can't be a true burkitshi until you hunt in the mountains, until you hunt in the winter. Your eagle has made you an eagle hunter. So you must stay with your eagle, and learn."

"Stay—?" Aisulu's heart skipped a beat. She looked at her brother, high and happy on the borrowed horse. "But Serik has to go—"

"I'll be back," Serik said. He sounded, for the first time, as if he meant that.

"Don't you need me?"

"What I need is for you to be happy." He leaned down. "I'm going to be okay, Aish. But I need you to be happy, for me."

"What will Ake say?"

"Yes," said Serik. "Duh."

"I can teach you," said Nursultan again. "You will stay with me. For the winter. For the year. Until your family comes back for you."

"Till you're ready for that university thing," said Serik. "You could go to a school in Oglii City. It's a good school."

Nursultan nodded. "I have three sons and three grand-sons living in my aul. There is plenty of room for you."

"But I already have a family."

Ker-honk, said Toktar.

"Aish . . ." Serik began.

"Not—" She was not sure how to say it. That family are the people who choose you. Kara-Kat-Kis with her fox-bright eyes and steady hands, Dulat with his kingly mustache and his drawings of power generators. "My aunt and my uncle. They will take me in."

"Eh," said Nursultan. "Eh, good!" He turned aside and spat, loudly, precisely, and with great satisfaction. "Yes. Good. That uncle of yours needs an eagle in his heart."

"An eagle or a windmill," said Aisulu. And thought, *Or a daughter.*

"You and your uncle will both come up here sometimes," said Nursultan. "And you will hunt with me."

"I'm wildly jealous," said Serik. "FYI."

"Oh, Serken . . ." And then she was crying again. A thought occurred to her. "Here, hold Toktar."

There was a moment's fuss as Nursultan fetched Serik an extra glove, and Aisulu passed Toktar up to her brother. The eagle spread his wings and peered from Serik to Aisulu and back.

Aisulu reached into her pocket and drew out the extra

ribbon. She felt down Serik's leg until she found the point where the pant leg fell empty. She unpinned it so that the pant leg dangled, and then cinched the extra fabric up and wrapped the ribbon around it.

She looked up at Serik. She looked at Toktar, who had turned his head upside down and was considering whether to eat the ribbon.

The white ribbon.

"Why?" said Serik, his fingers on her fingers, on the knot.

"So that you can't be captured," Aisulu said. "So you can never be taken again. So you can find your way home."

Glossary

Possibly Unfamiliar Things

aul: A group of gers belonging to one extended family. The word sounds like "owl."

balapan: An eagle in its first year.

baursak: Sticks of fried dough.

burkitshi: An eagle hunter.

dombra: A stringed instrument, like a guitar or a banjo.

ger: A round tent-house. The word rhymes with "bear."

khan: A ruler, a king.

kumiss: A drink made of horse milk.

shapan: A calf-length padded jacket.

shimin-airkh: A homemade alchohol.

tugreg: The name for the Mongolian currency, the way "dollar" is for the American currency.

Kazakh Words and Phrases

Ake: Dad.

Bold-da: Stop that, that's enough.

Eej: Mom.

Jok: No.

Ket: Go away, dog.

Köp Rahkmet: Thank you very much.

Tsai oh: Let's drink tea.

Arabic Phrases

Asalaam Aleykum: "God's peace be with you"; a greeting.

Bismillah: "In the name of God"; a prayer to begin things, including meals.

Inshallah: "If it pleases God"; a prayer said upon wishing for something.

Masha-Allah: "Praise God"; a prayer of joy and gratitude.

The Family

THE THREE BROTHERS, THEIR WIVES, AND
CHILDREN

Dulat (the oldest brother): "Riches."

Kara-Kat-Kis (married to Dulat): This name is Tuvan, not
Kazakh. It means "blackberry girl." Kara-Kat-Kis is also
called the Fox Wife.

Abai (the middle brother): "Careful."

Rizagul (married to Abai): "Bright Flower."

Serik (their son, age fourteen): "Hope." His shortened name is
"Serken.")

Aisulu (their daughter, age twelve): "Beauty of the Moon" (Her
shortened name is "Aish.")

Yerzhan (the youngest brother): "Hero's Soul."

Meiz (married to Yerzhan): "Sultana."

Temir and Balta (their twin sons, age six): "Iron" and "Axe."

Enlik (their daughter, age four): "Edelweiss."

Naizabai (their infant son): "Many Arrows."

Pazylbek, father of Dulat, Abai, and Yerzhan (deceased): "Generous."

Gulsara, mother of Dulat, Abai, and Yerzhan (deceased): "Yellow Flower."

The Others

Beskempir: An old widow and matchmaker; "[Blessed by] Five Old Women."

Chudruk: aka Sneering Muscles, Beskempir's grandson, Zhambyl's son; "Fist."

Nursultan: The oldest eagle hunter; "Shining king."

Oraz: an eagle hunter; "Fast."

Yrymbassar: aka Axe Thinker, an eagle hunter; "Has taken the name of the grandfather."

Zhambyl: Beskempir's son, head man of the neighboring aul; named after Mount Zhambyl.

Note to the Reader

Ever since I started writing this book, people have asked me how much of it is true.

Here is one way to answer that: The book you have in your hands is a work of fiction, which is to say, I made up the people in it, and the things that happen to them. Mongolia, on the other hand, is a real place. The Kazakh people are real people. And the eagles are entirely real.

I came to this book eagles first. I have been fascinated by falconry—the art of hunting using falcons, hawks, and eagles—my whole life, since I came across a hawk caught by its leash in the woods where I used to play as a kid. In my memory, that bird still hangs upside down, alternately limp and frantic, trapped and dangerous, tiny and huge. Ever since I started writing stories, I knew one day I would have to write a book with that bird in it.

About ten years ago, I started one. The hero was a boy whose sister fell ill. His parents were too distracted taking care of her to take care of him, and so he was left on his own—loved but cut adrift. The family were naturalists who ran a wilderness station, and the boy was left with the job of caring for a human-imprinted hawk—teaching it to be wild again so that it could survive on its own. I fiddled and fiddled with this story, but it would not come together.

Then, one day in April of 2014, I saw a series of images by photojournalist Asher Svidensky depicting young eagle hunters training in Mongolia. When I first saw Svindensky's photographs, I felt as if I had been hit by lightning. In North America, falconers will tell you that returning a trained bird to the wild is difficult, maybe even impossible. In Mongolia, the Kazakh people have been releasing their eagles back into the wild for thousands of years. That gave my story a whole new set of possibilities. It rearranged itself, came to life, and flew away.

I chased it. All the way to Mongolia.

Here is what you'll learn about the eagle hunters of Mongolia if you read books about them, which was, naturally, the first thing I did. They live on the western edge of Mongolia, in a part of the country called Bayan-Ölgii, east of Kazakhstan, north of China, and south of Siberian Russia. The eagle hunters are not ethnically Mongolian, but ethnically Kazakh—they have a different history from Mongolians and speak a different language. Most are nomads, moving with their herds every season in search of good grazing. They have ridden horses since at least the Bronze Age—they may have been the first people to tame horses—and they have, they say, always hunted with eagles.

Here is what you cannot learn: That when you enter your own ger, you should walk counterclockwise around the fire, but when you are a visitor, you should go the other way. That a ger might be plain on the outside, but on the inside, it is hung with the brightest embroidery you can possibly imagine—when a woman gets married and sets up her own ger, her mother gives her one hanging, so that her walls will never be bare. That when you are finished milking a string of seventy goats, you should never, ever wash your hands in the river—milky hands must be washed where the milk can fall into the ground in your camp, because milk is life. These are things that every Kazakh knows but few books will explain.

To learn those things, I had to travel to Mongolia and live with eagle hunters.

I am not a world traveler, but my friend Seánan Forbes is, so I asked her to travel with me. We found a guide, a young woman named Tansaya Khajikhan—a remarkable person who grew up as a nomad and now holds a degree in gender studies. She found a family of eagle hunters willing to host us. Thus it was that in July of 2015, Seánan, Tansaya, and I found ourselves rattling across the Altai Mountains in an old Russian Jeep, looking for the aul of Alimbai the eagle hunter.

I paid Alimbai and his family for their great generosity in letting us share their lives for the summer, however we asked them not to treat us as guests but as they might treat thirteen-year-old girls in their community. I knew my book would be about a teenage Kazakh child living in a Kazakh family—I wanted to get inside that experience as far as I could. Immediately there was a problem: Seánan and I were not fit to be Kazakh girls. The women of the family looked at us and then looked at one another, as if to say *These people can't milk* anything.

In the winter, Kazakhs eat a lot of meat, but in the summer, all they have is milk and cheese and baursak—bread fried in clarified butter. Milk is literally life and death, and milk is endless work. Men and boys take the herds out every day in search of good grazing, and women and girls stay close to their aul, in a world made of milk. They milk the yaks and cows at dawn; they milk the horses five times a day; they milk their huge herds of goats. There is no refrigeration, so they must also process all that milk every day. They churn butter for hours. They boil whey in hot little sheds. They make cheese.

And I couldn't do any of it. I did learn, but it was slow, and at first I could only do the jobs normally given to very young children. I collected yak dung and spread it out to dry so that it could be used as fuel for the fire. I swept the linoleum floors of the ger and nearly broke my back doing it—the broom was sized for a little girl. I carried water. That was the most difficult job—a big pail full of water is heavy, and the wire handles cut my hands. The girls of the aul—but not the boys—all had hard yellow calluses across their palms from those handles.

There was one girl in the family who was exactly the age of my own daughter Eleanor. Her name was Kumsai, and I fell in love with her. Seánan taught her origami, and she took to it like a mathematical genius. She taught me the local hand-clap game and the dice game played with the ankle bones of sheep—and proceeded to beat the pants off me. She brought me flowers. And she took me walking, as often as we could sneak away, to see Alimbai's eagles.

There were two of them: an adult eagle captured in the wild and a baby only recently taken from the nest. I think the baby was about nine or ten weeks old when we arrived—already full-size but scraggly looking, with a mix of down that was falling out and flight feathers that were coming in, looking like a seventh-grader's first sewing project. But in a single month, we saw that eagle grow up. Her feathers filled in. She experimented with her wings—she would tilt them, rubberneck her head around as if she could actually see the wind breaking over them, and make adjustments. She learned to sit on the glove and wear the hood. We were there the day she made her first kill. Alimbai's son brought her a live rabbit tied to the end of a rope. Alimbai, holding the eagle, whisked off her hood, and she paused for one heartbeat, locked on to that rabbit, and swooped down on it like a bolt of lightning.

While the eagle was growing and learning, I was watching and thinking. I already had the seed of my story—the brother and sister, the sickness, and the moment where the healthy child was cut adrift. Now I had a timeline: a single summer. And I had the scaffold of the plot: the training of a baby eagle. I saw the look on Kumsai's face as she watched the eagles—and watched the boys training with eagles—as if her heart were drifting up into the sky. Longing and the limits placed on girls—their hard work and fierce pride and great joy—these are what shaped this story.

My time in Mongolia is all over these pages: the goats and the milking, the water pails, the mountains, the smell of the dung fire, the summer weather, the Choco-Pies, the way the light seeps in around the doorframe of the ger at dawn. I even incorporated the bit from my diary where we had all the gers loaded into a truck, which was then intercepted by horsemen from a rival family. "It was a like a scene from a movie," I wrote. "Specifically, it was like the scene from a movie where people are killed by Kazakh horsemen." But in the end, I hope this story is universal: about family, belonging, adventure, courage, and love.

Ultimately this is my story. I was that child who was

loved but also cut adrift because I was the one not in crisis. I was that child spending endless hours with books of animal friendship and long days exploring the woods behind my house. They were just a series of vacant lots, really, where houses couldn't be built because the creek there flooded. But at the time they seemed huge. And one day I found a hawk there, hanging upside down from its own jesses. I was terrified and awestruck as if caught in a story. My heart rose into the sky. And then a falconer came through the trees.

It's all true. And I made it all up. And that's fiction.

Acknowledgments

During the drafting of this book, a flock of people lent expertise.

Birds first: Young falconer and YA book fan Harleigh Heese shared her experience with her golden eagle Thor and read two drafts. Friedhelm Hoesterey, master falconer, let me spend time at Golden Creek Bird Farm, which is where I got to meet and handle Murder Fluff, a newly hatched golden eaglet. The Mountsberg Conservation Centre, near my home, has adult golden eagles and is practically on speed dial.

Jason Palmieri shared his experience as an above-the-knee amputee and read my draft to help me look after Serik. Doctor J.P. gave me insight into the state of medicine in Central Asia.

Most vitally, I have to thank my readers in Kazakh Mongolia: Kanat and P. Z., who started as hired readers and became—in the Kazakh way—great friends. Their patience with me has been nothing less than saintly. A Tuvan shaman, who did not wish her name to be written down, answered many questions and listened to me read the scenes in which Kara-Kat-Kis appears. I owe her for much—including that reindeer skull. Also, did you know that you can Skype Siberia now?

Despite this all this help, I am sure there are mistakes. Those are my own.

Further tremendous gratitude to the following:

Region of Waterloo Arts Fund and Canada Council for the Arts, whose grants allowed me to spend part of the summer of 2015 living in the aul of a Kazakh eagle hunter.

Seánan Forbes—writer, photographer, adventurer, and friend, who traveled to Mongolia with me.

Tansaya—daughter of eagle hunters; holder of a degree in gender studies; translator and guide in the Altai; and ultimately a dear friend. You are an extraordinary person. Thank you for sharing your country with us.

Alimbai the eagle hunter and his wife Jibek, for opening their aul and their ger to us and letting us share their lives for the summer.

We did not meet Alimbai and Jibek's sons—it was haying season—but I thank daughters-in-law Bika and Cirku, for showing me what was what in a Kazakh family.

The children of the aul stole my heart—Ayrekai, the eldest, and Djursen, just younger, the prince of the aul. Chalatai and Quontai, who with Djursen made a band of three musketeers. Kumsai, eight, like my own little Eleanor, is brilliant and kind like her; Kumsai, who shone like the moon. Isolo, who sat like a tank of a kindergartner in my lap but never stopped coughing. Little ones Ayam and Tiku, who showed me that even toddlers can wrestle goats better than me.

Alimbai's eagles, to whom Toktar owes his existence. The wild-caught muzbalak, or eagle in its sixth year, was a magnificent killing machine. She had a crooked claw from tangling with a wolf. The nest-caught balapan, or eagle in its first year, was a dorky muppet killing machine.

To all of these people and animals: Ракмет! Rahkmet! Баярлалаа! Bayarlalaa! Thank you! I could say it in a dozen languages and it wouldn't be enough.

While writing this book, I was supported in part by a grant from Ontario Arts Council—and nearly entirely by my writer friends. I want to thank:

Karuna Riazi, who read my very earliest sample chapters—the ones that got me the travel grants—and made crucial suggestions.

My beloved in-person writers' group—Susan Fish, Nan Forler, Kristen Mathies, and Pamela Mulloy—who believed in me from the beginning.

My mother-in-law, the late Patricia Bow, also read the early stuff with her eagle eye. I am sorry she didn't get to see this book finished. She said it was going to be her favorite.

E. K. Johnston, who rescued me after the book got stuck, letting me join her at the Magic Cabin.

R. J. Anderson, who read along and provided weeping and cheering and general enthusiasm.

Seánan Forbes again, who read along and provided memory checks and specific enthusiasms.

My mother, Rosemarie O'Connor, and her husband Michael Allsopp, who loved draft three.

Ishta Mercurio, who provided fresh eyes and crucial ideas between drafts three and four.

Kristen Ciccarelli, who held my hand as this book was being sold.

And of course, my husband, the novelist James Bow, who was there through it all (except the amebic dysentery I acquired in Mongolia, and I'm sure he feels bad to have missed that).

A book like this is not just the words of an author, but the work of dozens of amazing professionals. Jane Putch, my agent, flew this book high and found it a nest at HMH. Cat Onder, my editor, has been generous, sharp-eyed, and brilliant—a wonderful support to me and a perfect fit for my book. Thank you so much, Jane and Cat. Colleen Fellingham did the copy edits and was a joy to mark-up